THE LAST CRUSADE

The Last Crusade

To Rupci
with complements

A novel

by

GEORGE MATHEW

George Mathew
6/2/25

BOOKS

Adelaide Books
New York / Lisbon
2021

THE LAST CRUSADE

A novel

By George Mathew

Published by Adelaide Books, New York / Lisbon
adelaidebooks.org

Editor-in-Chief
Stevan V. Nikolic

For any information, please address Adelaide Books
at info@adelaidebooks.org

or write to:

Adelaide Books
244 Fifth Ave. Suite D27
New York, NY, 10001

ISBN: 978-1-955196-21-5

Printed in the United States of America

Contents

CHAPTER ONE
Murder Most Foul **7**

CHAPTER TWO
The Sum of All Evils **23**

CHAPTER THREE
The Hunt Begins **38**

CHAPTER FOUR
The Plot **57**

CHAPTER FIVE
The Fox **72**

CHAPTER SIX
Financial Armageddon **86**

CHAPTER SEVEN
A Recce **99**

CHAPTER EIGHT
Target Practice **112**

CHAPTER NINE
Bavaria **125**

CHAPTER TEN
The Crusade **141**

CHAPTER ELEVEN
Harmagedon **153**

CHAPTER TWELVE
The Crusade—Finale **167**

CHAPTER THIRTEEN
Assassination! **180**

CHAPTER FOURTEEN
"Every Contact Leaves Its Trace" **195**

CHAPTER FIFTEEN
Captured! **208**

CHAPTER SIXTEEN
Counterattack! **230**

CHAPTER SEVENTEEN
Operation Brimstone **246**

About the Author **265**

CHAPTER ONE

Murder Most Foul

The truck was parked on the side of the road. Though a driver was inside, the lights were not turned on. There was no activity in the cabin, just a silhouette of the driver outlined against the dull streetlights from a distance. It was 7:00 p.m., the end of a quiet weekday on the Marienplatz in Munich. The pedestrian street opposite the Augustiner Großgaststätten beer hall had not yet become crowded. The driver in the darkened cabin of the truck waited patiently for his prey. He was a professional in matters such as this.

Then he saw her. She got off the bus and walked toward where he was parked. She came to a stop a few feet away from the truck. He turned on the ignition and kept the engine running. He did not turn on the lights, and she did not look his way. Instead, she stood on the curb and riffled through her bag, looking for something. She fished out her phone, punched in some numbers, raised it to her ear, and spoke excitedly. She stepped off the curb and into the crosswalk. He waited until she was nearly halfway across, speaking animatedly into the phone.

He revved the engine and released the huge truck forward. She began to turn her head toward the sound. The powerful 15.6-liter V8 engine of the Mercedes-Benz Arcos truck picked up speed and barreled toward her. Four headlamps came on full blast, blinding her temporarily, and she froze. She turned and dropped her phone as both her hands went up to cover her face in sheer fright. Her mouth opened as if to scream.

She simply did not stand a chance.

The huge ten-ton truck pummeled into her at full speed. Her body jackknifed into the air like a rag doll, her neck snapped on impact and then hung limply as her dead form flopped down into a crumpled heap on the wet cobblestones. He drove over her body. Bones cracked like matchsticks. The driver turned off the lights and thundered past the beer hall. By the time the first group of patrons of the Augustiner beer hall were rushing out to help, Amy Jordan, CIA operative working undercover at the G & H Bayerischer Bank in Bavaria, was dead.

No one had seen the license plates. The street cameras had captured only a darkened image of a truck racing past. The rest followed as it always does. The German Federal Police, the Bundespolizei, the crime scene experts, the reporters, and the TV cameras all came and left. The body was sent back to America, and the investigations by the German police and the agency went on for a year. According to the police, Amy Jordan was on the phone and had not seen the oncoming truck as she stepped off the curb and into the truck's path. The driver had hit her accidentally, panicked, and bolted. To the Bundespolizei, it did not seem premeditated. The agency concurred with the German Federal Police. The file was closed. Matt Jordan in New York had lost his wife of twenty-five years.

★

On the north side of Forest Hills, in a detached single-family home in Queens, New York, Matt stood looking pensively at the large picture of his wife, Amy, smiling down at him from her perch inside a frame high above the fireplace. More than a year had passed since that horrific accident in faraway Munich. He still could not come to terms with it. She had been a CIA operative who worked undercover in a bank to monitor financial crimes. This hadn't been cloak-and-dagger stuff.

You don't get knocked off for things like that. It was no longer the Cold War era when spooks from Russia from behind the Iron Curtain simply knocked you off. Something about her death did not add up. Amy could not have walked under a truck just like that. Matt did not buy the official story that she was killed because she was on the phone, distracted. He had a gut feeling that it was a deliberate act. But he had no way of knowing. It had been well over a year. He had grieved, every single day, every single minute of that excruciatingly long period. You had to love someone for a long time and spend a quarter of a century with them to know what it means to suddenly lose someone. He could not move on.

Matt Jordan, a decorated war veteran, was a tall, rugged outdoors type of a man. He was also a gentle soul. That was what had attracted Amy to him since their younger days. He was someone you could lean on. Someone you always looked up to when in trouble. He had served out his military service and returned home to lead a normal life with his wife and daughter. But life had been cruel, and now Amy was gone. Suddenly, the gentle giant was crushed from the inside. His soul was empty. Matt could not come to terms with losing his life partner. He was stuck in a place from which he had no escape. It was purgatory.

He and Amy had literally grown up together, gone to school together, and been inseparable since they were kids. Age had caught up with them, and the innocence of childhood friendship had blossomed into liking and then full-blown love. She had been the prom queen, and he had been the envy of all the other boys when he escorted her to the dance floor. He looked again at the picture on the wall, and his eyes were moist. He remembered that evening far back in time when, as a teenager, he was on top of the world. He still was when, years later, he dropped onto one knee and proposed to her. She had cried that day and accepted his proposal. They had hugged and laughed. They had married soon afterward and gone on a honeymoon to Africa. Nestling against each other in a tented camp in the Masai Mara Game Reserve in Kenya, they had listened to the lions roar outside.

Time had flown. Ashley was born soon afterward. Amy held on to Matt as she labored through the night, and finally little cries announced the birth of their beautiful baby girl, Ashley. Raising Ash had been fun. Amy was the perfect mother. No wonder Ashley had turned out to be the fine daughter she was. Matt had joined the military, and Amy had gone to work for the CIA. Between leave from tours and raising Ashley, time had flown, and now, suddenly Amy was gone. He looked up at Amy's picture once again as he had done a thousand times in the past year.

"We'll find out what happened in Munich that day, Dad," Ashley said reading his mind. She had come up from behind him. "Come on. Kareem should be here soon. I'm excited. He did say that he has some new leads. We'll still crack this case wide open!"

Ashley smiled. She knew her father's sense of loss was almost unbearable. Though he tried hard to hide it from her, she had woken up nights to find him seated alone in the dark, deep in thought. He hardly ever went out. In many ways, she suffered along with him. She loved her dad intensely and could not let him waste away like this. But she also knew how much her dad loved her mom. Her parents had been a match made in heaven. They were inseparable. You could feel the magic if you were in a room with them. One complemented the other. They knew what the other thought. She had grown up seeing the happiest parents any child could have. So, she understood what it meant for her dad to be so devastated, like a castaway adrift in an ocean of loneliness.

She worried about him. Losing her mother was bad enough. Her father may have physically buried her mother, but he carried the burden. He seemed lost between two extremes. He needed to act. But he was a hard realist and would do that only if he had evidence. He did not. He was stuck in between. At times she hoped he would bump into someone and move on in life and be happy. But there was no chance he would consider going out, let alone do it. He would not meet people. She could see that her father was digging himself into a hole.

Although he was devastated by the loss of her mother, he was still a strong person—someone she could look up to. His sorrow came not from an inability to act, but from simply not knowing what had really happened to her mom. The two of them just had this gut feeling that her mother's death was not accidental, as the authorities put it. But they had no proof to the contrary. Her dad's pain was from vacillating between knowing and not knowing. He was strong and would have taken anyone on if he knew who was responsible. If he ever found out who had harmed her mother, she knew her dad could be a dangerous opponent. He would act. Simple as that. It was not for nothing that he was a decorated war veteran. But right now, he was lost in a dark place, where he did not know which way to turn. That was why Kareem's visit today was so important.

"Grab the beers and the steak for the grill, Dad," she called as she pushed open the French doors to the deck to set up the barbecue and grill the meat.

"Sure, Ash," Matt said with a smile.

His daughter was perceptive and could read his mind. He knew she was worried. Since losing Amy, he had retreated into himself. He had not spent much time with his daughter. He felt bad. He would be in agony until he knew what had happened. His life and that of his daughter hung in the balance. Still, he was proud of Ashley. She was a strong and pragmatic kind of girl. Matt knew she missed her mother and was angry. But he felt she was internalizing it. Like him, she was waiting for some proof. She was a fighter, and fearless in her approach, taking life head-on. But he knew she worried for him. He felt guilty that he had not spent as much time with her as he should have. But he was in a quandary. He needed to find out what had really happened. He was a trained soldier, a hardened combat veteran who was not going to wallow in self-pity. He was also not a conspiracy theorist. He was uneasy, even sad, but that did not mean he would shoot at anything and everything. He needed concrete proof to act. Think. Plan. Act. That accounted for Kareem's visit. Kareem kept following up with all the agencies he could, for some concrete information about Amy's death.

"Lieutenant Colonel Matt Jordan!" a familiar voice boomed from the doorway. "Still missing Amy, I see." It was Special Agent Kareem Khan of the FBI, a colleague of Amy's and a good friend. Kareem's right palm shot up in a crisp salute, and his face lit up with a huge smile. Kareem was a big man, and his smile was infectious.

"Speak of the devil! I was just thinking of you," Matt exclaimed. "Come on in, buddy. Yes, it's hard to get over Amy. That's why we're both waiting for you. We need to do something about it." He pointed to the fridge and said, "Grab the steaks. Ash's out on the deck waiting to grill 'em."

Even when Matt tried to be lighthearted, there was a certain melancholic undertone in his voice. A tinge of sadness, Kareem noticed. In his opinion, Matt hadn't been able to find closure. But he knew his buddy was also a hard-core military man who didn't shoot at shadows, but wanted proof. Once Matt had that, he'd make his move. No wonder Matt had been awarded the Silver Star for his service during Operation Desert Storm in the Persian Gulf. Kareem remembered parts of the award citation: "For Captain Matthew Jordan's repeated acts of bravery in providing support to embattled Marines, flying into Iraqi ground and anti-aircraft fire at great personal risk to himself, resulting in the destruction of as many as a hundred Iraqi armored vehicles and saving the lives of his fellow Marines."

Kareem had something today that he hoped would throw some light on Amy's death. He looked at Matt and smiled.

Ashley gave the tall, well-built, black FBI special agent a bear hug. "Welcome! Been dying to see you and hear what you have for us." Handing the tenderizing hammer to him, she said, "Here, do the steak while I get the coals going."

She held the air blower to the already lit coals and got them burning, slowly turning them into glowing red embers.

Matt passed the beers around and remarked, "Still don't know how a routine undercover job in a German bank could be so dangerous. A desk job looking at figures cannot get you killed, KK. Something just does not seem right."

"I know what you mean, MJ," Kareem said. "I'm a federal agent, trained to believe a report in the absence of anything to the contrary." Kareem had hammered the steaks and seasoned them with salt and pepper. "But still, like you guys, I felt that something wasn't quite right, and I've been chasing anything and everything to learn more about Amy's death."

He continued, "Amy was good at finance, and she was stationed at that Munich bank as an analyst in direct lending. That job description suited the CIA eminently. It entailed performing detailed financials, market research, and analysis for investment decisions, preparing various complex financial models, and screening new investments. She would help close deals and monitor all new investments, just what the agency wanted. Under that cover, the agency wanted her to keep an eye on the dealings of G & H Bayerischer Bank in Munich. Amy was investigating the flow of money that might've had a bearing on terrorist activities linked to the United States. So, I'm certain that she must have looked into investments flowing to and from Europe and America through G & H." Kareem brushed a light coat of olive oil on the steaks and passed them on to Ashley.

"For some time, the agency had been onto a flow of millions of dollars out of Germany to the homeland. We didn't know what it was for—whether it was money laundering, drug money, or terror related. The agency had no idea which bank was involved, so they simply chose the biggest bank in Munich and inserted Amy there. I believe Amy was on to something in G & H. But before she could uncover anything, that accident ended it all. No one in the agency truly knows anything. They can't say if it was a case of sabotage or merely an unfortunate accident. They didn't have anything against G & H. It was just a wild card choice for Amy to go undercover. That's why no one thought twice about looking up the bank after the accident happened. It was treated as a hit-and-run, and the driver and vehicle were never found. They didn't have anything to work with—no vehicle, no driver, no witnesses, and no evidence. So, after a year of investigation, they closed the case."

Ashley placed the steaks on the red-hot grill, and the air filled with the smell of grilled meat. "From what you say, I can see that Mom was in the middle of something large and international in scope. That accident was not natural. My gut feeling, as you just said, is that she was *on to* something. Probably she saw or heard something. No one will ever know. Possibly someone wasn't happy that she was in the know."

There was a perceptible sense of anger in Ashley's voice. She took after her father and could sense the possibility of foul play in her mother's death. Ashley was no coward. In her career as an investigative journalist, she had come across some nasty customers. Some had tried to browbeat her or throw the odd threat her way. She had stood her ground and taken them on. She kind of switched on when faced with adversity. She was raring to go once she had some information and was counting on Kareem to give them some pointers.

"Maybe as part of her job of investment monitoring," Ashley said, "she bumped into some clients with shady investments or something bigger. I don't know. Mom was a tough girl. I cannot imagine her fading away into the sunset like that. She probably wasn't ready for a detailed report, hoping to tie up some loose ends, and got caught before she could put it down on paper. Possibly her cover was blown. Something *just* does not add up, Kareem. It just doesn't."

"You're right, Ash," Kareem agreed. "I worked with Amy, and she was a tough person and a thorough operative. She would not just shoot at shadows. She investigated and looked at things from every angle before she formed an opinion. So, in this case, if she had any doubts about G & H, she wouldn't have written up something and wasted the agency's time and resources unless she had rock-solid evidence. I assure you that in our line of work, we come up against highly suspect and sometimes downright shady situations, but usually we find a perfectly normal explanation for something that looks weird at first. Amy knew that a lot better than I did. I'm certain that she was on to something, but someone stopped her before she could put two and two together and report it."

"That's exactly why I wanted to go to Munich and nose around," Matt said. "You are so right. I don't think she absent-mindedly walked under that truck, KK. No, that's not my girl. You're damn right about her being methodical. That's why she ended up crunching numbers and chasing shadows in the agency, while I did straight military work. She was good at deciphering things. She could see beyond what a lot of people saw as mundane. In separating the grain from the chaff of the intelligence world, Amy was careful not to get it wrong. Yeah, buddy, she was very meticulous."

"Then she found something, and the chips must have fallen into place, but she didn't live to tell the tale," Kareem said. "Sadly, that's all we have."

"Despite my sickening sense of distrust and anger," Matt said, "there was pretty much nothing I could do. At first, I wanted to collect her body and ask around in case anyone had information, but the agency was against that, and they had a strong rationale for dissuading me. In her cover, Amy had been single and unattached, so the last thing they wanted was a distraught husband arriving to collect the body of a single woman. It would have ruined the agency's chances of planting another mole in her place. All the same, I really wanted to go, find the killer, and possibly wring his neck."

"Matt, I know that if you had found the culprit, you would've done precisely that," Kareem said. "But you are also right that a vendetta trip to Bavaria would've upset the apple cart for the agency and led to a scandal on foreign soil."

"I know," said Matt, sounding deflated. That was the very essence of his being right then, stuck between knowing and not knowing. Amy had been killed, but he had no evidence. He was angry.

"All the same, I like that part about wringing someone's neck," Kareem said. "Amy was my friend, too." This was a good family. Kareem had known them for a long time. They deserved to be happy. It was sad to see Matt and Ash stuck in limbo.

"I hope you have something for us today," Ashley said. She trusted Kareem. He had been a rock of support during this trying time. He was very analytical. The things that he had just said about her mother also described him—methodical, careful, and thorough. For a year now they had been pushing to see if he could come up with anything. He had not given them any false hope. He kept in touch and ensured she and her dad were okay.

"Okay, guys, let's see if this gets us anywhere," Kareem said, tossing a large brown envelope onto the table. "Ash, tell me if you know the person in that picture."

Ashley turned the meat over with a spatula, wiped her hands, and flipped open the envelope. A glossy picture slid out. She gasped. "Oh, my God, do I know her? Of course, I do! That's Cynthia. She's a highly respected journalist. We worked together at the *Daily Sentinel* in New York, a long time ago. I was a rookie then, and she was an assistant editor. She reminded me of Mom a lot, and I was close to her. She taught me the ropes, and I'm deeply grateful to her for helping to make me what I am today. But she went off to Germany or Holland, somewhere, and I lost track of her. Why do you ask, Kareem?"

"Because her boyfriend, Ryan, an IT consultant, worked for G & H Bayerischer." The steaks had formed brown grill lines and caramelized to perfection. Kareem handed Ash the last piece of steak, looked her in the eye, and said, "He was found dead in his apartment a month before Amy's accident. He was *murdered.*"

Matt was silently chopping greens for a salad. His knife froze midway through the lettuce, and his grip on it tightened. In that instant, he knew that his misgivings about his wife's sudden death were not unfounded. He did not say anything, but his steely countenance belied the storm in his mind. His daughter, however, was unable to be as calm as her soldier father.

Ashley almost dropped the spatula. She was always in control and did not easily show her emotions. But this was, by any measure, a shocker. "What?" she exclaimed. "Cynthia's boyfriend got killed? Working for the same bank Mom worked for?"

"Yes. As part of my role with the Terrorist Threat Integration Center, I coordinated with Amy and her handlers in Munich," Kareem said. "She reported to Mitch, the head of the Cologne station of the agency. He's a good friend, and I asked him to check out any suspicious deaths related to the bank for which Amy worked. I was hoping for any fragment of information on Amy's death that might have inadvertently been left out. Strangely, what he got me is the same thing the agency has already told you. Then Mitch gave me the details on Ryan's murder and some pictures. Somewhere there I read the name of that newspaper, the *Daily Sentinel.* After that, I remembered that Ashley had started out there, and I was hoping you might have known Cynthia. Honestly, I hadn't read much into it until I came here today. It was just a hunch, and if you hadn't known her, I wouldn't have given it much credence. But since you do know her, why don't you look her up? She might know something we don't. You can ask her. Not easy for me."

Matt was done with the salad. He had still not said a word. It was as if he was reorganizing his mind from a position of not knowing to absolute certitude. Until now Amy's death could have been accidental. But hearing that Ryan had been murdered lifted the veil of uncertainty. Amy and Ryan had been killed a month apart. They had both worked for the same bank. The clouds had dissipated. The skies were clear. If one of her colleagues was found murdered in a bank already under investigation, *there was reason to suspect foul play in Amy's sudden death.* It no longer could be merely accidental. Matt was considering a new course of action. There was no turning back here. This was the calm before the storm. First, accept the fact. Then analyze. Plan. Act.

"Sure, I can talk to her," Ashley said. "And yes, if she knows anything, she'll tell me." Like her father, Ashley's mind was in a state of turmoil. Her mother's colleague had been murdered. In the same bank? Within a month? *Something* was not right. Suddenly they had something to channel their collective investigative energies into—the G & H bank in Bavaria. She too wanted to fly to Munich that very moment and find out what had happened to her mother. She wanted to confront whoever it was in Germany who could have ordered her mother's death. She was willing to face anything to get at the truth and let the world know. She would unmask whoever was behind this.

She looked at her father. For the first time in a year, she could see a glimmer of hope on his face. The loneliness and the not knowing seemed to have lifted. She was pleased. In some ways, she was like her father, under control until some piece of news changed the status quo. Like right now. A murder. She was itching for action.

Kareem looked at his friend Matt, whose mind, he was sure, was in turmoil as it accepted this new bit of information. Matt had always believed Amy's death was not accidental, even though he had no evidence to back it up. But Kareem knew

Matt was a hardened soldier, a war hero who knew to hold his calm. In battle and in life, he did not show emotion. Despite his steely countenance, though, Kareem spied a slight glimmer of hope.

Although other people in Matt's situation might have been suicidal, it was a testament to his mental strength that he had not been, although he had suffered from loneliness, depression, and the uncertainty around Amy's death.

For the first time, Kareem could bring Matt some evidence of possible foul play, which seemed to give Matt some hope. Kareem was happy that he could at least do that much. But the increasing possibility that Amy's death was the result of premeditated murder might be worse than the previous uncertainty. He could see a steely resolve on Matt's face. Kareem knew he was planning some action.

"Good, Ashley, you do that," Kareem said. "Let me know when you hear from Cynthia. MJ, I need to get back to work now."

Matt saw Kareem out, but his mind was racing. For the first time in a year, he felt there was light at the end of the tunnel. Now more than anything he wanted to find out what had happened. He had to, or he would not be able to go on. Amy deserved better. Matt looked at the picture of his wife again. He smiled. He knew he was going to find out the truth. He had braved Desert Storm. He had seen the horrors of war in the Middle East. Taking on a German bank was the least of his worries. But he needed to know some more details before he acted.

"Let me dig into Cynthia's background, Dad. I'll find her. If Cynthia's boyfriend worked for the same bank as Mom and was killed around the same time, she may have something that will help us out. Who knows what we might come up with? I have a strange feeling that this will lead us somewhere. At least this is better than anything we have had up to now."

"I know you can hunt Cynthia down," Matt said. "We have nothing as of now, but Cynthia can surely unlock stuff and lead us to what might have happened. There's more to this than meets the eye. Your mother was a tough girl. You go and get Cynthia, and let's take it from there."

Ashley had a bit of both her parents in her. She was strong willed, thorough, and fearless once she got going. She had been an investigative journalist for over two years now and helped crack some pretty tough cases. Her best had been a class action lawsuit she'd helped bring against American Paints, a company accused of contaminating the waters in the rust belt of upstate New York with polychlorinated biphenyl. AP had used polychlorinated biphenyl in their manufacturing processes, leading to several cases of liver, nervous system, and reproductive health complaints from area citizens. She had found evidence of the compound's presence in waters that received waste from the company and in the paint sold on the retail market.

In more than fifty commercial paint pigments purchased from three local paint stores, she had been able to prove that American Paints had the greatest instance of polychlorinated biphenyl. The courts had ruled in her favor, and AP had been forced to make huge payouts to those affected. Soon after the incident, AP had filed for Chapter 11 bankruptcy.

She had faced stiff opposition in her work, and people related to AP had sent vague threats her way. Once a representative of the company offered her a bribe to back off and, when she refused, suggested that "accidents do happen." She had been expecting something of the sort and had agreed to meet the AP man in a restaurant while he made his pitch. She had recorded the conversation and later marched into AP's offices and confronted them with it. AP backed off from trying to threaten her after that. They knew she was a bad opponent to have.

Now she wanted justice for her mother. She was going to work with her father and Kareem and get to the bottom of it all.

"Let me go to the *Daily Sentinel* and ask around. Who knows? Cynthia may have left a forwarding address, or someone there may still be in touch with her. I'll get Cynthia. You have my word on that." She smiled and waved a mock salute at her soldier dad.

Matt smiled. He knew his daughter was a fighter. They had raised her to be one. Amy would have been proud of her. As Ashley went to her room, Matt again looked at his wife's picture and said quietly, "I will find out, I will."

CHAPTER TWO

The Sum of All Evils

Deep in the Bavarian countryside, set against the backdrop of the majestic snowcapped Alps, the towering castle-like chateau shrouded in the evening mist stood like a lonely sentinel against the night sky. Clinging to the rugged hills, the towering structure rose high, jutting into the air as the land fell sharply away down the rugged mountains to the lush green plains far below that unfurled like a green carpet to the distant red rooftops of the village of Schwangau, beside Lake Forggensee.

In the bowels of this massive abode, six men were seated in a large room that looked like something out of a medieval castle, a veritable museum of Renaissance art. A replica of the mural of Leonardo Da Vinci's *Last Supper* was painted on the high ceiling, and another part of a wall was devoted to a rendering of Michelangelo's *Creation of Adam* and Caravaggio's *Salome with the Head of Saint John the Baptist.* A replica marble sculpture of the *Pieta*, the seated Madonna holding the body of Christ on her lap, stood in one corner of the room, and the marble rendering of *Moses* in another. Ornate chairs sat on richly embroidered oriental carpets, and lush red drapes with opulent tassels, tiebacks, and fringe adorned the numerous large stained-glass, lancet windows.

"This gentleman," Father Englebert Volker said, pointing a remote-control device at the large-screen, flat-panel television on the wall, "is *evil incarnate*!"

The screen came alive in blazing high-definition color showing Mohamed Bouhlel, a Tunisian Frenchman, plowing a truck through and killing eighty-four people celebrating Bastille Day at Promenade des Anglais and then switched to gory images of the brutal mass murder of fifty partygoers at a gay nightclub in Orlando, Florida, by Omar Mateen, son of an immigrant from Afghanistan. The screen displayed the senseless terror attacks at the offices of *Charlie Hebdo* magazine, the slayings at the Hypercacher kosher market, and the shootings that killed more than ninety innocents at the Bataclan theater in Paris. They were replaced by equally gruesome sights of the dead and decapitated at the Brussels airport and the fourteen Americans butchered by Tasfeen Malik, a Pakistani woman, and her American husband, Syed Rizwan, in San Bernardino, California. Grisly scenes of Jihadi John decapitating Western journalists James Foley, Steven Sotloff, British aid worker Alan Henning, and Christians of many nationalities filled the screen.

If the intention was to evoke repugnance and hatred against Islamist terror, it seemed to have its desired effect. Some of the seated men looked away, aghast. They had seen it before, but each time, it created a deep sense of revulsion in them.

Aleixandre Thierry Devereux, the sixty-five-year-old chairman of France-Net and a member of France's far-right party, the National Front, said, "Last week a nineteen-year-old ISIS supporter forced an eighty-four-year-old priest to kneel at the altar of his church in Normandy, and then slit the priest's throat." Consumed with righteous indignation, Aleixandre continued, "They have no mercy. In fact, their religion permits and encourages such actions. Hassan al-Banna, the founder of the Muslim Brotherhood with branches in seventy countries worldwide, clearly said, when he formed the party in 1928, 'It is in the nature of Islam to dominate, not be dominated, to impose its law and to extend its power to the entire planet.' We are looking at a religion that is determined to wipe out our civilization. We must put a stop to this, here and now."

Aleixandre poured generously of his host's £122,000 Chateau Margaux wine in a glass, settled down into one of the plush sofas, took a mouthful of the limited-edition wine, and slowly swirled it in his mouth, enjoying its rich taste. His indignation seemed to calm down a bit.

"That was a horrible way to die," said Volker, an excommunicated Jesuit priest. He was enjoying piling hatred on the Muslim faith. "I guess the founder of the Muslim Brotherhood foresaw this onslaught. Here they come, the hordes that can multiply and quadruple radical Islamic terror."

Volker clicked on the remote control again. Images of Syrian, Afghan, and African refugees streaming across the borders at Calais, Greece, and Italy filled the large screen. Although the images did not show the deaths of the migrants trying to make the perilous journey across the Mediterranean, it dwelled in detail on far-right media reports of the danger of the Islamization of Europe and an increasing number of attacks on Christians by ISIS in Syria and Iraq. The images of terrorist attacks on Europeans seemed to connect Islamic fundamentalism to migrants from Muslim countries.

Volker concluded, "Gentlemen, welcome to Gunther's chateau and our special meeting to discuss the many evils that afflict our world."

"Yes, Volker, we need to put an end to this kind of Islamization of the West," said Christian Hannes, the middle-aged CEO of Vastgoed NV, a Dutch real estate company. "Whether it's Nidal Hassan, the military doctor in Fort Hood, Texas, who shot thirteen of his unarmed colleagues; Richard Colvin, the shoe bomber; Tsarnaev, the Boston Marathon bomber; or Dahir Adan, the Somali immigrant who stabbed nine innocents in Minnesota, they are all adherents to a violent religion who are intent on wiping out Western civilization. Europol, the European police body, reports that as many as five thousand jihadists trained in terror camps around the world may have returned to Europe to stage terror attacks."

Christian flipped through a sheaf of papers and said, "That's why Geert Wilders, of the Party for Freedom, addressed the Dutch Parliament with this." He proceeded to read. "'Many Dutch citizens experience the presence of Islam around them. And I can report that they have had enough of burkas, headscarves, the ritual slaughter of animals, so-called honor revenge, blaring minarets, female circumcision, hymen restoration operations, abuse of homosexuals, Turkish and Arabic on the buses and trains as well as on town hall leaflets, halal meat at grocery shops and department stores, sharia exams, the finance minister's sharia mortgages, and the enormous overrepresentation of Muslims in the area of crime, including Moroccan street terrorists.'"

"Spot on, Christian!" Raymond Webster Coleman, the tall, aristocratic, and flamboyant CEO of Webster Coleman Brokerage London, concurred. "Over fourteen hundred of our non-Muslim English girls, some as young as twelve or thirteen, were raped over a period of twenty years by British men of Pakistani origin in Rotherham and London. Our sick anti-bigotry laws and political correctness stopped social workers and others from bringing this to light, and the police kept quiet out of fear of stoking Muslim riots. By some estimates, over *ten thousand girls* have been groomed and sold into the sex trade by these Muslim men."

Raymond continued, "In the UK, we have a large population of Muslims who have been radicalized, follow sharia law, and have created literal no-go zones for Christians like us in London. You all know that the real reason for Brexit was to stop this uncontrolled immigration. If they keep coming, our problems in the UK will reach the boiling point and tip over into sheer anarchy. I agree with you, gentlemen. We need to stop this looming menace of Islamic domination!" His friends cheered as Raymond walked over to a couch and sat down.

Herr Gunther Otto Heinrich, chairman of G & H Bayerischer Bank, Munich, and their host for the evening, stood up and said, "A deranged Afghani youth armed with an ax and a knife injured several passengers on a train in Bavaria recently. They raped our daughters in Cologne on New Year's Eve. In Sweden during a music festival, large groups of young immigrant Muslims sexually harassed girls as young as twelve." Gunther could see that everyone in the room shared a hatred for Muslims. Now was the time for him to drive the point home and present the course of action for the evening. "I can see that we all agree that we need to find a solution to the threat from Islamic fundamentalism on our shores, but may I add that the threat from Islam is not the only danger that faces Western civilization today."

That grabbed the attention of his audience, who looked to him as if for direction.

"First, I warmly welcome you, the members of the cabal, to my humble abode."

That put a smile on everyone's faces. Herr Gunther Otto Heinrich was a man of great means, and the owner of the chateau where they sat was anything but humble. His piercing blue eyes seemed to bore into the very soul of his assembled guests. His voice was detached and sounded like that of a priest conducting Mass.

Gunther was forthright: "If we believe that life as we know it in the West is being threatened by these barbarian hordes, homegrown or imported, then we are all sorely mistaken. It is my assertion that our civilization, our culture, our values, and our very existence as a race is threatened by forces other than Islamic terror." Gunther's fingers touched the remote control in his hands as he waved everyone's attention to the large screen and intoned gravely as if he were prophesying the end of times, "See for yourselves!"

The screen came on again with images of Chinese military jets landing on the runway at Fiery Cross Reef, China's man-made islands, created from reclaiming close to three thousand acres in the Spratly Islands chain in the South China Sea. The TV showed images of deployment of surface-to-air missiles on the Paracel chain of islands and Chinese reclamation activities on the Scarborough Shoal, Pratas islands, and Macclesfield Bank. Despite a ruling brought against it by the Philippines in the International Court in The Hague, China was not just ignoring it but had also threatened to declare an air defense identification zone over the South China Sea to monitor foreign military aircraft entering "Chinese territory."

The correspondents went on to describe how the Chinese flew a highly provocative sortie of more than forty fighter planes and bombers through the Miyako Strait between the Japanese islands in a show of force and saber rattling.

One reporter put it succinctly when he said, "With this illegal 'nine-dash line,' the People's Republic of China is now laying claim to a nearly 1.4-million-square-mile swath of the

South China Sea. If this is allowed to happen, they'll control nearly five trillion dollars' worth of merchant and military shipping lanes, plus a large portion of its fishing catchments!"

Aleixandre said, "This is not just naked aggression. It's bloody daylight robbery by the Chinese."

"It gets worse, Alex," Gunther said. "China also indulges in cyber warfare on a large scale. The notorious Unit 61398 of the People's Liberation Army hacked the Pentagon's joint staff email system, exposing more than four thousand civilian and military employees and the Office of Personnel Management of the USA, including personal details of more than twenty-two million people."

Gunther went on, "China takes advantage of Western democratic values and trade with us yet refuses entry for our products into their markets. They make it difficult, almost impossible to succeed. They work within our system and at the same time *outside* of it to rig the economic world to their benefit. Cyber warfare may be one of the many tools they use to get whatever they want at any cost. Unlike our governments, their state sponsors this crime."

Gunther's bass voice intoned, "These attempts of aggression by China in the South China Sea or cyber warfare are the tip of the iceberg in China's grandiose schemes to dominate the world. As of now, China's GDP is second only to that of the United States. But in barely fourteen years, China will surpass the United States as the largest economy in the world."

"That cannot be permitted." Christian was vocal in his disgust. "How is it that our governments stand by and watch as the Chinese do this? Is it even legal to snoop on friendly countries and take over territory? No one says anything. Why do we have a United Nations and ambassadors or even a military? What guarantee do we have that the Chinese won't someday walk into any of our countries and just decide it belongs to them?"

"Christian, our governments have become weak and ineffective." Gunther was enraged. "Yes, we stand and watch. The UN is a toothless tiger. The possibility you speak of is very real. China has territorial claims against just about every neighboring country, including India, Korea, Burma, Vietnam, Nepal, Thailand, Singapore, Taiwan, Laos, and Afghanistan."

Gunther looked at his friends and upped the ante. "China is not the only aggressor we have. Watch this."

The large TV screen showed images of Russian soldiers fighting in the Ukrainian territory of Crimea. Reporters described how Russia had shamelessly annexed Crimea in 2014 in broad daylight and conducted a sham referendum to justify the real motive. In Vladimir Putin's words, the annexation was actually "the return of Crimea to Russia." He was referring to the fact that Crimea was originally part of the Russian Empire and had been handed over to Ukraine only in 1954.

"You're right, Gunther," Ray said. "Russia walked into Crimea, annexed it, and issued Russian passports to the Ukrainians living there. One minute they were Ukrainians—the next, Russians! Our governments stood by and watched, and now they're doing it again. Russia may not have taken over Syria, but they're there, effectively running Bashar al-Assad's war and planning to build permanent bases there. Meanwhile our governments look on impotently."

Gunther drew their attention back to the TV screen.

News reporters and talk show hosts of the major media channels alleged Russian state-sponsored support in the shooting down of Malaysian Airlines Flight 17, with Russian Buk anti-aircraft missile systems, from the pro-Russian, rebel-held territory in Ukraine. The imagery on the large-screen TV played into Gunther's diatribe against the enemies of the free world as his small group grew increasingly agitated. Volker had set the agenda with Islamic terror.

Gunther was now carefully igniting the flames, adding Chinese and Russian malevolence to the list. The list was growing. Something had to be done. This elite group seated around him had the money and the means to pull off the most diabolical of plots. All that was required was to fuel the conflagration of naked hatred and intense fear. He was a master at that game.

Gunther continued, "Our weak attempts at isolating Russia from the world scene, in retaliation for the Crimean annexation, have served only to get our two biggest enemies, China and Russia, to cozy up and become friends. Recently, China and Russia signed a four-hundred-billion-dollar natural gas deal for Russia's government-controlled Gazprom, to supply state-owned China National Petroleum Corporation with up to thirty-eight billion cubic meters of gas a year from 2018 to 2048. That means Russia doesn't have to depend on gas imported from Europe, so there goes our bargaining chip in this geopolitical warfare. The cards are stacked against us."

Gunther looked at his friends, who looked increasingly agitated. He said, "Chinese banks are willing to finance Russia in the absence of Western funding. China abstained from voting against Russia on the Crimean Security Council Resolution. Russia and China vetoed UN attempts to sanction Bashar al-Assad of Syria. China and Russia have valid reasons to scratch each other's backs. Russia is having problems in Ukraine, Georgia, and Moldova, and the Chinese have their hands full with Taiwan, Vietnam, Japan, and the Philippines."

Gunther stopped to refill his glass with a generous shot of schnapps, downed it in one gulp, and turned to his fellow associates.

"In the midst of all this, we have the ultimate clown of all, Kim Jong Un of North Korea, with his proclivities toward nuclear annihilation of South Korea and America."

The screens showed the portly figure of Kim Jong Un inspecting missiles and then switched to large columns of goose-stepping North Korean soldiers marching, holding aloft phalanxes of red flags in Kim Il-sung square.

Gunther raged on: "North Korea has more than twenty nuclear warheads and missiles with a range of more than fifteen hundred kilometers, making them a grave danger to South Korea and our other allies in that part of the world. They mock the world community by continuing to conduct nuclear tests and ratcheting up tensions in the Korean peninsula, threatening to bomb all and sundry, including the USA. Again, the Chinese back them up as in the case of Russian impunity in Crimea and in Syria. The Western world is impotent when it comes to finding a way to stop this evil despot."

"Finally,"—Gunther was in his element— "we have an archangel of evil: the Islamic Republic of Iran. With its mullahs, ayatollahs, and the Islamic Revolutionary Guard, Iran is the world's leading sponsor of terrorism. Their leader, Ahmadinejad, once threatened that our strongest ally, Israel, would be wiped off the map of the world. Iran also supports Hezbollah and Hamas, brutal terrorist organizations whose committed goal is to destroy Israel. A US judge blamed Iran for the 1998 bombings of the US embassies in Kenya and Tanzania. It was also widely reported that the Iranians helped train the 9/11 attackers with heavy weapons and explosives training in Tehran. Iran supports the Taliban in Afghanistan and the anti-American cleric Muqtada al-Sadr in Iraq, who is responsible for large-scale deaths of American soldiers."

Gunther piled on Iran's atrocities. "Though the list of Iran's complicities in exporting terror or harboring terrorists is endless, it did not stop the US and five world powers from lifting the trade embargo, refunding over fifty billion of the nearly one hundred billion dollars of its frozen assets. Russia plans to build eight nuclear power plants in Tehran. Interesting to note is that *one* of these reactors will be able to produce plutonium and uranium. I am not convinced by the argument that the plutonium or uranium produced here will not be of weapons grade."

Gunther was fuming when he said, "What stops a country that has existed on guile, cunning, and subterfuge, once they lay their hands on more than a hundred billion dollars in frozen funds, from developing nuclear weapons? Iran has already violated the tenets of the agreement and test-fired ballistic missiles. The ayatollah routinely lambasts the nuclear deal, and Iranian armed forces harass American ships in the Persian Gulf. Gentlemen, the threat of a nuclear Iran is a clear and present danger."

There was a pregnant pause. Gunther then looked at the small group of power brokers from around the world and said in measured tones, "In conclusion, gentlemen, radical Islamic terror, the danger from Russian imperialism, Chinese aggression, North Korean saber rattling, and Iranian nuclear ambitions together form … *the sum of all evils!*"

Gunther was pleased with himself. He had built a picture of gloom and doom. Muslims and Communists were planning to take over the world. Democratic nations stood by and watched idly. Something had to be done, or evil would reign. He had dexterously channeled the men's emotions and thought processes to the end game he had in mind—*revenge*. Between the six of them, they had the power and the means to rain death and destruction across both sides of the Atlantic. He wanted them to *feel* the pain, and act. The images of terror, the tales of horror, and the image of impending doom seemed to have done the trick. The assembled members of the cabal were incensed.

This was the moment Gunther was waiting for. He looked at the faces of his colleagues. The iron was hot. It was time to strike. His words were ominous. "It is now eminently self-evident that neither our governments nor the United Nations are able to do anything. It now behooves right-thinking men like us, the Cabal of Christian Crusaders, to take up cudgels against these forces of evil and create a *new world order.* For close to a year, Chuck and I have been working behind the scenes to finalize our plans. It has not been easy. There were a lot of things to be put in place. But gentlemen, I can now proudly report that all our plans are complete, and we are ready. Permit me to welcome Chuck Scott, who will outline the course of action."

Gunther walked back to his seat, to loud cheers from his colleagues.

Robert Chuck Scott Jr., the vice president of the United States, slowly got to his feet. For his age, Chuck looked remarkably well built and commanded a powerful presence. His eyes, voice, and demeanor were suggestive of the high office he held. When he stood up, others took notice. Chuck scanned the faces of those seated around the room. They were rich and powerful men from different parts of the world, all united by a common cause-to rid the world of evil against the West. Between the six of them, they commanded resources and wealth that were beyond the realm of mere men. Chuck raised his glass to his friends.

"First, thanks to Gunther." Chuck's voice resonated around the room. "He has been a huge support in the work that has gone on behind the scenes for quite some time now to put together the project I am about to unveil. During this time, I have also had the proud privilege to work with some of you in this endeavor. I must agree, I have had nothing but excellent support. Thanks, all!"

Chuck spoke in a lofty tone, "The free world looks to us to make a change. The collective might of everyone seated in this room can move mountains. We can, we must, and we will. This must stop! Toward that end, today I unveil Project Harmagedon. To explain the context of the project, I welcome you to see this passage from the good book."

Chuck clicked on his remote control. A baritone voice-over read out the verses from the Book of Revelation Chapter 19, the Apocalypse of John……

"'I saw heaven standing open and there before me was a white horse, whose rider is called Faithful and True … He is dressed in a robe dipped in blood, and his name is the Word of God. The armies of heaven were following him, riding on white horses and dressed in fine linen, white and clean. Coming out of his mouth is a sharp sword with which to strike down the nations. Then I saw the beast and the kings of the earth and their armies, gathered together to wage war against the rider on the horse and his army. But the beast was captured, and with it the false prophet who had performed the signs on its behalf. With these signs, he had deluded those who had received the mark of the beast and worshiped its image. The two of them were thrown alive into the fiery lake of burning sulfur.'"

Chuck switched off the TV, let the ominous Biblical prophecy sink into the minds of the assembled group. Then pontificated. "Gentlemen, as you all know, Jesus Christ will vanquish the beast, the Antichrist, and Satan the devil in the battle of the ages at the Meggido mountain range, and fire from the heavens will devour them and the unholy will be thrown into the Gehenna, the lake of fire! *That* is the Armageddon that our plan today is based on. We will rid the world of the beast—*the sum of all evils*, as Gunther so evocatively described it. Our avowed aim will be to vanquish the enemy and rain death and destruction in the form of a cataclysmic annihilation of Islamic terror and godless Communism and create an apocalyptic change of world order. Hence our project will be known by its Hebrew word—*Harmagedon*!"

The assembled guests applauded loudly. After seeing images of death and destruction against Western interests, it was good to hear of a retaliatory attack. What Chuck had described was cataclysmic. It whetted the men's appetites for revenge: an eye for an eye. They wanted to spill the blood of Muslims and Communists. Chuck was making them feel good. Yes, they would throw their enemies into the fiery lake of burning sulfur. They were eager, as Chuck described, how Harmagedon would play out.

"Our plan will commence with one seminal action. First *we assassinate the president of the United States*."

There was stunned silence in the room.

Chuck continued, "As vice president, I will automatically ascend to the presidency. I will use my executive privilege to declare war on the enemies of the Western world. I will sign executive orders to bomb the Muslim hordes in the ISIS strongholds, nuke the Chinese islands in the South China Sea, and bomb the Russian Black Sea Navy fleet at the shipyards of Sevastopol, Ukraine, and wipe out both the North Korean and the Iranian nuclear sites back to the Stone Age!"

"Yeaaaaaaaah!" They loved every word of it. It was exactly what they wanted. They could smell blood in the air.

Chuck did not miss a beat. "Just when the world thinks it has had enough of the apocalypse, we will engineer a stock market crash in America and Europe to pummel even the strongest to craven submission. Then, with the world on its knees, we will *reset the Western world back to its Christian roots*!"

He raised his glass with the aplomb of a master showman.

The men rose in a standing ovation. This was the retaliation for all the brutal murders they had watched on the TV screens and the tales of Communist artifice and guile against Western interests. They wanted revenge. They wanted blood. Not just an eye for an eye. They wanted total damnation of their enemies. The slate had to be wiped clean. No more Muslims and Communists in their lives. They should pay for their sins tenfold. After all the gloom of the evening, Chuck had described a truly magnificent plan, something that would change the world order. They liked it. It truly suited the aims of the Cabal of Christian Crusaders as evinced in their insignia, which hung high above the fireplace—a blue pyramid within three red *C*s. The cabal guaranteed a completely new world order.

It was their sacred duty to reshape the world as they saw fit. Back to a Christian way of life. They had to reclaim the world from other religions and return it to how it used to be, run from the capitals of the Christian, Western world. Not by Communists from China or Russia. Not by Muslims or followers of other religions. They had waited far too long on the sidelines, watching the so-called liberals bargain away every Western value and kowtow to political correctness, which dictated that one said "Happy Holidays" and not "Merry Christmas," lest it hurt the sensibilities of people of other religions that had been imported into America. That same political correctness meant that those who spoke against Muslims in Britain risked being arrested for racial bigotry. Other faiths had come to the West and effectively changed the Christian way of life that had existed for generations. But all that had to come to a stop. They were going to act. They were going to create a new world order.

"Welcome to dinner, everyone." Gunther was the perfect host.

CHAPTER THREE

The Hunt Begins

"I have located Cynthia." Ash was elated as she looked at her father. "Not much sleuthing there, Dad. As I guessed, a call to the *Daily Sentinel* did the trick. She did leave a forwarding address. But she had moved and I had to follow several addresses until I found her right here in Kings, Brooklyn!"

"Well, isn't that smart of my investigative reporter of a daughter," Matt said. "So, when do we get to see her?"

"Ah, thanks, Dad. All I have is an address. I need to look up 1134 Manhattan Avenue, Brooklyn. Let me go check it out. I hope she hasn't taken off to some other European location. If I get to see her, I can assure you, it will blow her away to see me. She'll be surprised when I tell her about Mom. Obviously, I couldn't tell her about the CIA part of her job earlier."

"I'm sure she'll understand why you couldn't."

"One thing I can assure you, Dad: you *will* like her. Something about her inspires confidence and great love. She was one heck of a helpful person. For someone like me starting out, Cynthia was a lifeline. If not for her, I would have been doing something else now. I owe it her for what I am today. She showed me the ropes. She was almost a surrogate mom to me when I was at the *Daily Sentinel.* If she hears about what happened to Mom, she is going to be shocked. If she knows anything at all, she will help us."

"If you can say that about someone other than your mother, then I am already looking forward to meeting your mentor."

Matt was honest. If this woman had been such a strong influence on his daughter, then she must be a good person. Ashley would not let anyone close to the high pedestal on which she kept her mother's memory. If Cynthia was close enough to Ashley to have been a surrogate to her, then she must be special. He looked forward to meeting her.

"See you soon, Dad."

After she left, Matt picked up his phone and called Kareem. They spoke at length, but there wasn't much to go on. Kareem promised to drop by that afternoon.

Matt hoped Ashley would find Cynthia. That was the best possible lead they had. Cynthia had been in Germany with Amy. Her boyfriend Ryan had worked in the same bank. He had been murdered. That was a smoking gun. Matt was certain Cynthia would be able to shed some light on Amy's death.

While he waited for his daughter, Matt thought it was time he learned a bit more about the G & H Bayerischer Bank in Munich. This bank where people got killed needed some looking into. For the past year, he had assumed the circumstances of Amy's death were suspect. But even as he had waited for the agency and the German police to complete their investigations, it had never crossed his mind to connect G & H to her death. Now that Kareem had dropped the bombshell that Amy's colleague Ryan had been murdered, his mind was in turmoil.

If there were any murky dealings going on below the shiny surface of this monolith of a Bavarian bank, he was going to find out about them. He was going to unearth them, even if he had to pick the entire edifice apart, brick by brick. If it took all his life, he would do it. Amy deserved that. Nothing else mattered. Life had no meaning if he could not get justice for Amy. He sat at his computer and searched for anything and everything he could find on the G & H bank, from its inception to the board of governors, their activities, subsidiaries, employees—anything he could read up on. At first, all he found were the glossy stories of how it was a powerful German bank established in 1840, with subsidiaries in more than sixty countries, more than a hundred thousand employees, and an asset base in excess of €2.8 billion. Impressive, Matt thought.

G & H's core business, he read, was in investment banking, with 50 percent equity and 85 percent of leverage assets. It offered services such as sales, trading, mergers, acquisitions, derivatives, fund management, insurance, wealth management, and corporate management. With an operating income of more than €10 billion, G & H revenue for the previous year had been €54 billion. That was the grand façade of the bank. Matt searched for scandals related to G & H. He hit pay dirt. Recent investigations by the German Federal Financial Supervisory Authority and the German Public Prosecutor's office pointed to financial irregularities.

He was shocked at the reports. G & H was facing accusations of financial malfeasance. There was an allegation of severe tax evasion, money laundering, and collusion with other banks to manipulate the key global interest rate, the Libor. There was also some talk of insider trading in stocks, and publication of falsified financial reports that inflated revenues and assets and understated expenses and liabilities. Matt read that G & H had effectively battled all this with a multimillion-dollar PR campaign while at the same time tearing down the allegations in the German courts with an army of lawyers.

Amy had been stationed inside this bank! She had gone nosing into the spider's web. She may have thought it was merely a routine investigation she had been asked to carry out, about alleged improprieties at the bank in relation to American interests on behalf of the CIA. Her terms of reference were to track illegal money, drug or terrorism related, and figure out if it had emanated from the United States or was being funneled back home from Germany The CIA would treat that as information that could help the FBI track and prosecute perpetrators in the United States. It was quite possible she had been looking at large transactions and the accounts of the bank's top-tier clients.

But although her principal job may have been exploratory, Matt could now see that Amy had been working for a bank that was involved in shady dealings. That information hadn't been made public at the time, but he could see that she had walked into a lion's den. What did she unearth at the G & H that had warranted her not living to tell the tale? Was it information about the bank? One of their large investors? Was it some other reason that he could not fathom? Matt did not know. But one thing he was assured of: Amy had *not* died accidentally. Whatever had caused her death, it was connected to G & H Bayerischer Bank. How he wished he had looked up the bank a long time ago. He had waited close to a year for both the CIA and the German police to complete extensive investigations. Not once during that period had he had any suspicions about the bank. If he had, he would have pushed the authorities to do something about it. Matt checked the dates of the reports he had just researched. All the information was fairly new, having been made available long after Amy's death. No wonder the agency and the German police had not investigated them.

The bank was big. Although this new information gave him some hope of zooming in on his search for answers to Amy's death within the bank, it was as good as saying the murderer was on a mountain. Where in this giant monolith of a bank was, he going to start searching for answers? It was like searching for the proverbial needle in a haystack. Who could have had her killed? Matt leaned back in his chair, closed his eyes, and thought deeply. Whoever had the ability to decide to snuff out someone's life could not have been on the lower rungs of the echelon. Whoever held the say over life and death was no ordinary clerk or manager. Whoever had played God in such a situation was an omnipotent deity or someone close to such a figure, in an organization as large as G & H.

He sat up at his computer again and scrolled down the screen to the board of governors. He skimmed through the list of the board members, read their brief bios, and looked at their images. He went through several of the seemingly eminent pillars of German society, their financial acumen and unimpeachable standards of integrity described in glowing terms. He scrolled through them several times and finally came to rest on the face of the chairman of the bank, Herr Gunther Otto Heinrich. Gunther was a seventy-year-old man with steel-gray hair, sharp Slavic features, and the piercing light blue eyes of a shark. Matt looked at his eyes. They seemed to be devoid of life, empty of emotion, and eerily looked right through him. He exuded the quiet power that comes with great wealth and the assured calmness of a man who controlled a vast empire—a god, to lesser mortals.

Matt wanted to investigate Gunther first. Then he would work his way down the ladder, through each member of the board, the CEO, the vice presidents, and so on. For now, Gunther was *numero uno* on his list. Gunther was the highest authority in the G & H bank—the equivalent of God in that organization. Was he the god who had given the order to have Amy killed? Matt didn't know. He looked again at the icy blue shark eyes. Something deep down his psyche seemed to stir. He felt the raw emotion of a hunter in the wild. He could smell blood in the air. He was back in the field. It was Desert Storm all over again.

"Hi, Dad. Guess who's here."

"Ah, dear, this must be your mentor at the *Daily Sentinel*. Cynthia, I presume."

Matt was on his feet, walking toward the woman beside his daughter. She looked to be in her mid- to late thirties and was tall, slender, and attractive. Despite her faded jeans and plain T-shirt, she had a commanding presence. Her bright blue eyes sparkled with an inner glow as she smiled broadly and stuck her hand out toward Matt. There was something about Cynthia that Matt could not put his finger on. Something familiar. Something that harkened to Amy.

"So, I finally get to meet Ashley's favorite person in the world. She never stopped talking about you." Cynthia did not take her eyes off Matt. She was impressed, seeing the man who was such a huge influence on his daughter. Such men were few and far between. "She hardly spoke about her mom. Well, I now know she could not, because of Amy's work with the agency. But you were always tops. She never got tired of telling me how fortunate she was to have a father like you. So, I must say, the pleasure to meet Ashley's role model is all mine!" Her handshake was firm.

"Thanks, Cynthia. Having Ash has been a gift. I hear you have also been a great influence on her. She speaks a lot about you."

Cynthia was good at reading people fast. She noticed that Matt had a charming personality with an infectious warmth that spread to those around him. He was not only tall and good-looking, but also sported the calm demeanor of someone who was in control of his life. She guessed it was not wanton pride that he exuded but a sense of control over his destiny and those around him. She could tell he was the type who knew where he was going and how to get there. He had that sense of quiet power that comes from knowledge and years of training and not the brash arrogance she had seen in so many men she had come across in life. If Cynthia was impressed, she did not show it. But the semblance of a smile on her face belied her otherwise featureless expression.

Ashley noticed that smile or something close to it on Cynthia's face. It was a fleeting expression, but if it was real, nothing would please Ashley more. Her father had been lonely for a long time. She was even worried for him. And there was no one more eligible to fill that gap in her father's life than Cynthia. She had been like a mother to Ashley. She was a genuine person. She had also suffered the same fate as her dad when her boyfriend was killed. They were both lost in a well of despair and gloom. She smiled to herself. Cynthia had barely walked in, and here she was matchmaking. Well, she loved her father intensely. What daughter would not dream of a happy life for a dad as wonderful as hers?

"Thanks, Dad. Let me get you guys some coffee while you get to know each other." She was genuinely not matchmaking but letting them be. *Just offering coffee*, she told herself, but she smiled wickedly anyway. She didn't care. For now, these were her best two people, and they were going to find out what had happened to her mom. She could see that they had hit it off on a good note, chatting away, being warm and friendly in a short span of time. She did not push her mind to imagine anything more.

She smiled again and added in a conspiratorial hush, "Cynthia has some great news, Dad. She gave me a heads-up on our way here. From the little I got to hear, it's explosive! Let me get the coffee. I want to hear the details."

"Let's sit outside." Matt led the way to the deck and helped Cynthia to a chair.

"I am sorry about Amy," Cynthia said. "I truly am. It must have been hard on both of you. I, too, as you are aware by now, have had to contend with the loss. Ryan was good to me. I was very happy. I knew he was hoping to pop the question. I found an engagement ring in his pocket. But that was after he was murdered. Ryan never got to ask me to marry him. That hurts, Matt. And I am angry. So, I know you and Ashley are in a bad place."

She did not cry, but Cynthia felt strangely at peace confiding in Matt. He had been a total stranger to her until just a moment ago. It was either that he had suffered the same loss she had or that he was the type who instilled confidence in people around him—Cynthia did not know. But she felt at ease unloading her mind.

"Yes, Cynthia. It's not been easy. I have been away on active duty in the Middle East and had finally come home. It was a dream to come back home. Time to spend time with Amy. More so with Ashley. We had missed being with our daughter for long periods of time. We had planned on doing so many things together. Amy had always wanted us to travel to Europe as a family. She also loved hiking and trekking in the woods—camping and all sorts of simple stuff families get to do together. We just wanted time for ourselves after all the wars and the cloak-and-dagger stuff. Losing Amy has not been easy. So yes,

Cynthia, I can feel your loss. It must have been hard. I am so sorry for what happened."

"Thanks, Matt."

"Here's the coffee." Ashley handed out the cups and curled up on one of the deck chairs "Okay, Cynthia, I am dying to hear it all."

Cynthia took a sip of the coffee and said, "G & H Bayerischer Bank is not what it seems from the outside."

"I learned as much from a few hours of online research about its murky business dealings," Matt said. "I was looking up its board of directors, starting from their chairman, Herr Gunther Otto Heinrich, when you guys came in. So, go right ahead, I am all ears!"

"You could not have been more right, Matt," Cynthia picked up again. "Gunther, that cold bastard who runs the bank, is as shady as they come. Under that thin veneer of cultured sophistication and that smug, wealthy countenance is a deathly cold person. Someone who can easily eliminate anyone who dares cross his path."

"He sure looks it," Matt agreed as the word *eliminate* evoked ugly images of death in his mind. Death and Amy.

Cynthia began, "To better understand how and why they killed Ryan, I need to give you a little more background."

Cynthia's eyes were moist when she spoke of her murdered boyfriend, but she was a strong woman and held an even tone. "Ryan was an IT consultant for the bank. He was an expert at the Scorecard, created by the *Wall Street Journal* and Dialogic, that keeps track of investment banking revenue by product, region, and bank worldwide. For G & H that was big, as it was in investment banking across several nations. He also managed the bank's IT security, use of magnetic ink character recognition, imaging technology for check clearing, networking and building real-time databases to help forecast liquidity."

She went on, "It was that part of investment banking that brought him close to Amy. Both Americans working in a German bank, they became good friends, and all of us had some great times together. But I must be honest: I had no idea your wife was working for the CIA. In fact, when Ashley told me that this morning, I was shocked. God, I did not even know she was Ashley's mother. Looking back now, I know she could not confide in us about her cover. Just like Ashley could not tell me."

Matt just raised his eyebrows, tilted his head sideways, and smiled at Cynthia with a telling look that said it was understandable that Amy could not disclose the real nature of her employment at the bank.

Cynthia sipped at the coffee and said, "A few months into the job, Ryan felt uncomfortable about something, and he confided in me. As part of his job, he often had to work in the offices of the chairman and other senior officers of the bank. On one such occasion, while setting up some security systems on Gunther's computer, Ryan noticed several election leaflets on his table. Ryan could not help noticing that they were all from extreme far-right parties, some of which actually advocated for violence against Muslims and immigrants. He saw brochures from the Alternative für Deutschland party, the neo-Nazi German Reich party, the National Democratic Party, and the ultra-right-wing Patriotic Europeans Against the Islamization of the West. Have you heard of them?"

Receiving blank expressions from both, Cynthia continued. "The AfD party is an extreme far-right-wing party that advocates against immigration, especially Muslim immigration. It is alleged that Frauke Petry, one of its leaders, twice advocated for shooting refugees at the borders to Germany. Xenophobic and leaning toward Russia, the AfD had recently called for a ban on all Islamic symbols, including burkas, minarets, and their call to prayer, because they thought Islam was not part of Germany."

Ashley said, "Like I said before, that is blatant xenophobia in a man holding such a high office!"

"Yes, it was, Ash," Cynthia said. "That was why Ryan was shocked to see the election materials on the table of the most powerful and influential man in the bank. He did not give it much thought at the time, though. Later that evening we saw on TV that Frauke Petry, the AfD leader, was planning to speak at the famous Hofbräukeller beer hall, where Adolf Hitler had spoken. The reporter was making a connection between the two. That's when Ryan told me about the AfD election pamphlet and the brochures of the numerous other parties that he had seen in Gunther's office. Again, we did not think much of it at that time."

Cynthia finished the coffee, placed it on the table, and continued. "Several other unrelated incidents then brought Gunther's name back into focus. The head of the IT department at G & H was a very jovial guy called Gerhard. From the time they met, Ryan and Gerhard hit it off, and they often went out for beers together. One day when Ryan was on his way back from the vice president's office, he saw Gerhard storming out of Gunther's office. Gunther had fired him, and Gerhard was livid. That evening they had a few beers, and Gerhard got drunk and blurted out, 'Gunther, that bloody Nazi son of a bitch! Where do you think he got his surname Heinrich from? He was sired by Karl Wolfe and Hedwig Potthast!'"

Cynthia smiled when she described that part. "Gerhard was suggesting that Gunther was the offspring of Hitler's confidante Karl Wolfe and Hedwig Potthast, mistress of his Nazi party colleague, Heinrich Himmler. We were unsure about the alleged relationship and whether Gunther was their illegitimate child. But he easily could have been, for he surely behaved like a Nazi animal, if not worse."

Cynthia went on. "Ryan spent several weeks in Gunther's office while he was setting up a private email server and a videoconferencing facility. This was to help Gunther stay in touch with his divisions worldwide as well as retain a secure portal that only he had access to. Ryan would spend hours in his office and other times working on the several banks of computers and servers in his private back office. On one such occasion, Ryan walked in from the server room to Gunther's office. Gunther was on a scrambler phone speaking to someone in English. Ryan heard him say, 'Yes, Chuck, we will meet at my chateau. Yes, Christian, Englebert, Aleixandre, and Raymond will join us. Harmagedon is on! The timing will depend on you getting the Fox ... Yes, yes, I know it may take a few months. Sure, I'll await your word. Agreed, will inform others only when I have a confirmation from you. Thanks, Chuck ... Bye for now.'

"Suddenly Gunther noticed that he was not alone. He quickly disconnected the phone and looked away. Ryan left soon afterward, but not before he had noticed the look of guilt on Gunther's face—as though he'd been caught in the act. Ryan had no idea why Gunther would feel that way. He did not know who Chuck was or any of the others he was talking about. The strange thing was the scrambler. Gunther had secure phone connections and a heavily secure, private email server. All he had to secure were banking secrets, and for that, the IT setup Ryan had built for him was foolproof enough. Scramblers on phones are used by security agencies, the FBI, and the like. Ryan was surprised that Gunther would use one to arrange what seemed to be some sort of a party of friends. What was a Harmagedon? Some sort of German sauerkraut? And 'get a fox'? Was it a hunting party? He had no idea."

"Can I get you some more coffee?" Ashley asked.

"No thanks, dear," Cynthia replied before resuming. "So, in the evening, Ryan and I would discuss this powerful German chairman of a bank, allegedly sired by Himmler's mistress, who was planning some kind of secret meeting at some chateau. Gerhard did confirm that Gunther had a chateau in the Bavarian countryside. On one of those occasions Amy was dining with us, and we told her the story. She too had a good laugh. But a few weeks later, Ryan got something explosive. He was so agitated. He called me and said he was actually frightened. In an apparent effort to cloak the name, he said that 'Potthast's son' was deadlier than he had imagined. Amy was not at work that day. He asked me to bring her along and meet him at the Augustiner Großgaststätten beer hall, which we often went to."

Cynthia's expression turned somber, and her tone mellowed. "I changed and rushed there. I called Amy and asked her to join me, and she arrived just a little while later. We discussed what Ryan had said as we waited for him. We waited for a long time that night. But he never turned up and calls to his phone went unanswered." Cynthia looked down, paused for a moment, and then, looking Matt in the eye, said, "I never saw Ryan alive again. Just like that. He calls me, says he is frightened, and suggests that Gunther is dangerous. And then he is gone. Amy and I went to the apartment where Ryan and I lived." Cynthia swallowed hard and said in a resigned tone, "We found him lying on the rug. He was dead. Someone had shot him, brought his bullet-ridden body to our place, and thrown it there."

Cynthia bit her lip and looked away. There were tears in her eyes. Matt shot up instinctively and reached out and placed his hand on Cynthia's shoulder.

"I am sorry to hear that. You don't need to continue. We can do this later. I'm sorry."

"No, no, I'm fine." Cynthia had regained her composure. But she looked up at Matt. Though she did not show it, she felt safe at that instant. "I need to be strong. I need justice for Ryan. Crying will not help me. That's why when Ashley called me, I came. I wanted to tell you this. So together we can find out who killed our loved ones and why and make them pay!"

Ashley had brought her a box of tissues. She wiped her eyes and went on.

"I was devastated, seeing Ryan's body tossed on the rug like a rag doll. Amy was with me throughout and was a great help. She advised me to pack up and leave immediately. Ryan had found something on the chairman of the bank and was dead within hours. She thought the fact that his body had been left at our place was possibly a message to me. Someone wanted me to be afraid and run. They might have thought I did not know much and would be safer out of the way. She did not think it was safe for me to stay. After I finished with the police, Amy helped me pack and go back to America with Ryan's body."

Cynthia said, "I don't know what Ryan saw. I don't know who killed him. In all probability, Amy may have cranked up her investigation when she saw Ryan killed. And the same forces that eliminated Ryan must have had her killed her as well. I am certain that whoever did this is directly connected to Gunther, the chairman of G & H bank. A year later the German police informed me that they had no clues and were forced to close the case.

"I did not believe they had done a good job." Cynthia was clearly upset. "But I was alone and helpless. I tried talking to a lot of people here about my hunches. No one would believe me. I remembered Amy's warning and decided against returning to Bavaria to investigate. Whoever had killed Ryan would not have had much difficulty getting me out of the way. I tried calling

Amy. Her phone went unanswered. If I had known she had a family, I would have come to you right away.

"I'm angry. Ryan and my friend, both killed? We have to get them, Matt. Ash, we have to get all of them. We must get all the sorry Nazi bastards who did this to Ryan and Amy. I am ready to do anything to help."

"A meeting in some chateau in Bavaria and a bunch of names is all we have." Matt heaved a sigh as he began to see some light at the end of the tunnel. "But it's something that I intend to work on."

"And a fox hunting party?" Ashley asked. "What or who is that? Har- *what*?"

"Harmagedon," Matt said. "No idea what that is. Until now all I had were accident reports and hunches that led nowhere. Amy died a few weeks after Ryan's passing. Interesting that the investigating agencies did not see a connection between two Americans working for the same bank dying so close to each other. But now, thanks to you and Kareem, I firmly believe that Amy was *eliminated.* Just like Ryan was. Amy probably upped her investigation and walked in somewhere and was caught in the act. Or someone assumed Ryan told Amy something, and silenced her. I think it's about time I paid Herr Gunther Otto Heinrich, the chairman of G & H bank, a visit."

"Matt, for Ryan's sake and for Amy's, I want in." Cynthia looked determined. "I don't know how I can help, but please make me a part of your team. For the first time in a year, I feel close to Ryan. Like I am doing something to help bring his killers to book."

"I'm in too. This is for Mom. And I will not take no for an answer, Dad!" Ashley looked even more determined than Cynthia.

"Now, that's a team!" Matt felt he was back in the army and putting together a dream team to cross behind enemy lines.

Though he worried that he would be placing Ashley's and Cynthia's lives in danger, he also knew there would be no stopping them on this particular hunt. With Kareem to help, Matt was confident he could ensure their safety on a dangerous mission like this.

"Who's talking about a team?" Kareem could not have entered at a better time.

"Yes, KK, just the man I was thinking of!" Matt sounded excited for the first time. "Meet Cynthia. We have just formed a team, buddy. All of us! By the time you are up to speed with the events, be ready. We are going to Bavaria, Germany!"

"Hi Cynthia," Kareem introduced himself. "Matt, I have just been drafted into the presidential security detail for his upcoming visit to the United Nations. So, I am grounded in the homeland, buddy."

"But I thought the Presidential Protective Division of the Secret Service decided who did that. Since when did the FBI get to do the job of the Secret Service?"

Matt was already worried. Without Kareem, the trip to Bavaria with his daughter and Cynthia had just gotten trickier. He had agreed to take the women along because he had banked on Kareem and his FBI background to help keep them secure while sniffing around in Bavaria. Now he suddenly felt very alone in the enterprise.

Kareem responded, "Exceptional situations call for exceptional changes to the norm. There has been some intel from the Terrorist Threat Integration Center that occasioned my inclusion with the Secret Service. The law book also guarantees that in the event any harm befalls the protectee, the jurisdiction of the investigation falls upon the FBI. Nothing is bound to happen, but my director wants me in on it, just in case. This is the most powerful man on earth on the move, buddy. No one wants to take any chances!"

"He is my commander in chief, too," Matt said, accepting the situation. "You better stick to your call of duty. I planned this trip to Germany with you, and now I'll have to manage. Don't worry—we will figure it out. Promise me that as soon as your temporary duty is over, you will hop over to Munich and help us in the investigation. I am so looking forward to having you on our team. Feels a lot safer."

Kareem was quick to respond to that. "That, Matt, is not just a promise, but my duty. As soon as I'm free, I'll apply for a week's emergency furlough and fly to Bavaria. But for now, let me make some calls and ensure you have some help while you're there. Remember this, though: be very careful. Do not go snooping around in the wrong places. Losing Amy was bad enough. I will not let you get yourself, Ashley, and this lovely lady in trouble."

"No sir, Special Agent Kareem Khan." Matt at least had a smile for a change. Kareem was happy to see his buddy in a jovial mood after a long time. "Now let me update you with what Cynthia told us. Trust me, it will blow your socks off." They all sat down over a beer as Cynthia went through her account. Kareem listened carefully.

When Cynthia was through with her narration of the incidents, Kareem sounded very serious. "This seems quite a dangerous situation, Matt. I am aware of G & H bank and its nefarious activities. For several reasons, I cannot go into all those details. I was aware of Ryan's death. Mitch had told me. But Ryan was not an agent, and the only interest we had was the fact that it was the death of an American on foreign soil. We informed the embassy, and they managed the case. The local police investigated Ryan's death for a year but didn't end up with any arrests. G & H is a large corporation with thousands of employees, and much as it strikes us as strange that two Americans died so close to each other, the German police did not see any connection in that. One was a murder and the other was a hit-and-run."

Kareem went on, "In hindsight, it seems like both cases should have been investigated as one. But trust me, at that time there was no apparent connection between the murder of an IT contractor and the accidental killing of a CIA operative. In Ryan's case, there were no fingerprints, no eyewitnesses, and no enemies, and there was nothing to follow up on. Ryan's file was closed after a year. Amy's case was similar in that there were no clues and it was closed after a similar amount of time." Kareem looked at Cynthia and said, "Sorry, ma'am. I honestly am."

Cynthia dipped her head in gratitude.

Matt suggested what he thought could have happened. "Already scared that Ryan had overheard something, Gunther and his team must have been on edge when they possibly caught Amy riffling through something. Poor Amy probably wanted to corroborate some more facts, but that German bastard surprised her and snuffed her out." Matt's lips curled inward. Anger was writ large on his steely countenance.

Ashley walked out of the room. It was hard to imagine someone "snuffing out" her mother. Cynthia followed her out.

"Sorry, buddy," Kareem added. "I am so sorry. There was no way we could have known. We did not know about Cynthia. How I wish now that someone had looked up Cynthia and gotten her version about Ryan's disclosures. Things would have been different. That German bastard would not be sitting plum like he is right now. Anyway, I must report this matter. I know I am not supposed to let you handle this investigation, especially on foreign soil. But I know you, Matt. You will go anyway. So, I am going to look the other way. But remember, this looks a lot more dangerous now than it seemed earlier. So please, for my sake and for Amy's sake, be very careful. Do not put Ashley's or

Cynthia's life in harm's way. I will speak to Mitch in Cologne to offer you some cover. But please just investigate from afar and report to Mitch. Let him handle it. I will join you as soon as I am through with my duties here."

Cynthia and Ashley came back in. Ashley's eyes were bloodshot. It was evident she had been crying.

Matt looked at Kareem and said, "I will, KK. I can't lose Ashley. I am sure Ryan won't forgive me if I put Cynthia in harm's way. We'll be careful, KK—very, very careful."

"Thanks, Kareem," Cynthia said. "I know you are a federal agent and that allowing us to travel to foreign countries to play spies is not something your bosses would approve of. But from what I hear, Amy was a good friend of yours. If Amy's death was not accidental, but a result of someone's conscious design, then I am sure you too would love to bring the culprits to book. But for now, all we are doing is going there to learn more. We have lost our loved ones. Amy and Ryan are both gone. All we want to know are some more facts. We assure you that we will not play cloak-and-dagger schemes. We will just look around and try to pick up anything that tells us if there was foul play. I am sure Matt here will report to you. You can pick up the investigation from there."

"Thanks, Cynthia." Kareem felt better. "I trust Matt. He is a soldier and knows the rules. I know both you and Ashley are safe with him. I also know all of you will be careful. Thanks for assuring me. Okay, guys, let me make some arrangements in Cologne. I will be back before you leave. See you all soon."

As he walked away, Kareem kept thinking of one of the names Ryan had heard Gunther mention. Something nagging at the back of his mind was telling him he had heard it before in connection with something else. But he could not quite put his finger on it. It would come to him, Kareem knew. Still scratching his head, he drove off.

CHAPTER FOUR

The Plot

"I present … the Fox," Chuck Scott said, waving his remote toward the large TV on the wall. The darkened silhouette of a man's face appeared on the screen, and the Fox's metallic robotic voice boomed across the room:

"Good evening, gentlemen It is in our best interest that we not see each other. Contact with me has been made through intermediaries, and I do not have the foggiest idea who you are or where you are based. I have been given a contract. And that contract comes with a price. I have been paid half the agreed amount, and the project is on. I will now ask the host to screen the image of the target, so we are all clear in our objective."

Glasses were being refilled. Wine and whiskey were being downed. There was an air of excitement in the room. The Fox's image faded out, and the screen filled with images of Hollywood's glitterati, beltway insiders, federal officials, lobbyists, and the jet set of the corporate media, all assembled in the Washington Hilton. Then against the backdrop of the strident drumbeat of military music from the United States Marine

Band and the Joint Armed Forces Color Guard, the baritone voice of the master of ceremonies announced, "Ladies and gentlemen, please welcome the president of the United States and first lady Elizabeth Harrison."

The men in tuxedos and women in designer dresses stood at the Washington correspondents' dinner to applaud as the marines marched in through the aisles to present the colors and played the "Star Spangled Banner." From behind the curtains in strode Andrew William Harrison, the president of the United States. He walked to center stage and stood with his right palm on his heart. The camera panned over the crowd and slowly came to rest on the face of the most powerful man on the face of the earth, President Harrison.

"That, gentlemen, is my target," the Fox said. "Trust me, he will be eliminated." With that, the screen went dark.

Chuck continued, "In a career that has spanned a little over three decades, this elusive, shadowy figure, the Fox, whom you just had the rare honor to hear from directly, has been responsible for more than fifty assassinations across several continents. That list includes prime ministers, chief justices, journalists, and presidents. It is rumored that he has not failed in a single mission. Some say he learned his trade from Carlos 'the Jackal' himself—the notorious Venezuelan terrorist Illich Ramirez Sanchez. So, he came highly recommended when we sent out the word. It took us a few months to hear from him and negotiate the deal. A payment of five million has been made. We will pay the rest upon completion. He needs some information on the POTUS. I don't know what, exactly, but I am willing to help."

Gunther said, "He probably needs to know where the president will be and when, and information about his security detail and such that I am sure you can help with. Be careful: we do not want you involved directly in the situation. You are, after all, to be the next president of the United States."

Chuck nodded gratefully and said, "I'll be careful. I have never spoken to the Fox. He does not communicate via phone. All I get are encrypted emails with fake names. So, I will ensure he has all the information he needs for the job. Unless he completes his contract, we do not have a project. Between getting the Fox and setting up Harmagedon, it has taken us close to a year. So, rest assured, the Fox will get what he wants. I am at his service."

Gunther was impressed. "I am sure the Fox will succeed. His credentials are sterling, and we have no cause for concern. When Harrison is out of the scene, Chuck, the VPOTUS and first in the presidential line of succession, will ascend to the presidency of the United States. Join me, friends, in proposing a loyal toast to Robert Chuck Scott Jr., the president of the United States!"

There was loud and raucous cheering. "To the president!" Gunther said, and everyone raised their glasses. Chuck stood up, raised his glass to his friends, and smiled.

Gunther continued, "We will then change the face of this world once and for all. We will set the clock right. We will get things done and take the country back to the way it was, to a Christian order of things and a way of life we were all used to. With executive power guaranteed to the president under Article Two, Section One of the American Constitution, Chuck will have his way, even if it means he may be impeached later." Gunther clicked on his remote, and the large screen displayed maps of Syria and Iraq. "He will sign executive orders to carpet-bomb the ISIS morons in Syria and Iraq, nuke the bloody artificial islands the Chinese built in the South China Sea to kingdom come, and wipe out that fat pig Kim Jung Un."

Gunther's voice matched the fire in the eyes of his colleagues, who sat in rapt attention, gloating over the description of the death and destruction of all the enemies of the free world as they saw it. Gunther's list rattled on—choke Crimea, bomb the Russian Black Sea Navy fleet and shipyards at Sevastopol, Ukraine, bomb Teheran's suspected nuclear sites, stop illegal immigration, deport Muslims back to their countries of origin, and make the West "pure" again.

"To the president of the United States!" Volker was happy to hear about the "purity" of the West and prophesied, "This will be the Second Crusade to stop westward-marching Muslim hordes," referring to the eleventh-century call to arms by Pope Urban II in support of Byzantine Emperor Alexios I's battle to stop westward-migrating Turks in Anatolia.

Gunther went on, "Yes, Volker, history seems to be repeating itself centuries later with the present Muslim invasion of the West, and yes, we need to reclaim Christendom once again. Just as Pope Urban II assured, God will forgive us for all our sins, the plenary indulgences and even time spent in purgatory. That is why we are known as Christian crusaders."

He went on, "In the hope of getting mass support for Chuck's unilateral call to arms, we need to get the people of the world to support us. The only way they will do that and not rise against American intervention in these countries is if we put the masses in a sea of misery. It's only when a man has a pain of his own that he will stop to ignore the common cause and search inward to serve his own interests. To explain how we hope to make the populace turn inward to their own selfish needs, permit me to invite the CEO of Webster Coleman Brokerage of the United Kingdom, our dear friend Raymond Webster Coleman!"

There was loud applause for their host's impassioned pitch and a warm welcome for Raymond. For his sixty-odd years, Ray had a large frame and a commanding presence.

"When they said Chuck is a heartbeat away from the presidency, the Americans probably did not know that he would make it come true!" Ray said.

Everyone had a good laugh. Raymond raised his glass toward the president-in-waiting and mouthed silent cheers, and then turned to address his colleagues. "Selfishness is at the core of every human being. When people fear losing what makes them feel safe—their houses or money in the bank—their world tends to crumble inward. When they face the possibility of penury and being thrown onto the streets, the average mans will tends to buckle. Survival becomes the driving force. Brother will rise against brother. Cain will kill Abel. That is why, when Chuck lets out the dogs of war, we cannot afford for public opinion to be swayed toward impeachment or pause the carnage we have started before we've achieved our goals. We want people to think about themselves and not have the rationality to form public opinion. Toward that end, we will engineer a stock market crash across the Western world!"

"Really?" Christian was clearly impressed and egged Ray on. "You mean, we can *engineer* one?"

Raymond was in his element. He explained the historical parallel. "Oh sure, Christian, we can and we most certainly *will*. On September 3, 1929, the Dow Jones Industrial Average stood at 381 points. But by November, the Dow had lost 89 percent of its value, leading to the Great Depression in the US, the worst stock market crashes the world has seen. If history has taught us anything, it is only that *we do not learn anything*. In 2008, we repeated the same mistakes as the subprime loans and credit default led to the collapse of Lehman Brothers and more than fifteen banks in America."

Christian seemed impressed. The others listened in rapt attention as Ray built his case. "Panic by any name is just that—panic. If we can fuel it appropriately, we can engineer a meltdown of the markets. Human beings will behave like animals if they are pushed to extremes. Because unlike the stock market crashes of 1929 and 2008, which were natural, what we hope to unleash now is a *systematically planned crash* aimed at creating panic, resulting in more selling, further panic, and a crash. In today's climate, this is not hard to achieve. As I said, history teaches us only that we learn nothing. To put that in perspective, gentlemen, you may remember that when Lehman Brothers filed for bankruptcy at the height of the 2008 stock market crash, the American default rate was only 2.96 percent! Today the US corporate default rate stands at 3.3 percent!"

"Why, then, have markets not already crashed?" Volker queried.

"Because after the 1987 Black Monday event when markets around the world crashed, the Securities and Exchange Commission, Financial Industry Regulatory Authority, and exchanges installed curbs to stop panic selling," Raymond explained. "Known as circuit breakers, these curbs temporarily halt trading for fifteen minutes when markets drop below certain levels and for the rest of the day if indexes dip below 20 percent."

"How will we pull off a market crash, if trading is stopped?" Volker asked.

"Simple," Ray said. "We need to prepare to engineer a crash *within* these circuit breakers."

Gunther was happy he had asked Raymond to lead the stock market project. As the head of a brokerage house, Ray had the knowledge, but he was also a master at the game. He knew not only the history of the market but also how to bend the rules, to achieve their devious ends. He looked around at the faces of his colleagues. If there had been a sense of impassivity until then, it was gone now. The room had suddenly gone quiet.

Ray continued, "Early this year, the Chinese stock market lost 7 percent overnight, the Dow dropped 911 points, more than 5 percent, and the Nasdaq fell by 3 percent. Derivative contracts, we know, are basically securities that are dependent on the future value of underlying assets such as stocks, bonds, market indexes, commodities, interest rates, and other factors that tend to fluctuate. Right now, just five US banks have in excess of 247 trillion dollars in derivatives, and globally that figure stands at a mind-boggling 552 trillion dollars, leading influential stock market gurus to see a looming crash and an economic meltdown. If banks worldwide can indulge in this type of gambling on the presumed value of paper assets, we can play our own little game."

"You mean 247 trillion dollars in assets held by US banks is not worth its face value?" Christian was clearly shocked.

"Let me put it like this," Ray said. "The banks may have insured the contracts, but if these banks fail, then even claims under Chapter 11 may net, say, only 20 percent on the dollar. If all five of the large banks that hold this colossal number of derivatives were to fail, almost 200 trillion dollars would be wiped out in an instant. If a 158-year-old company, the Lehman Brothers Investment Bank, could go bust with a debt of 619 billion dollars, leading to an erosion of more than 10 trillion dollars in the markets, need I say more?"

The men could see that natural causes of negligence could lead to failures and believed in Ray's capacity to engineer a collapse.

Assured that he had everyone's undivided attention, Ray said, "All we have to do is a bunch of fairly simple things." With that, he switched on the TV. The words *Pump and Dump* appeared in large letters on the screen. "We have all done this before, only this time around, we will do it on a much larger scale and across continents. We will buy heavily into previously unknown corporations, spike their stock prices by assuring massive profits in the offing through internet chat rooms, stock message boards, and use email spamming. People will start investing in it, hoping to make windfalls. We will wait until it's superheated enough and then, just before it comes to the notice of the SEC or other regulatory agencies, dump these stocks on the high."

Ray expounded, "We will make tons of money for ourselves while routing the market. Of course, markets will initiate circuit breakers and temporarily halt trading. We wait and do the same as soon as these curbs are lifted, pump and dump, over and over again, until we have not just milked the markets dry but also created enough carnage to cause the first ripples of an impending market crash. Trading curbs cannot be in place for ages."

Aleixandre Thierry agreed with Ray. "We must manipulate the trading curbs by sustained attacks. I am sure we can pull it off. Market curbs are temporary and meant to halt spikes such as fat-finger trading when a trader accidentally punches in more zeroes and causes panic. But markets have to function. After fifteen minutes or daylong breaks, markets will open. We attack again. We are, as Ray says, engineering a crash. This is not some wild fluctuation of the market. No one expects a large group such as ours to systematically play the market for days and weeks on end. No curbs will stop us."

"Thanks, Alex," Ray said. "We will create hundreds of boiler rooms," he said, a reference to a rented room where hundreds of stockbrokers, seated cheek by jowl, sell bogus stocks over rows of telephones to unsuspecting investors all over the country. "We will operate these from several countries and over the internet, so detection will be difficult. We offer microcap, thinly traded penny stocks of, say, five-dollar value in companies with less than 250-million-dollar market capitalization, pre-IPO stocks, and over-the-counter stocks. These companies are not required to file their financial reports with the SEC or other regulatory bodies. So, investors cannot check the veracity of the stocks that we are pumping up. They will be useless pieces of paper by the time we have dumped them."

Ray's voice rose as he concluded, "We have plans to 'short and distort,' driving down prices of good stocks first, buying them at the low and later selling them at a high. I will explain in detail how we also plan to rip off large institutionalized brokerages that account for half the combined wealth of their countries. All these schemes, carried out consistently for weeks on end and across the Atlantic, will lead to a meltdown of the markets. In 1929 it took just three days—Black Thursday on October 24, Black Monday on October 28, and Black Tuesday on October 29—to bring America to its knees and lead to the Great Depression." Ray stopped for a moment, looked at the faces of his colleagues, and said in measured tones, "A three-week engineered stock market crash that we have just discussed will bring the mighty governments on both sides of the pond to an *apocalyptic collapse*!"

"You are a past master at this game, Raymond." Alex raised his glass to the loud applause of all present.

Ray added, "Alex, Christian, and I will meet at my house in London next week to finalize plans to set up boiler rooms in several countries. We hope to rope in a massive number of potential clients, both individual and institutional ones. The idea is to wipe out the wealth of nations, not pinch a few coins. This will require a lot of skill to set up. With a background in the internet and real estate, Alex and Christian are both uniquely placed to provide the perfect support that I need to pull this off. Thank you all."

Raymond walked back to his seat amid thunderous applause from his friends.

"That," Christian Hannes added, "could be worse than the popping of the Dutch tulip bulb bubble that sent us into a depression lasting several years."

Gunther took the stage and said, "A lot worse, Christian, but unlike the Dutch Tulip Mania or the Great Depression in the US, we will destroy *so we can create again.* Unlike those years of pain, ours will be short lived. Remember, ours will be an engineered collapse. Like a phoenix, we will raise up the Western world in the Christian tradition from its death after the collapse of its markets. Our populations will see us as saviors of the market. But everyone in this room will be absolved of the vagaries of the destructive force we unleash. Our own corporations will reap unimaginable profits. We can run the Western Hemisphere from the conference rooms of our companies. *We will own the bloody world.* The cabal will rule."

Carried away by Gunther's words, Christian prophesied, "Strike down the nations, raze the high and mighty, vanquish the Muslim hordes and slaughter them. Like Christ appearing from among the clouds, riding on chariots of fire, we will descend upon our enemies and annihilate them. Our battle of the ages to forge a new world order, our Armageddon, is *now*!"

The applause was deafening.

★

"Game day is T minus seven days from now," Gwen Sanders, special agent in charge of the New York field office of the US Secret Service, said. "I believe our security advance is in full operational readiness."

She looked around the command center that had been set up in a downtown hotel. The room had been completely taken over by the Secret Service. All the furniture had been moved out and the bedrooms retrofitted as offices. Office equipment from Secret Service headquarters filled every available space. Gwen was a twenty-year veteran of the Secret Service and had come up the ranks. She had great respect for the fifty or so Secret Service agents who formed the Presidential Protective Division who sat facing her. They were the best type-A personalities, handpicked for the job of providing cover for the commander in chief, the first family, the vice president, and visiting heads of state.

They had been at this command center for three weeks now, putting together a security preparation—the "advance," as they called it when the president of the United States was on the move. All of them had worked hard. She was pleased. But she also knew no amount of preparation was good enough in today's day and age. All it took was one deranged person to upset their well-laid plans and take a potshot at the president.

"We have gone through the route POTUS will take several times now," Gwen said. "State and local police have worked with us in sweeping the entire route from the White House, where he will take off on Marine One, to his destination. Every possible sniper position or bomb threat, on land, air, and the river that runs this route has been neutralized with countermeasures. All of you have your positions along the route. The security bubble is airtight and impregnable. But it's precisely at moments like this that we need to question ourselves again—be our own devil's advocate. Is someone out there who is one step ahead of us? Is the bubble really impregnable? Are we being cocky?"

She looked around the room. No one spoke. No amount of preparation was ever enough. Anything could go wrong. All of them seated there knew about the failed attempts in recent history. If Lynette Fromme's Colt pistol had had a bullet in the firing chamber, Gerald Ford would have been killed in September 1975 and history would have been different. Within seventeen days of the first attempt on his life, another woman, Sara Jane Moore, had tried to shoot Ford from across the road. Ford was again saved when a bystander grabbed the shooter's hands and deflected the shot.

The agents facing Gwen knew only too well that there were many such instances, where the best-laid plans could fall painfully short. Like when John Hinckley shot at Ronald Regan and punctured his lungs, or when Francisco Duran fired twenty-nine times at the White House, assuming he was firing at Bill Clinton. Anything could happen. This was the most powerful man on earth on the move. A lot of people out there wanted to harm him. It was their mandate to protect the president, the symbol, and the office—with their lives, if need be.

"It is for this purpose that I have invited an FBI agent to be part of this advance." Gwen looked toward the back of the room and called out, "Please welcome Special Agent Kareem Khan." The crowd applauded as Kareem walked up to the front. "Kareem is part of the Interagency Terrorist Threat Integration Center, formed after 9/11 as a storehouse for intelligence information gathering from sources within the US and around the globe and shared with all agencies. Threats can emanate from within the homeland or from abroad. Terrorist threats can come from ISIS-inspired local Americans as well as from hostile nations."

Gwen continued, "There is one more reason for Mr. Khan's attachment to our team. Since the FBI has investigative jurisdiction over us in the event that a protectee of the US Secret Service is killed, the FBI director thought it was vital that we had someone on our team. We do not expect anything unlikely to happen on our watch. But it is equally vital that we be prepared for it. We need to be one step ahead of a potential assassin. Today, I understand, Kareem has something to share with us."

Gwen looked at Kareem and waved her hands to the front saying, "Welcome."

"Good morning, ladies and gentlemen," Kareem said. "I am very proud to be standing in front of the best in the business. In your hands, I am certain President Harrison will be completely safe."

The agents' faces reflected their pride in hearing Kareem's words. It always felt good when another agency recognized their work and when they could avoid intergovernment rivalry and criticism. Kareem seemed to bridge that divide easily. He had not lied. The Presidential Protection Division was the best. These career officers had been handpicked after years of toil in the field for being the very best. Their loyalty was absolute. One had only to think of Agent Tim McCarthy, who shielded Ronald Reagan's life when he took a bullet for him during a 1981 assassination attempt. Kareem meant every word of his praise for the team. But he also wanted their support in this venture and had no time to dabble in interagency rivalries.

"We listen to a lot of chatter over the telephone and the internet, and share information from our allies across several nations," Kareem went on. "We also share information with your own Global Threat Assessment Center in Washington, DC. For some time now, we have been hearing some chatter about someone seeking an assassin. At first, we thought it was a business rivalry or even a crime of passion, but it's the amount of the contract that caught our attention. Ten million dollars was on offer."

"Ten million bucks?" Samantha, one of the agents could not hide her disbelief. "That sure is no aggrieved lover."

"Yes ma'am, ten million is quite an amount," Kareem said. "We have no idea who is paying this amount for a contract, in which country, or even who the intended target is. For all we know, it could be the head of state of a foreign country or it could be some business mogul. With the increase in ISIS-inspired terrorist attacks in Europe and the ones we have faced in the homeland in San Bernardino, Orlando, New Jersey, Minnesota, and other places, there is cause for worry. We cannot take any information lightly. We know such organizations are always looking for a prize victim."

Kareem looked around the room and continued. "So, whenever POTUS is on the move, we take the advance that you have planned for very seriously. I like the term Gwen used. Let's play devil's advocate and relook at all we have planned and prepared for these past weeks and look for any loopholes. Have we missed anything? Can we form two groups, one a set of assassins and one a bunch of agents? Try to outdo each other. Do it over and over again, until you have a watertight security bubble that no one can breach." He looked at the agents. "Any questions?"

No one spoke. Any suggestion of redoubling their efforts to guarantee their mandate to their commander in chief was welcome. No one in the room wanted to fail. Everyone there was a Tim McCarthy. Everyone there was prepared to stand in the line of fire if someone should attempt to shoot at their protectee. Everyone there was willing to do anything that was required to fulfill their mandate. Protect the president, protect the office, and protect the symbol—or die trying.

"Thanks, Kareem," Garcia, one of the other agents said. "We will do exactly that. We look forward to future briefings on this subject. This has been truly very informative. Thank you, sir."

Kareem tipped his head gently and walked back to his seat.

Gwen added, "In addition to brainstorming on this issue, let's check gun sales, especially long-range weapons, terrorist or other threats received by any of our field offices countrywide, and any arrivals of people on our watch list in the past thirty days. Check out anything and everything you can. Speak to your local and state police and their army of informers, drug peddlers, hookers, fences, whoever. They live in a parallel world and hear a bit more than we normally do. Whatever you hear, the tiniest shred of information, share with the team, and then let's collate and see if we can get an image from the bits. Something has to be out there. Nothing lives in a vacuum. You are the best. Remember, we don't have the liberty of time. As I said at the opening, we are T minus seven days to game day, when we move the president. Whatever you can get, I want it *now*. Let's move, guys."

CHAPTER FIVE

The Fox

If the followers of al-Hassan Ibn-al-Sabbah, the eleventh-century Old Man of the Mountains, were called Haassasins, the hashish users, from which the word *assassin* is alleged to have originated, then Gabriel Marquez Lopez, the Argentinean man known only as the Fox, was an improbable disciple. Gabriel neither smoked hashish nor was a follower of any sect, religion, or family. He was a loner. He did not have a wife, a lover, or a child. He was almost as nameless to himself as he was to anyone else in his world. He was no public figure like Lee Harvey Oswald, who had shot John Kennedy; or Gavrilo Princip, who had killed Archduke Franz Ferdinand of Austria, which led to World War I; or Prince Felix Yusupov, who assassinated Grigori Rasputin; or Carlos "the Jackal," Illich Ramirez Sanchez, his mentor. Unlike all those hugely public names, Gabriel Marquez Lopez lived as a shadow under his nom de guerre, the Fox.

He had a deep-seated aversion to the limelight. He left no "calling card," as it was known in the trade, where assassins would leave some object at the scene of a crime to taunt law enforcement agencies. He preferred to carry out his craft quietly and disappear. He did not have any one type of modus operandi but worked in a myriad of ways. Possibly that was why in his thirty-odd years in the profession, he had never been caught. No police record. No fingerprints. No pictures. He was practically a ghost. He was invisible. He did not exist. It was not because law enforcement officers were weak and inefficient. The Fox had come up against the most powerful and the smartest of the smart in his long career. The CIA of the United States, MI6 of the United Kingdom, even the powerful Israeli Mossad had tracked him at various times of his life. He was simply better than the best they could throw at him. He was always one step, sometimes several steps, ahead of them. He left long before anyone even had an idea who had struck or where he had gone.

He enjoyed the craft for itself. He liked the fact that for a fee, he could aim his weapon of choice, be it a long-range gun or a fast-acting poison and snuff out a life in the fraction of a second. The harder the target, the greater the challenge, the more intense the pleasure—akin to sexual gratification for some. He savored the game of being hunted as he outwitted the best in the trade.

There was a rider, though. He liked it when someone told him that it would be impossible to take out the person or people they wanted killed. That the odds of success were a million to one. That the prize for them was immeasurable. That was when he felt a surge of fire flash through him. That was when he felt like God. He would decide. That's why the latest contract to take out one Andrew William Harrison excited him. Only he was called upon to take out the president of the United States.

He did not look like any swanky villainous character out of the movies. Not some glamorous chap who rode in Alfa Romeos and bedded the most beautiful lasses. He did not play Russian roulette in the glitzy casinos in Macau or lounge in beach hotels in Monte Carlo. He was a lackluster, bespectacled fifty-year-old man who walked with a slight slouch. Nobody who passed him on the streets would know he was the Fox, someone who had carried out assassinations the world over. He was just another old man. He was a nobody who could easily melt into the background. That suited his profession, as he could strike and fade away into the drab picture of an everyday crowd.

He remembered his last contract and smiled. Each time, he came up with something different, something unique, some style meant just for the occasion. It was not necessary to invent the modus each time. He researched a lot. That time he'd had help from something the KGB had used to take out an enemy in the United Kingdom. But no one could foresee his plan. The cops knew that an assassination plot was planned. The greatest security blankets of all time were spread across the podium where his target stood as he addressed the huge crowd of people. Not even a flea could get near him. But the Fox had neutralized him so swiftly and so neatly, no one knew. No one had noticed until long after he had left the scene and the country.

His target had been the president of a South American nation embroiled in a civil war with his political opponents. He was a brutal dictator and did not deserve to live anyway. But that was not the Fox's concern. He would have killed the pope if he'd been asked to. He did a job. He did not think about right or wrong. The greater the risk, the greater his sense of accomplishment and readiness for the next job. That was why now, as he planned to take out the American president, he savored the memory of his previous job. It egged him on. He felt like God.

He ran through the events of that day a year ago. To gain entrance to the event where his target would be the guest of honor, he had managed to kill one of the invited guests, a military attaché of a friendly country. And had taken his role. He did not carry any weapons, though he was dressed in full military regalia. Not that he would have been allowed to. All he had was a ballpoint pen. When John Jacob Loud invented the humble ballpoint pen more than a century ago, he could not have imagined how his writing instrument would be remodeled by the Fox to assassinate a head of state!

The Fox had replaced the ink holder of the pen with a steel tube that held little pellets filled with the deadly poison ricin. A few grains of this highly toxic protein could easily kill an adult man. Armed with a spring mechanism that he had perfected to shoot the pellets as much as ten feet, the Fox had arrived at the marquee where the guests sat. The KGB's hit man had used an umbrella gun filled with ricin pellets to kill Bulgarian exile George Markov at a bus stop in Waterloo in London. The Fox had switched the umbrella for a large ballpoint pen that held the same ricin-filled pellets. Thanks to the KGB.

He was disguised to look old, and he hobbled, displaying great difficulty in climbing the steps. He worked his charm, and the ushers, seeing this great old military hero with an array of medals strung across his chest, had helped him to the second tier of chairs from where the main dignitary would sit. The first tier was for the dictator's ministers of state and elaborate security. That suited the Fox. He did not want anyone to see him use his weapon. He could easily do it behind the cover of the military brass seated in front of him. He was barely five feet away from his prey. He waited until the president stood up when they played the national anthem. The guests in the front row stood up in a phalanx, giving him the perfect cover.

The Fox seemed to scratch his chin with his thumb. But his four fingers were wrapped around the deadly ricin pen. Just when the president was in his line of fire, the Fox's thumb dropped from his chin to the top of the pen and depressed the plunger. The ricin shot out and hit the president's neck. He repeated the action thrice and dropped the pen, wiped his face, and stood to attention as if in honor of the military band's strident beat of the national anthem. He looked very respectful. The president slapped his neck as if he had felt an insect bite. The band kept playing. The president made his speech, the army made a glorious march past him, planes flew in formation over the crowds, floats rolled by, and other events followed. The function came to an end, and everyone left. The president fell ill the next day and was admitted to a hospital. Four days later he was dead. By the time the doctors diagnosed ricin in his system, the Fox had already left the country. The ballpoint pen that had delivered the ricin lay on the concrete steps of the stadium, crushed by the boots of the military brass and other guests.

The Fox smiled at his success and returned to the job at hand, planning the assassination of Andrew William Harrison, the president of the United States. This job was far more complex than the dumb dictator and his lax security in the southern nation. This was the American president, and the blanket of security thrown around him would be impenetrable. When the president moved, a fortress of security moved around him, with him. The Fox smiled. That is when his adrenaline flowed—when it was impregnable, seeming impossible for the ordinary man. But not for him. He was the Fox. He was the master craftsman at his game. He was second to none. He was going to plan his game. He would get his prey. He would kill the most powerful man on the face of the earth, the most closely guarded man on the planet, the American president.

He sat at his desk in what appeared to be a run-down, nondescript apartment filled with electronic gizmos of every kind and shape. A battery of computers covered the workspace on two tables placed on either side of his chair. He switched on his computer and clicked on his email inbox. Sure enough, there was an email message to one John Smith, an innocuous enough American name, from one Joshua Taylor. He knew it was from one among the group that had hired him. Joshua Taylor, like John Smith, was a fake name. He knew it was someone important. Though he did not disclose it to Joshua, the Fox had some idea who he was. But he did not want to dwell on that connection right now. He would use it if it became necessary for his enterprise. The Fox always did thorough research and was one step ahead of everyone else. It was his survival instinct. He decrypted the attachment and printed the list. Few people could lay their eyes on the list he now held in his hands. It had come from someone deep inside the American political establishment and very high up the pecking order. It just mentioned places, dates, and times.

It was the president's itinerary for the next month—where he would be, at what time, and the several possible routes he could take to get there. Of course, the Secret Service would choose the routes and might change it several times; they might even come up with a completely new route at the last possible moment. But right now, these were, for all intents and purposes, the most recent ones. They must have reconnoitered intensely, covered several of these possible routes, and thrown a blanket of security around them that they simply would not have the time to change on short notice without causing too much of a disruption to the president's itinerary. He might have been short on time, but the Fox knew he had to pick a route that was close enough, but also gave him ample time to prepare. But first, he had to thwart the Secret Service and ensure they chose what he chose. That was going to be difficult. But that is why he was the Fox. He smiled. He was in his element. Like the wily animal he was known by, he set about to play his mind games.

He stared at the printed copy of the list. After what seemed an eternity of considering each of the various locations, he suddenly rose and switched on a large TV screen on the wall. He typed in locations on Google Street View and stood up close, studying various aspects of several of the locations from all possible angles. The images were from multiple locations as far apart as a White House state dinner, a state visit to Buckingham Palace in London, a schoolbook-reading session in Massachusetts, and a charity event in Alabama to raise funds for fighting Ebola in Africa. He paced up and down, pondered over some, checked details on others, went to his battery of computers and punched in locations, went back to the list, keyed in more locations, and studied more street views. In between, he stretched out on his chaise longue, shut his eyes, and went into a lengthy period of introspection. He lay like that for a long time.

Something seemed to strike his fancy, and he jumped up quickly and clicked on the browser, skipping through all the locations he had just viewed until he reached one and stopped. He stared long and hard at it, closed his eyes, sighed deeply, and slowly opened his eyes again. His lips curled into a gentle smile. Almost like seeing something that had been right under his nose all along. You look but you don't see it. Then it suddenly stares at you right in the face. It was so obvious. The perfect one. Where else? It was something that could not be changed by the White House. Because even though it was in New York, it was technically not in the United States. It operated by its own rules, and its itinerary could not be changed even by the president of the United States. It was sovereign to 193 nations of the world—the United Nations in New York!

The president was scheduled to address the United Nations General Assembly. That was fixed. Could not be changed on short notice! All he had to do was figure out the route POTUS would take on that day and a vantage point from which he could pick his target. That was not going to be easy. But as he stood by the giant images of the United Nations building and the street views from every angle, he smiled. He had his target pinned down to a *location*. All he needed was a spot to shoot him from. This was better than any pleasure known to man. The ultimate challenge. To play God. He felt he was the chosen one.

He went back to his battery of computers. He pressed various switches, and the screens showed images of wiping the hard drives and the browsers of the TV of any connection to the sites he had just visited. The email Joshua had sent and the fake email address he had created in the name of John Smith were deleted. Then the hard drives were wiped clean again. Moving to a corner of the room, he opened the steel trapdoor of the mini-incinerator, threw the list in it, and watched it curl up into a ball of flame. He smiled. The Fox had his prey cornered. Now all he needed to figure out was his weapons of choice, which depended on the location and distance to his target.

★

Robert Chuck Scott Jr. was descended from a long lineage of wealthy ancestors. Chuck's grandparents and parents were from the cotton-growing belt in the Deep South. He had had an affluent upbringing, attended Ivy League schools, married into a rich family, and owned several large oilfields in Rusk County, in East Texas, and businesses dealing in aerospace, munitions, and communications. He had stepped into the political limelight when his late father, Robert Scott Sr, passed on.

During his formative years, he was influenced by the British occultist and writer Alice Bailey, who suggested that the Masters of the Ancient Wisdom were preparing the world for the second coming of Jesus Christ and that the Great White Brotherhood of Masters, would ensure a new world order. This world was destined to be run according to divine interpretation—a Christian order of things. That is why he had joined the Cabal of Christian Crusaders. The battle lines had been drawn. The Western world was teetering on the edge of Islamization and Communism. That *had* to be checked.

He passionately believed William Carr's theories of the threat of godless Communism, H. G. Wells's claims that the new world order was a technocratic world state, and David Rothkopf's assertion that an elite of six thousand people, the *superclass,* ruled the world of six billion people. He knew deep down he was one of the six thousand. He was a chosen one. His father had been on the Council on Foreign Relations, under President Woodrow Wilson. He knew that the council grew from the Round Table Group and was influential in the creation of the UN's predecessor, the League of Nations, which had also hoped for a new world order. Chuck himself was a member of the Trilateral Commission, an elite group of three hundred members from the USA, Europe, and Asia who sought economic cooperation to harbinger a new order. Chuck was also a permanent invitee to the elite Bilderberg Group of power brokers from Europe and America who met to discuss mutual understanding among politicians, media, governments, and business czars of the Western Hemisphere.

In his stately mansion, the three-story brick house at Number One Observatory Circle, the official residence of the vice president in Washington, DC, Chuck was pouring himself a drink from his crystal decanter as he thought of this post. The influence of his late father, his readings, and membership of all the groups that advocated a new world order was not enough. It didn't take him to that new dawn he had dreamed of since his youth. The cabal was the answer to his dreams. He was pleased that for the first time in his sixty-eight long years on this earth, the cabal was going to act.

He dropped a few cubes of ice into his glass, strode across the room, and sat down with his $1.4 million Master of Malt whiskey from the Aisla T'Orten distillery. He sipped at it slowly and closed his eyes to taste the rich, woody intensity, a smoky, thick, creamy essence with elements of coffee, hay, and mahogany leather, a masterpiece in the art of distilling. But as he felt the robust malt whiskey with a touch of oak grains, chestnut, and black pepper trail its way down his throat, his mind was far away. He was finally on the road to some action. He took a generous sip of the choice whiskey and thought of his present job.

The vice presidency was all pomp and splendor, but no substance. Many would have been proud to have ascended to the second-highest office of the most powerful democracy on the planet. He was the president of the US Senate. He was also the only one who had the authority to vote as a tiebreaker. He also presided over the joint session of the Congress when it convened to count the vote of the Electoral College. But that was it. Despite that oft-quoted misnomer, "a heartbeat away from the presidency," in reality he was nowhere in the great scheme of things. He decided nothing and influenced nothing. Even the Senate did not stop in his absence as a president pro-tempore; a temporary president is normally chosen from among the longest-serving members of the Senate. Life went on. Chuck knew his office had no influence in the great momentum of US politics. He was merely a spectator as the great moments of history passed him by.

He attended funerals of foreign dignitaries or other state functions when the president simply did not have time to go to or the event was not of much significance to the presidency. The president had matters of state to attend to. Some of his predecessors had choice names for it. John Garner, a former vice president, said the vice presidency "isn't worth a pitcher of warm piss." Harry Truman had described it "as useful as a cow's fifth teat." Then there was Thomas R. Marshall, who said, "Once there were two brothers. One ran away to sea and the other was elected vice president of the United States. And nothing was heard of either of them again." Chuck poured himself a tall shot of whiskey and swallowed it down in one gulp as he considered his insignificance.

But not anymore. Once the Fox pulled the trigger and Harrison fell, he would ascend to the highest office of the land. He would be the president of the United States! As commander in chief, he would rewrite history. He would stop being someone who only attended weddings or funerals. The world would remember him. He would change the course of the world. Islamization of America had to stop. This senseless violence by some crazed Muslim shooting innocent Americans in theaters and shopping malls had to be stopped. As the president, Chuck would ensure that it was not the norm as it was now. He would deport them to their countries of origin. The others who were born in America would be held in segregated communities so that they could be monitored and did not have the freedom to walk in anywhere and unleash carnage in the name of their religion.

There was a greater and real danger from the Communists. China could not be allowed to wreak havoc on the free market economy of the West by hacking into opponents' computers to gain a competitive edge in bidding for international business deals and artificially controlling the value of their currency. Nor could he brook that fat North Korean pig Kim Jung Un threatening to nuke America testing nuclear weapons at will. He would pummel North Korea into a nuclear wasteland. Ever since the sanctions had been lifted, the mullahs of Tehran were footloose. Chuck was sure they were developing a nuclear weapon. The "death to America" chanting Iranian dogs could not be allowed to develop a nuclear weapon. Of course, they would aim it at America. Again, they had to be taken out.

He also would not permit the Russians to annex Ukraine. Otherwise Russians would march into Estonia, Latvia, Lithuania, Kazakhstan, Kyrgyzstan, and all the other Baltic states. The Russian bear would effectively redraw the map of the world, alter the balance of power, and crumble NATO. Such imperialist designs could not be allowed to see the light of day. Chuck threw the rest of the whiskey down his throat as he considered all the changes, he would effect to help create a new world. He would make a difference as the president of the United States.

But that was when the Fox had killed the present incumbent, President Harrison. Chuck looked at the printed copy of the email that he held in his hands. It was from John Smith, the fake name the Fox had chosen just to send this email. It was a set of instructions, terse and to the point.

"Rent an office on the twentieth floor of 55 Water Street in New York. I have already checked the property. There are several vacant offices available on that floor. It should be one that faces the Downtown Manhattan Heliport. Furnish it as a birder's studio. It should look like that of a professional birdwatcher, not an ornithologist, who studies for scientific reasons. The office will be used by one Rusty Newman who enjoys birdwatching and sketching birds. Have loads of bird pictures set up: kestrels, bald eagles, merlins, northern harriers, and especially many of peregrine falcons. Since 1999 a pair of peregrine falcons has been nesting on the fourteenth floor of 55 Water.

Rusty will like watching the falcon pair named Jack and Jill and their offspring."

Chuck smiled at that. For a professional assassin, the Fox seemed to know a lot about birdwatching. Or possibly that was his style—to create an elaborate cover.

"Fill it with paints, easels, brushes, canvases, frames, paintings, and the furniture to go with it. They should be exclusive and done tastefully. Get it done within a fortnight. The person who draws up the rental agreement should be someone who cannot be traced back to you. And it should be someone we can dispense with. After he has signed the lease, send him to Hunters' Lodge in Santa Clara next weekend. Tell him it's up for sale and that a prospective buyer wishes to check it out. I will ensure all loose ends are tied up."

The hairs on the nape of Chuck's neck stood up at that. He could feel the assassin's icy cold words *someone we can dispense with* and *tie up loose ends*. He wanted Chuck to choose someone far removed from himself to carry out the exercise of renting the property. But he still did not want to take any chances. He would "dispense" with the real estate agent once he had done his bit. No loose ends. The enterprise at hand was way too big to leave any loose ends. So, Chuck understood. Still, he did not wish to be in the crosshairs of this killer. He felt safer hiring the Fox. Not being on his wrong side. He did not wish to be a "loose end" to be dispensed with. He also worried about why the Fox had asked for the real estate agent to be sent to Hunters' Lodge. Was it a sheer coincidence or had he chosen a remote spot far removed from 55 Water Street? Well, he would check it out later.

He read and reread the note several times, then strode over to the large fireplace and threw the sheet of paper into it, watching it coil up into an orange ball of flame, then curl into a darkened ephemeral ball of ash. He was not going to be somebody who only attended weddings and funerals or was "a pitcher of warm piss," an inconsequential vice president. He would be the president of the United States of America—the most powerful man on the face of the earth! And the godless Communists and Muslims were in for a rude shock.

CHAPTER SIX

Financial Armageddon

Looking out of his £100 million Edwardian home on Bishop's Avenue in Hampstead, the north London suburb of the super-rich, Raymond Webster Coleman, CEO of Webster Coleman Brokerage, smiled as he saw the limousines arrive with his friends, Christian Hannes and Aleixandre Thierry. He closed the drapes of the living room with a remote control and set up the mood lighting to a gentle amber glow that made it look like an evening bathed in the golden rays of the setting sun. *Just the mood of the discussion at hand*, Raymond thought to himself, crossing the expansive living room to meet them just as Henry, his butler, ushered them in.

"Welcome." Raymond was warm and shook their hands, smiling broadly. "Henry will serve you with drinks of your choice." They all sat down on the plush white sofas. Raymond waited for Henry to serve his friends and then waved his man-servant away.

"Things seem to have moved on at a steady pace," Aleix-andre said as he placed his glass on the side table beside him.

"Chuck tells me the Fox has already asked him to rent an office in New York."

"Yes," Christian said. "He knows his tradecraft and will be successful. We need to be ready with our plans to manipulate the market, just as the Fox eliminates the POTUS and Chuck as the new commander in chief lets loose the dogs of war."

"That's the idea, Christian," Raymond agreed, raising his glass to support his claim. "We need to have our operation in place. It's not an easy task. It will take some time to build, set in motion, and bring down an established market. That is why, gentlemen, I must extend my warm regards for your visit today, so we can finalize the elaborate scheme to engineer a market crash across several nations." Turning to the chairman of France-Net, Raymond said, "Alex, I know you have already done a lot of work to get this scheme off the ground. Let's hear from you."

"Thanks, Ray," Alex said. "We have identified two sets of players in the stock market, the institutional ones that have shares in very large corporations and another set of individuals—retirees, wealthy spinsters, widowers, and heiresses. My team managed to obtain these lists of wealthy investors from both sides of the Atlantic, but also went to great lengths to ensure these were the most gullible ones. We want a bunch of moneybags who are prone to throwing their money around with the least amount of caution. We hired spooks to track them down and get their histories. Unlike normal boiler rooms that blindly call in a hit-and-run operation, we want to have a list of prey who have not only the means but also a history of falling easily. We also chose the loners, the gambling types, the ones who live far away from big cities, and the alcoholics—the ones who won't give a rat's ass if they lost a few millions."

"What kind of numbers are we talking about here, Alex?" Ray asked.

Alex smiled as he reported, "In the US, Germany, France, Holland, and the United Kingdom, we have cobbled together a list of over sixty thousand idiots, the best moneybags there could be."

"Over sixty thousand, Alex? Now, that calls for a drink. Henry, over here." Christian was obviously happy about the prospects of their operation becoming a roaring success. He raised his empty glass as Henry hurried across to replenish it.

Alex raised his glass in humble acceptance of the praise. "Having an internet company does have its benefits. We can carry out more background checks than your average Joe. I have some professional hackers in my employ, so the spooking work was easy. We hacked into records of stockbrokers and downloaded their lists of investors. Then we did a little more. We went into the personal backgrounds of everyone on those lists and picked the most gullible ones and the types with shady records. In some cases, we know more about them than their own spouses or close family members do. This includes ill-gotten wealth stashed in the Grand Cayman Islands and other tax havens that could prove an embarrassment if reported.

"Here is the best part of all." Aleixandre paused a moment for effect and said, "Over half of them are institutional investors who have shares in the largest corporations in their respective countries. In short, they represent the combined value of nearly half the wealth of their countries. So, should their wealth be suddenly wiped out, half of those mega-corporations, banks, pension fund institutions, hedge funds, and the like will crumble. It will be a meltdown, and the economies of these countries will face financial Armageddon!"

"Alex, you know you have a future in brokerage," Ray said. "You have not just picked off names but chosen the institutional ones that could bring the economy down. Thanks, Alex, for those numbers. Now let me show you how we rip off those sixty thousand dolts. We will set up more than a thousand boiler rooms in Spain, Paraguay, Serbia, Bosnia, Croatia, Kazakhstan, Bhutan, Venezuela, and of course the People's Republic of China. Because these countries lack proper laws, our governments won't be able to follow us to track these scams. Christian has already set up offices in all these locations. Thanks, Christian!"

"My pleasure, Ray." Christian Hannes, the CEO of Vastgoed NV, the €148 million turnover Dutch real estate company, was in his element and raised his glass toward both his friends.

Ray continued, "Our idea is not to lose any of our own money. Half of these boiler rooms will attack the retirees, the loners, and such people and fleece them of their money. We will invest the money that we skim off individual investors to seduce the institutional lot in a creative manner. I shall refer to these individual investors as the idiot lot. Most large corporations consider themselves scam-proof because they will not fall for the hundreds of wild calls that our operators make to the idiot group that result in easy gains. The institutional lot will check on the source of the call and the companies we claim to represent. They'll just want to be sure that the new ventures we wax eloquent about are truly about to go big league and that it's worth their while to invest millions of dollars in them to quadruple their earnings. So, let's refer to them as the smart ones."

Ray stopped to take a drink and went on. "To the first idiot lot, we will easily hawk imaginary shares in eco projects, telecommunications, carbon credits, tech start-ups, consumer hygiene, wine, or real estate. Basically, we will pump up the value of the penny stocks with share values of less than five dollars a share. These companies are quoted on the Over-the-Counter Bulletin Board pink sheets and will be snapped up immediately by these gullible loners, depending on the skill set of our teams hawking them. Our teams will claim we are part of Nasdaq, though we are not. It's done all the time. Some of the microcaps we choose will be the ones that don't have to file reports with regulatory bodies under an exemption known as Reg D or Reg A offerings in the US, so our idiots will not be able to validate the companies' assets and liabilities."

Ray picked up some brochures and said, "We have made these appealing glitzy brochures and marketing materials for our teams and have trained them to put high-stakes boiler-room pressure on these idiots—the unsuspecting, half-drunk, loners, retirees, spinsters—and the bored, rich lot. We'll pump it to astronomical heights of possible returns, wait for their money to roll in, dump the stocks, and make a killing."

Aleixandre was impressed and said, "Ray, you are a genius. That's quite a pile we will make there."

Ray turned toward Aleixandre and said, "Thanks, Alex. We need your help in this. We need to set up internet chat rooms across the length and breadth of the stockbroking websites that speak highly of our shell companies, filled with our teams on live chat oozing praise of the millions they made and the fake rags-to-riches customer testimonials on internet boards and through email spamming. We will also use a new variation—the misdialed number trick, where one of our stockbrokers will leave a hot investment tip for his friend, as if by accident, on our intended victim's answering machine. Six out of ten times, it works to a tee. More than 60 percent of our teams across these countries will do this type of scheme. As I said earlier, they have been trained in this. They have the brochures and the glib talking expertise to skim money out of this idiot group of gullible investors."

Aleixandre responded, "I'll do anything you wish me to, Ray. And why not? We are going to rip off these idiots."

"Yes, Alex, we will. However, the second group, the smarties, will take more convincing." Ray took a deep gulp of his drink and continued in earnest. "The rest of the team is made up of hard-core stockbrokers. I decided to handpick that team myself. This group will target large institutional brokerages. This is the most vital part of our enterprise. They will offer real offshore investments in, say, a large gold mine in South Africa, with a real South African office, an address, and people working there who send out brochures and churn out prospectuses, financial statements, paper clippings, and even television coverage. It will be an elaborate cover. We will even make large payouts of dividends to maintain the fantasy."

Ray was in his element now as he expounded on his Machiavellian scheme. "There are some new products that large corporations will throw large chunks of money at without a moment's hesitation. How about controlling shares in a company that manufactures a pioneering breakthrough product from a Paraguayan shrub known as *Stevia rebaudiana* that's 150 times sweeter than sugar? Extracted from the leaves and used by the Guarani peoples of South America for over fifteen hundred years, *ka'a he'ȇor*—which means 'sweet herb'—is natural and has none of the side effects of the sugar that we use. The European Union and FDA have approved it. Soft drink companies the world over are craving it, although because of the bitter aftertaste, stevia has not performed well. The initial hype that it would replace sugar is not there anymore. Of course, we are not going to dwell on its failure. We will simply say that it will replace sugar. No more obesity. Eat all the sweets you want in any form. No side effects. It will blow your mind away. But just to give it more appeal, we have a Paraguayan office that will build on stories of a rare genus of the stevia shrub that was just discovered and is being cultivated in a secret lab."

Ray said emphatically, "We'll sell shares of that company to some large stock brokerage houses. We will present samples of the product—which will, of course, be normal sugar that will not have the bitter licorice-like aftertaste of stevia. This industry-shattering news will be well received. We have actual companies in Paraguay selling stevia-based sweeteners. This scam alone will bust at least ten or fifteen large stock brokerages.

"Friends, I won't bore you with more stories," Raymond said. "We have a hundred such products and ventures that these large companies will easily flip for. As I said before, this scheme has been carefully planned. Only the best and real stockbrokers with well-researched prospectuses, real offices, with staff who truly believe that such a venture does exist, actual company sites, and real payouts will help build our elaborate fantasy of huge payouts. News of dividends paid will be circulated widely, but each person will be told that they're among the 'select few' who are fortunate to be in the know."

Ray smiled broadly as he foretold the effects of his scheme on the markets. "We'll set all of this up at great cost for a month or so, and once we ensure huge inflows of investment, we'll shut down and disappear, bringing down large stockbrokerages and companies that invested in it. It is my belief that with this venture, we will bring down half the largest companies in all the countries we hope to hit. And the tsunami of panic selling by others will wipe out the stock markets of the US, UK, Netherlands, France, and Germany and have a severe ripple effect on economies worldwide that depend on them."

As the magnitude of the scheme dawned on Alex's mind, he said in measured tones, "American banks have over two hundred and fifty trillion dollars of exposure to derivatives, which is essentially a security with a price that depends on the value of assets. To my mind, most of the assets are currencies, bonds, and stocks. So, if the value of the stock's crashes, then the securities held in the banks also crash. Ray, our enterprise will bring down large banks, just as in 2008."

"Spot-on, Alex," Ray complimented him. "You've hit the nail on the head. Warren Buffet reportedly referred to derivatives as 'financial weapons of mass destruction.' China lost a hundred and eight billion dollars in December, at a whopping rate of three and a half billion dollars per day! Twice they used circuit breakers to stop the market from bleeding more than 7 percent in a single night. The domino effect was that the Dow dropped 392 points, the S&P lost 2.4 percent, and the Nasdaq was down by 3 percent. The panic selling that followed saw the Dow losing 911 points, the worst since 1897! That's what sheer and unabated panic does to a market, friends." Ray downed his drink. "All we are going to do is set a match to the tinderbox." Then, with the smile of a magician's flamboyant showmanship, like yanking a rabbit out of a hat, he signed off, saying, "In this case, all we are doing, gentlemen, is building that elaborate tinderbox ourselves."

"Superb, Ray," Alex said. "I have no doubt that with you at the helm, we will have no trouble pulling off a stock market crash across America and Europe. This is truly a path-breaking enterprise."

"Alex, we will not be doing anything that has not been done before," Christian said. "But with Ray's experience, we have planned it on a much grander scale. *Verenigde Oostindische Compagnie*, the Dutch East India Company, established our Amsterdam Stock Exchange, the oldest in the world. Many of these *Voorcompagnieën* companies formed private partnerships like our cabal, financed expensive voyages to the Eastern worlds to cash in on the spice trade in 1602, and made massive profits. They shared the costs, just as we are planning to, and made joint profits just as Ray plans for us to reap while the masses suffer."

Christian said, "They were so successful that the Dutch state granted the Dutch East India Company a complete monopoly for more than two decades—the first mega-corporation that had complete control over all major trade and sold its stocks to investors. It is my wish that once we have complete control over the markets of the world, we too can control the markets for our own benefit. For the success of Christendom, we need the wealth to maintain it with sweeping control over all arms of the governments, the defenses, and the minds of its people."

"Christian has said something that we need to raise in our next meeting in Bavaria," Ray said, clearly impressed. While he had spun the techniques of pulling off a stock market swindle, Christian was suggesting a post-Harmagedon new world where the six of them would control all the stock markets of the world. That was mind boggling. They would be the elite six of the six-thousand-member superclass that, according to David Rothkopf, ruled the six billion inhabitants of this world. "I am aware of the trading clubs the Dutch had in the seventeenth century, meeting in pubs or coffee shops to discuss financial deals. Today's politically correct establishment would call that insider trading. I am in complete agreement with Christian and think we need to institutionalize this plan of ours and set it as the new norm in the new world we hope to set up. We need to control the minds of our populaces to maintain control. Thank you, Christian! You are a star!"

"This is from hard experience, Ray." Christian was humble in his response. "We are rightly known as a nation of thrifty people. The reason is the painful experience of the 'Tulipomania' of the seventeenth century, when speculation over the tulip bulb rose from a humble guilder to more than sixty guilders per bulb. Dutchmen sold all their belongings to prospect in tulip bulbs as prices skyrocketed and went beyond everyone's wildest dreams, and then suddenly it popped. One trader had defaulted on his contract. Just as you said earlier, Ray, panic sets in. People started selling them just as wildly as they had snapped them up. Prices crashed. The Dutch economy was driven into a depression of sorts. To date, its effects reverberate in the Dutch habit of frugality. I want us as a cabal to go back to a market that we can control and profiteer from. There will be no more about the effects of Tulipomania but profits from an engineered market or the future of our new world. We will be the new *Verenigde Oostindische Compagnie*, a much more refined cabal than the Dutch East India Company."

"To Christian and the Cabal of Christian Crusaders," said Aleixandre, toasting the cabal. The men rose to their feet, downed their drinks, and shook hands enthusiastically. They spent the rest of the afternoon drinking and fine-tuning their plans. Ray introduced his friends to his senior team who would manage the boiler room and other scams. He showed them the numerous prospectuses of companies that were tapped to grow exponentially. They made phone calls to various parts of the world from which some of the schemes would be run and calculated the billions of dollars they hoped to make as well as the vast amounts they would wipe off stock markets across the continents.

Ruthless in their enterprise, they plotted only for the success of their cabal and its heinous plans to shape the world order according to their narrow-minded outlook. They were modern-day gods who molded the lives of entire nations and populations. They decided who lived and who died. They decided who had wealth and who did not. Christian, Alex, and Ray drank and laughed as they reveled in their Machiavellian plans. They laughed at the misery they were about to unleash on the unsuspecting masses around the world.

★

Cynthia was in her apartment, thinking about all that had happened. Thoughts of Ryan filled her mind. She loved Europe and had really been hoping to move there. Ryan had been hopeful about making Germany home. Life had been looking great, and then it had all come crashing down when he was murdered. She was devastated. When she'd heard from Kareem earlier that day that the investigation in Germany had not unearthed any clues, she had been angry. Two Americans who worked for a bank had died within the space of a month. But the German police did not see fit to assume it was suspicious enough to question the bank.

Someone very powerful had not only had Ryan killed, but had also managed to wipe the slate clean. He was powerful. He could do anything. That thought made her angry. How trivial was human life for such demons? She remembered the past year and how she had cried herself to sleep for several months until she'd found the strength within to get up and get back to life. She knew Ryan would have wanted her to cope. He was such a gentle soul. Without that love, she would have given up on life a long time ago.

Then Ashley had come looking for her. She had met Matt and Kareem. She still could not believe all that had happened today. It was a real stroke of luck that someone she had worked with years ago turned out to be Amy's daughter. It was sad to know that her friend Amy was also dead. She felt sorry for Ashley and her father, Matt. But she was grateful for the acquaintance and the possibility of finding Ryan's killers. It had been a lonely and drab existence for her until now. She would plod through the day, come home, eat, sleep, go to work, and repeat that dull routine over and over again. That had been the story of her life for a year now. Although several men had made advances, she had carefully sidestepped all such offers. She had just gone through her featureless life more like a machine than a human being. She had existed, not lived. Until today.

Suddenly life had changed for the better. There was a chance to seek retribution for Ryan's death. She was happy that Ashley had found her. From a lonely existence in which she had no answers, suddenly she had support in the form of an FBI agent, a decorated soldier, and his daughter, who were eager to go out of their way to hunt down the murderers of their loved ones. Cynthia suddenly had a reason to be alive. She had reason to wake up every day. She was going back to Bavaria. She was going to hunt for the truth with Matt, Kareem, and Ashley!

She looked at the picture of Ryan on her nightstand. He seemed to smile at her. She smiled back. In her mind, she told him she was going to find his killers. She looked into his deep eyes and thought of her life without him. Then her mind raced back to the events of the day, and she went through every word that had been said and all the plans they had made. She thanked her lucky stars for having met Ashley, Kareem, and Matt.

Matt was a purposeful, driven person who seemed to know where he was going and what he was doing—precisely the type of guy with whom she could trust her life on a mission fraught with dangers. From what she had gathered from Ashley, Matt's grind through life since he'd lost Amy was pretty much like hers. Ashley had described how her father had retreated into a shell and was suffering. He had been indoors most of the time, had no relationships, and spent most of his time living in the past. Cynthia felt sorry for Matt. Unlike her, Matt had Ashley to think of. His pain must have been doubly worse. He had to nurse his internal pain while trying to put on a brave face for his daughter.

Cynthia had noticed his inner loneliness, the sense of hollowness he faced. She knew he missed Amy very much. A soldier in the Middle East and his wife in Europe make plans to settle down with their daughter and lead a normal life. But someone snuffs out the life of one of them. That was a story in pain. To lose someone you love after twenty-five years must have been unbearable—and not easy to get over. She could feel Matt's pain as it mirrored her own.

Ashley seemed to be suffering even more. She too was caught in a time loop, working, trying to keep her father happy, and, as a result, not having the time or desire to get into a meaningful relationship. She liked Ashley. From her days at the *Daily Sentinel*, she had seen in Ashley a daughter that she would have loved to have. Ashley had lost a mother and was living in pain as she watched her father waste away. Cynthia shared in Ashley's pain.

As she walked to the kitchen to fix herself some dinner, her thoughts were still on Matt, Ashley, and Kareem. Matt's calm nature belied his strong will and great strength. She knew he would lead them to the killers. Something in his nature told her that whoever had given the orders for Ryan and Amy's murders better be prepared for a very dangerous man. For the first time in almost a year, Cynthia smiled with a genuine sense of satisfaction. She stayed up late, and when she finally hit the bed and fell asleep, she dreamed of Matt kicking the shit out of a German banker who looked a lot like Hitler. She smiled in her sleep and hugged a large pillow to herself.

CHAPTER SEVEN

A Recce

Peering out of his high-powered telescope from the window of the largest office building in the world, the fifty-four-story skyscraper 55 Water Street, in the financial district of Lower Manhattan, the Fox surveyed the majestic East River and smiled. He moved his scope along FDR Drive, which hugged the East River coastline as it snaked 9.44 miles from the Battery Park Underpass to Harlem River Drive. He then focused the lens of his powerful scope north of the Staten Island Ferry above the Battery, stopped at the image of Pier 6, and smiled again as he looked down at the 84,000-square-foot Downtown Manhattan Heliport.

He swung his scope to the heliport just south of where FDR Drive began, opposite the Vietnam Veterans Plaza. He peered at the heliport, zoomed in, and spent a long time checking the entire two acres, the L-shaped area that had landing bays for eleven helicopters, offices, a control tower, and lounges for passengers. Choppers landed and took off at regular intervals, ferrying sightseers, private charters, police officers, hospital staff, and military personnel. The Fox spent some time watching passengers as they got on or off the choppers. He knew that executives of New York's financial district and tourists wishing to view the spectacle of the New York and New Jersey skyline used the heliport extensively. But most important of all, when he wished to visit New York, Downtown Manhattan Heliport was *a landing area for the president of the United States!* And the Fox smiled again. He zoomed in once more, checking the heliport with the intense devotion of a researcher peering through a high-powered microscope at lifesaving microorganisms.

He went back to his office and locked the door behind him. He was alone in the office block. But the Fox was not one to take chances. He secured his private office, setting an alarm for the locked main door to warn him against accidental or forced entry. Not that he was expecting anyone. But that was his style. He did not make mistakes. He looked at the CCTV images on the large screen on the wall. It showed every part of the office. Nothing moved. There was absolute silence. When he was thoroughly satisfied that he was alone, he opened a wall cabinet, lifted a large, heavy canvas bag out, and placed it on the small conference table.

He unzipped the almost five-feet-long bag, reached in, and took out four long-range rifles, complete with scopes, ballistic computers, and numerous accessories, and placed them beside one another on the table. He handled each of the guns and the trappings that went with them with the loving care a mother would her baby. He looked through the scopes at times, felt the trigger, or ran his fingers across the entire twenty-six inches of the barrel. He spent the next ten minutes setting up all four guns with their long scopes, then mounted them with highly elaborate adjusting equipment and tested each of them by viewing the framed picture of a bald eagle that hung on the distant end of his office. He moved from one specialized gun to the other.

The first one was a Custom 375 Cheyenne Tactical with a Schmidt & Bender scope. It came with armor-piercing Magnum .505 elephant rounds. He picked up the rounds for the Mighty Gibbs, as it was called, after the British rifle maker George Gibbs, who developed it in 1911 to fell elephants in the African bush. This could fell another elephant of a personality seated in the White House. From where he was seated on the twentieth floor, this CheyTac could easily pick its target at distances over a mile and a half. A New Jersey rifle enthusiast had pulled off a shot at a thirty-six-inch target from two miles away, hitting it within 7.2 seconds. That is precision! But would he have his target in his sights for 7.2 seconds? Did he have to contend with a two-mile distance, hence reducing his probability of hitting his target? He needed to consider these questions. He looked at the other weapons on the table.

The second was the long-range Steyr-Mannlicher Infantry Weapon System 2000. This semi-automatic bullpup anti-material, high-explosive tank gun with its 9.75-inch-barrel and a muzzle brake to reduce recoil seemed to be a pretty good choice for the job at hand. The Fox picked up the fin-stabilized, discarding sabot ammo. *Impressive*, he thought. These bullets made of depleted uranium could pierce through forty millimeters of rolled homogeneous armor from about a mile and a half away! He threw one of the dart-shaped projectiles into the air and caught it in its downward spiral just as quickly in his open palm as he imagined how its secondary fragmentation would blow his target's head away. Traveling 4,757 feet, this ammo made of tungsten carbide could hit a target a mile away in a *second*! That was a lot better than what the CheyTac had to offer. *All the more impressive*, the Fox thought. He had two more guns to check out.

The Arctic Warfare Super Magnum was the third on his list. British sniper Corporal Craig Harrison had used a similar gun in Helmand province, Afghanistan, to eliminate two Taliban insurgents from a mile and half away with repeated shots within three seconds. That was the longest recorded sniper shot! The rounds must have exited the barrel of the gun at three times the speed of sound! Now, that was the kind of distance, accuracy, and speed he was looking for. He sat down, raised the bipod of the gun, and peered through the Schmidt & Bender telescopic 10× variable sight. The Fox picked up the .338 Lapua Magnum armor-piercing magazine of bullets. It was a specialized rimless, bottlenecked cartridge he knew had been developed for the specific purpose of long-range sniper rifles. The Lapua Magnum anti-material rounds could penetrate body armor at great distances and were widely used by military and big-game hunters. *Not bad*, he thought. *Not bad at all.*

He liked the Arctic Warfare Super Magnum, which was vital for self-preservation. This rifle produced less recoil, sound, and muzzle flash and was the perfect weapon for a concealed shooter like him. He did not wish to give his location away to the FBI by the telltale wisp of smoke after a shoot. After he pulled off his operation, the Fox needed time to sneak away unnoticed. He did not want the Secret Service agents in helicopters overhead and rooftops to pick him off from the muzzle flash. He would be history in three seconds flat. He picked the steel magazine and counted five rounds, enough to take multiple shots at his target in case of a miss the first time around. But he knew that was not a luxury he could count on. He would have time for only *one shot*. That was it. After that, all he would have time for was to make his getaway. Designed for accuracy at sixteen hundred yards, this was his weapon of choice.

But it was the last weapon on the table that caught his fancy the most. He opened the sleek gun case and picked up the TrackingPoint XS1.338 Lapua Magnum Precision Guided Firearm. The PGF was a long-range, laser-guided robot rifle. This smart gun fitted with a Linux-powered scope used a jet-fighter lock-and-launch technology and guaranteed a kill at first shot even for a rookie shooter. He sat down at the table, viewed through the scope, and saw a computer-generated image of the picture of the bald eagle on the far wall on the gun's heads-up display. The 110-mm telephoto lens created a perfect 14.6-megapixel image thanks to the internal measurement unit streaming at fifty-four frames per second. He could see the deep yellow beak and sharp eyes of the majestic American bird in detail.

He looked at the eyes of the bird of prey staring ferociously into the distance. He ranged the eagle's head and pressed the red tag button on the side of the trigger guard. Sensors and gyroscopes on the weapon measured the temperature, barometric pressure, and relative humidity, and determined the inclination, cant, shot direction, muzzle velocity, launch dynamics, and drag coefficient. A red tag was placed on the eye of the bird in the display. The target had been marked.

The Fox moved the TrackingPoint XS1 a bit to simulate a moving target, and a blue X reticle appeared on his scope. He moved the gun back in line and squeezed the trigger. He knew the gun would not fire until the reticle sat squarely on the red tag on the bird's eye. The squeeze of the trigger only lined up the shot and the computers in the scope released the bullet only when the red tag and the reticle coincided. So even a twitch that occurs when a weapon recoils, which would normally upset one's aim in other firearms, would not affect the TrackingPoint XS1. A small electronic solenoid got power from the scope to block the firing mode as an internal safety system. The Fox was pleased.

The Fox knew that in real life when he scoped a target and squeezed the trigger and, even if the bird suddenly flew off its perch, the tag would stick on the bird as the tracking algorithm computed its velocity and developed an expected position predicted for the next 18.5 milliseconds, even at speeds of ten miles per hour. Now, *that* was precision—jet-fighter lock-and-launch that even a dummy could fire with. He was no dummy. That made his experience as a crack shot and a precision gun the perfect mix for a fail-free shot.

He carried all four weapons to the table set at the window of the office. He placed them on the bipods, adjusted them for the perfect angle, and one by one went through the motions of scoping random targets such as the helipad at the Downtown Manhattan Heliport. With more than twenty-seven flights per day, the heliport provided him with numerous subjects to target. Choppers were flying off or landing most of the time. Busy executives and sightseers had no idea they were in the crosshairs of one of the most professional assassins in the world. He looked at an excited young girl clinging to her father's hands, her blond hair flying in the wind. He adjusted the scope and caught her head in the crosshairs of his gun's telescopic sights. He could pick out the individual strands of her hair.

He moved on to another subject, a woman in high heels walking to a waiting chopper, her body swaying sideways as she stylishly pirouetted on her way. The Fox studied her head as it bobbed up and down as she strutted along gaily. He concentrated on the movements of her head and measured where it would be in the next three seconds, aimed at the spot, and held. He released the safety lock on the bolt and activated the trigger. She began to move. He released the two-stage trigger, depressed the half-pound slack, and adjusted his cheek firmly against the gun. He pushed the bolt safety to forward, the fire position. The firing pin shot out. He took a deep breath and held it as he saw her raise her feet as if in slow motion to move forward. He pulled the trigger. When three seconds were up and she appeared dead center of his crosshairs, the bullet would have impacted her head and blown it apart. That would have been a dead woman. The Fox smiled. The gun had no bullets. This was practice.

The choice of the weapon was one part of the job. It was vital to learn the distance from his vantage point on the twentieth floor of 55 Water to his target at the downtown heliport, the wind conditions, and the time of day, and to plan the rounds he would use, the speed at which he could hit his target, and his escape. He knew he would not get a second chance. *It was one shot or none.* So, he spent hours going through the machinations of scoping his target, using the ballistic computers and weather gauges to get his readings for elevation and wind conditions for a perfect shot. He calculated the downward slant, the possible movement of the target, the speed at which the target could move, the height of the target, the spindrift of the bullet, and the Coriolis effect caused by the earth's rotation, and jotted down multiple firing solutions. He knew if he was shooting from this one location, some of the basics would remain the same, barring weather conditions. He created a Target Range Card with several firing solutions for each of the guns.

After what seemed like hours, he returned all four weapons to the canvas bag and put them away. He returned to his window seat, removed the table and chair he'd set up there, and scanned the room to check whether it looked like someone had been scoping a target through the window. When he was sure that it looked like nothing more than a plain birder's studio, he went back to his office and sat at his computer. He keyed in all the firing solutions and calculated for some time. He knew he had more work to do. He would choose two weapons from the four and test-fire them at Hunters' Lodge in Santa Clara, in the northern part of the state. He would test with a Magneto Speed Chronograph to obtain a foot-per-second standard deviation of the bullet. The last time he'd tried, the bullet speed had been 2,995 feet per second with a standard deviation of ten feet per second. When he thought of Hunters' Lodge, he smiled to himself. He knew he had a target. He would kill two birds with one stone. But that was for a different time.

For now, he needed to study the wind conditions from 55 Water to the helipad. Even the smart gun, the TrackingPoint XS1, could not shoot itself, and depended on a user to determine the adjustment of its wind rocker buttons for the aggregate crosswind. He planned to take a ride on a chopper from the Downtown Manhattan Heliport. He needed to see the heliport at close range as well as measure actual wind conditions, not use the assumed ones he had been entering for today's practice. He went to the bathroom, where he spent an hour or so. By the time he came out, he had an altered persona. A gaunt, bespectacled, sixty-year-old man with steel-gray hair emerged. He walked with a slight stoop and seemed to be lost in his own thoughts. His new lean and haggard figure were a far cry from his earlier self. The Fox was a master in the art of camouflage. He should have been called the Chameleon instead of the Fox. But the Fox was not a bad metaphor.

He picked a simple cross-body sling bag and put in items that a sightseer would carry—a camera, a zoom lens, a bottle of water, and what looked like a pair of binoculars. Along with it, he added what he would need the most that afternoon, a Kestrel weather meter with applied ballistics, which could measure up to fifteen environmental parameters and allowed him to select from either G1, flat-base bullets or G7, long boat-tail bullets.

The weather meter would calculate and adjust for, among other factors, gyroscopic spindrift, wind speed, air velocity, wind chill, barometric pressure, density altitude, wind direction, crosswind, headwind, and tailwind. It was quite a beast of a meter and took out the hard work he would have otherwise had to do using loads of instruments. He would need it to take that shot from the twentieth floor of 55 Water. If he got any one of those wrong, the bullet's drag would take it away from the target. He had only one chance. This was his biggest contract ever. The president of the United States! His reputation in the dark world he lived in would outrival that of his peers.

He locked the office behind him and hobbled slowly to the bank of elevators. He reached the Downtown Manhattan Heliport and paid for a helicopter tour. He was in the company of eager sightseers taking pictures. He merged into the scene and strolled around, taking pictures of the area. He clicked hundreds of shots of the entire area and while facing 55 Water from where he stood on the helipad. When he was a little distance from the others, he took out the small weather meter and took copious readings from every possible angle and more while facing his office. He looked around at the people in his group. They were still lining up to take pictures against the choppers or the East River.

He slung his camera around his neck, picked up what looked like binoculars, and kept looking aimlessly around as any gawking sightseer would do. No one seemed interested in a wiry old man with his binoculars. But what the Fox was holding to his eyes was a 2500-meter handheld laser distance meter. He was gauging the distance from the helipad to the twentieth floor of his 55 Water office. That was vital. He had to know the distance his bullet had to travel. He replaced all his equipment into his sling bag and slowly ambled to the chopper where his group was about to board. He smiled again, only as the Fox did whenever he knew he had succeeded in his objective. It was the wry smile of a cunning Fox. But it was so subtle, few saw it under the elaborate disguise of a haggard-looking old man.

Everyone got on board and was strapped in, and the blue chopper lifted off. The sound of the wind and the rotor blades of the chopper were deafening. The pilot handed out voice-activated headsets through which he described the Big Apple's attractions. The Fox looked down at the wide expanse of the East River as the chopper went around Battery Park and then flew past Ground Zero, the 9/11 Memorial. Near Ellis Island the pilot intoned, "This is the island of hope and tears, where millions of immigrants came to America more than a hundred years ago."

The Fox was bored with all the sights and the history he was being fed. He could have hired a chopper on his own and seen more of what he wanted to see—the heliport and its distance to the twentieth floor of the 55 Water offices. But he did not want to attract any undue attention. Some pilot would remember that a scrawny old man had taken a VIP ride. That would be bad for him. He wanted to blend in. So, he had opted for the $199 ride with five eager-beaver sightseers in tow.

He played the part of a tourist, grabbing his camera and taking pictures of the Statue of Liberty on Liberty Island, and even drab Times Square, Madison Square Garden, and the Museum on Pier 86. He took pictures of the Staten Island Ferry, and the gaily colored cruise boats and speedboats that churned up a long, frothy white wake as they sped across the azure waters in every direction. He was treated to more of the endless skyscrapers of the New York financial district. Outwardly he appeared to be a gleefully picture-snapping old man enjoying the ride of a lifetime. Inwardly he balked at the endless façade of concrete as he saw it. Given a choice he would have loved to have been on a big-game safari somewhere in the African bush, felling an elephant with one of his prized long-distance tactical guns.

But this was his job. This was what he did. So, he smiled and took more pictures. Eventually the chopper made a turn and flew back to the heliport. When most of the sightseers were feeling low that their fifteen minutes was coming to an end, the Fox was excited. He imagined Marine One, the president's chopper, landing here in a week's time. He clicked more pictures of the landing area and 55 Water, which he could clearly see up ahead. This was perfect.

He needed to get back to his office and work on the pictures, and download all the information about the weather, wind conditions, and distance that he had captured with his equipment. He would then feed it into his ballistic computers and be able to get a much more precise firing solution. He had loads of works to do. But on one matter, he had made some progress. From the four weapons that he was working with, he had already cut his choice down to two, the Arctic Warfare Super Magnum gun and the TrackingPoint XS1. After live trials at Hunters' Lodge, he would choose one. When Marine One landed here with the president in exactly a week's time, he wanted to be ready. Only *one* of them would walk away from that confrontation. That someone would be himself. The Fox smiled inwardly.

The final part was to perfect a getaway plan after the assassination. He brought up the architectural plans of 55 Water and studied them at great length—the various floors, fire exits, offices, elevators, parking spaces, and utility rooms. He looked at the coffee bars, Veterans Plaza, the falcon cam, and the Elevated Acre. He studied them for a long time. A getaway was as important as the actual assassination itself, if not more so. He was the Fox. He did his act and got away. Always. He left no traces. No calling cards. No proof. Nothing that could be connected to him. After a lot of back-and-forth between the various plans, he finally decided the best way out. He checked out his escape route and decided that was it.

He looked around the room he was in. Nothing could be connected to him. He wore latex gloves, and his shoes were covered with boot covers whenever he was in the office. He did not touch anything with his bare hands. He did not leave any fingerprints. Before he left the office every day, he retraced his steps and carefully wiped the room clean. He sterilized the area using Oxy cleaners and invisible sprays that either erased or cloaked DNA. Some of the products he used were state of the art and not only hid his identity but replaced it with the genetic material of someone else's DNA sample. He shut his office and tried the getaway plan he had just worked out. He took the elevator down the way he had planned, slipped out of the 55 Water building, got into a cab, and took a ride. After an hour he got out and took a cab back. He went through his plans once again and fine-tuned it. He had a getaway plan.

He was expecting an email message from Joshua Taylor to John Smith. Josh was the same man who had hired him and sent him President Harrison's itinerary. John Smith was, of course, the Fox himself. Today's work studying the wind conditions and firing solutions at the Downtown Manhattan Heliport and all the weapons he had tried out depended on actual target practice. And Joshua's email would confirm his plans to carry out target practice with the weapon of his choice in the open at Hunters' Lodge. He opened his mailbox and sure enough, he had mail. If Joshua promised, he always delivered.

"Jason Goodman, the real estate agent I hired to rent your office at 55 Water, will meet Rusty Newman tomorrow at Hunters' Lodge."

To Jason Goodman, the Fox would be Rusty Newman. Joshua Taylor had just signed someone's death warrant. As always when his machinations went as planned, the Fox smiled.

CHAPTER EIGHT

Target Practice

"Mitch will meet you in Cologne." Kareem had been unable to come over and was on the phone with Matt. "He will provide you with as much assistance as he possibly can without putting himself in trouble. As I said, you are not officially permitted to carry out an investigation. Being on foreign soil is bad enough. Carrying out a personal vendetta with Mitch's help can put all of us in a spot. The agency will not want their cover blown in case they want to send in another agent in Amy's place. You are a soldier first, Matt, and you know where I am coming from."

Kareem was a federal agent above all. Being Amy's friend and now being close to Matt and Ashley did not take away from his fierce fealty to the agency or its basic tenets. If anyone heard what Matt and the team were up to, it would be Kareem's head on the chopping block. He could not condone it. But Matt and Ashley wouldn't be able to move on with their lives until they knew how and why Amy had died. Now Cynthia was also in the mix. It would be untrue to say that Kareem did not wish to know what had happened to Amy. He was willing to look the other way as long as they were all safe. But it was his duty to draw a line in the sand.

"I do, KK," Matt said gratefully. He was pacing up and down his outdoor deck as he spoke to Kareem. "My assurance to you, buddy, is that we will investigate only from afar—just pick up anything that may not have been seen before and pass it on to you. I do not plan to get directly involved in anything. I have Ashley and Cynthia with me and will not put their lives at risk. That is why I had so hoped you could come along. But I know you have your duties with the presidential visit to the UN. I still want you to come as soon as you can make it."

"I really wish I could come," Kareem said earnestly. "Amy was my friend too. I am as angry as you are about her death. But thanks for saying you'll be careful. Yes, you need to worry about Ashley and Cynthia. I am so sorry that you are alone in this battle, Matt. Gunther is like a wounded animal and may be a dangerous and powerful opponent of great means to have right now."

"You are right," Matt responded. He was worried about the trip but knew he had to go. He could not stop Ashley and Cynthia from coming but was concerned about their safety. He felt like he was putting them in harm's way for his personal vendetta. But he also knew there was no stopping those women. They were made of tougher stuff and would not be dissuaded. Something about Cynthia kept nagging at the back of his mind. He had felt it before. He felt it again when Kareem asked him to be careful. He would protect his daughter, Ashley. He wanted to protect Cynthia too. That was strange. He hadn't felt like that about anyone else after meeting Amy. He wiped the thought from his mind.

"That is exactly why I have asked Mitch to offer you whatever cover he can," Kareem said. He had done his best to help.

"Meanwhile I have reported what Cynthia told me about Ryan's death. The bureau will investigate. I suggest you leave before they call her in."

"Thanks, buddy." Matt was genuinely appreciative of all the help he was getting from Kareem. He knew KK was a hard-core professional who would not do anything illegal. But Amy had been his colleague. Kareem trusted him to be professional and just get leads. He felt sure he wouldn't do anything illegal. That is exactly what he hoped to do: find out what had happened to his childhood sweetheart and wife. He hoped he would be able to keep his word to his friend and not do anything rash if he came up face-to-face with the murderer. He hoped and prayed he would be able to keep his word to Kareem.

Kareem assured him, "As soon as I'm through with my duties, I'll put in a request for a week's emergency furlough and come join you guys. I'd feel better that way. Among the names Cynthia listed, something struck me. It's nagging away at the back of my mind, but I simply can't seem to put my finger on it. Anyway, not to worry now. I know it will come back. Promise I will call you and share. Okay, gotta go MJ. Bye."

"Call me if you come up with anything." Matt was unsure what Kareem meant. But he guessed that possibly Kareem did have enough to figure out what was worrying him. "Thanks again, buddy." Matt got off the phone.

"There, we're ready to go now!" Ashley looked very pleased as she set down two bags packed for their journey.

"That's my girl! What would I do without you?"

Ashley smiled and said, "That's the least I could do for getting you to agree to take me along."

"I am still worried." Her father looked at his wife's picture above the fireplace and added, "Your mother will never forgive me if I put you in harm's way. But then I guess she knows how stubborn you can be. You do take after her. She was a tough woman. I liked that about her. I like that about you, too. Kareem was on the phone just now, reminding us to be careful. Now that we know we are in this situation and things could get tricky in Bavaria, it's wise to be prepared."

Matt picked up a small bag and dumped its contents on the table. "Simple things, really, just to help us keep in touch in case we get lost in a strange place. These are very cleverly disguised tracking devices. As you can see, this one here looks like a button you can sew onto your clothes. This pen that sends out a signal of a person's location has a six-hour battery life and doubles as a miniature camera."

"Now, that's a pretty cool thing." Ashley was impressed by the gizmos.

"We are going to Munich to hunt for your mother's killer. Our only lead is the chairman of the most powerful banking corporation in Munich. We will be walking into a lion's den. As Kareem said just now, we are not the law, nor do we have anyone to back us up in case we run into trouble. We will meet Mitch, the CIA head, at Cologne just so that he knows we are in his territory. I am sure he is bound to stop us from doing anything daft. I still know we will do some snooping of our own. For all intents and purposes, we are on our own in a foreign land. These gizmos are just a few things for our protection."

"Mom would have made me have much more than this, Dad. Like I said, they are cool. You have lunch while I download our tickets and call for the cab."

She looked at her mother's picture and smiled to herself. At last, she knew she was doing something to get justice for her mother. That was a good feeling. This was better than fighting for justice against a paint company or exclusive scoops. This was personal. This was going after her mother's killers. For the first time in a long time, Ashley felt like her life had a purpose. Just like her father, who had sunk into a loner's life, Ashley had her own bouts of depression. She did not show it to her father. She did not want to make it any worse for him. But it had taken a toll on her life, too. She could not think about being in a relationship, though many eligible men had showed an interest in her. A man and a relationship were the last things on her mind. She wanted to know what had happened to her mother.

★

It was going to be a long ride. As he headed out on Highway 187 north to Santa Clara, 336 miles away, the Fox knew it would take him a little over five hours to reach Franklin County and the private Hunters' Lodge. He had only one major aim. Many would have found an easy way through it, put a bullet through his subject's head, and disposed of the body. No one would have been the wiser. But the Fox was a wily, creative animal who chose subtlety over brute force. He loved exploring forbidden paths and pulling off feats that required superhuman dexterity and great perseverance. He always won. And he always got away. He was the Fox. He could not afford to make mistakes. He would not. He was a born hunter. He needed to dispense with someone who could lead back to his lair. And he wanted to do it in characteristic style.

Creature of the night that he was, he drove in the darkness to the private six-hundred-acre Hunters' Lodge in Santa Clara. He knew the lodge was a well-appointed log home with all the trappings of a holiday retreat. He was not going there to view the scenic beauty of the Adirondack Park but to use the private wooded land to test his Arctic Warfare gun and the TrackingPoint XS1. He wanted a subject. He had one. He smiled at the prospect and stepped on the gas.

He reached the lodge and carted the bag with the weapons, bipods, ammo, ballistic computers, magneto chronographs, and other gear inside. He set them all out on the table, pleased with himself. He was tired. He showered, warmed some takeout he had brought, sat down, and ate in silence. He spent over two hours cleaning the weapons with great care. After he had checked every item he had come with, he packed them all up again and put the bag away. He switched off the lights and retired for the night.

After an early morning breakfast, the next day he was seated on the deck facing the Adirondack Park when he heard the car pulling up into the grassy courtyard. He went down and opened the screened porch and let Jason, the real estate agent, in.

"Good morning, Rusty!" Jason shot out his hand. "Jason Goodman! I arranged for the lease of your offices at 55 Water. It is one of the best in New York, and I am sure you will be happy to see the peregrine falcons on the fourteenth floor."

"Rusty here." The Fox shook Jason's proffered hand. "Oh yes, that's a good office block. Thanks for the help. I would also like some farmland to further not just my interest in watching birds, but also my hobby of hunting. I was told this property comes highly recommended."

He walked Jason to the living room, where they settled down on the sofas. "You said it, Rusty: this is one heck of a property. You need to go past the northern hardwood and conifer forests and check out the internal trails. You'll love it!"

Jason was a salesman. It bored the Fox, but he was forced to listen to this stupid oaf as he reeled off the values of the six-hundred-acre farm, the view of the Adirondack Park, the wildlife, the trails, and the prime hunting locations.

The Fox had other plans. "Yes, I would love to go on a trail right now and do some target practice. No firing today. I just want to scope and test the locations, then come back with my buddies in the fall and spend some time hunting deer and bear."

"Sure, why not?" Jason was ready to agree to anything. At 6 percent standard commission, Jason would pocket a cool $51,600 on the $860,000 listed price for Hunters' Lodge. Chloe would be happy. He hoped to propose to her. This commission would help make a handsome down payment on the mortgage he had lined up for her as a wedding gift.

The Fox could see that Jason was taking the bait hook, line, and sinker.

"Done, Jason," the Fox said. "If I find the hunting spot is good, then I'll be ready to ink the deal by the time we get back here." He watched Jason's eyes almost pop out of their sockets. "So, what do you say? Shall we?"

"Whatever you say, Rusty." Jason was fawning. "I am here to get the best deal for you. Trust me. Do you want help with your hunting gear?"

He was ready to bend over backward if he could earn fifty grand in an hour's time. His client had arranged for the 55 Water lease over the phone. He had been instructed to come here today to meet a potential buyer for Hunters' Lodge. Jason hadn't had any time to study the property in detail. He had read up a bit on its selling points and had already said all that to Rusty. But this chap seemed ready to sign on the dotted line right away. This would be the fastest fifty grand he'd ever made. He would have to stay overnight in Franklin County to draw up the paperwork and go through the sale procedures. His mind was already in a whirl.

"Thanks," the Fox said. "We are going to drive to the target site first. You can help place these wind flags at intervals on our way there. That's to help me get an estimate of wind speed, which will be converted into a lateral minute-of-angle point-of-aim correction." He handed Jason what looked like streamers fixed on small plastic poles.

Jason said, "Oh, these aren't flags. But I guess they'll help you figure out which way the wind is blowing, huh?" His mind was working overtime, figuring out the commission, paperwork, and mortgage, and seeing the huge smile on Chloe's face when he dangled the key to their new house in her face. He wanted to scream.

"Yeah, they are pennants, really," the Fox explained. "That long, pointy tail flies in the wind better and is great for my purposes. This, as you can see, is a human silhouette that we need to fix at the target site." He gave Jason what looked like a cutout of a human figure in black metal, with clearly marked white rings painted around a large X on the head and another on the heart.

Jason did not know why this prospective real estate client wanted a human figure to train on for shooting bears and deer in the fall, but something told him not to ask too many questions. Much as he appeared to be friendly, something about this bird-watcher-turned-hunter gave him an uneasy feeling. He did not seem to be the type who liked being chatted up. Jason was a salesman and had met all sorts of clients and could gauge the different types. Some were gregarious, others were like an odd female client who regaled him with raunchy jokes he did not approve of, and then there were the types like the man he was dealing with now—the quiet, self-assured ones like Rusty Newman. They did not speak much, and even if at times they appeared to be making small talk, he knew all they wanted was someone to just take instructions and not expect much in the form of a response.

"Sure thing, Rusty!" If he was going to sign the deal, who the hell cared what this rich bum shot at? All Jason cared about was Chloe and their little home.

Jason grabbed whatever he could and carried it to the Jeep. The Fox brought out a large bag that Jason presumed held the weapons and dumped it in the back. Jason wondered what kind of weapons required such large bags, but anyway, that was none of his concern. He hopped into the Jeep with his client and they drove off downhill.

It took them the better part of an hour to drive past Jennings Brook and the wetlands and almost two miles to get to the target site, stopping to place wind flags along the route. The Fox stopped when he saw a perfect site, a small hillock in a clearing. The silhouette target came with an A-frame, and Jason watched as Rusty anchored it, using a steel stake tie-down.

"That's it, then." The Fox hopped into the car. "Let me get back and scope this target." He handed Jason a bunch of knock-over animal silhouettes shaped like chickens, turkeys, and prairie dogs. "Hang on to these. After I'm finished scoping the human silhouette, I want to check if I can see these small fellas from a small hill near the lodge almost two miles away. I have some darn good scopes I paid a fortune for, and I want to see if I can see these small targets. If so, I may be able to do some small-game hunting without having to go far out into the woods. I'll call you on the radio and ask your help to move them around. Shall we?"

He waved at Jason as he started his vehicle and drove back to the lodge without waiting for a response. He knew the fawning idiot of a real estate agent would have run buck naked if he had asked him to.

"As you say, Rusty!" Jason tried to look excited and waved his two-way radio. "Give me a shout, and I'll hold up these animals for you to scope."

This guy's a knucklehead, Jason thought. The animal silhouettes were so darn small that you couldn't see them at a thousand yards. How the hell was this crazy lout hoping to see them from two miles away, no matter what kind of scope he had, let alone take potshots at them?

Jason knew this chap only barked orders and did not wait for responses. He knew people did his bidding. There was that something about him. That quiet power. Jason felt queasy about this guy. But if the stupid bugger had money to throw away, who was he to question him? This world was full of all sorts of loonies.

The Fox drove back to a small hillock that he had planned to shoot from. He wanted to test downhill shot angles, since that's what he would be doing from the twentieth floor of 55 Water. He hoped to replicate the downhill bullet drop—the angle at which a bullet drops during trajectory to target. He lifted the heavy bag and placed it on the ground, rolled out the shooting mat, and set up the weapons. He fixed the bayonet-style Magneto Speed chronograph on the barrel of the Arctic Warfare, appended the bipods and the scopes, and set his ballistic computers, weather meter, and range cards close at hand.

He loaded both weapons, since he planned to test-fire both. First, he would test the Arctic Warfare to obtain a standard deviation of ten feet per second. Then he would try out the TrackingPoint XS1. Finally, he would choose one for the job. He already had an idea how he was going to do the trials. His plan was as perfect as it was devious. He was going to wipe out any connecting line between him and the rental of 55 Water Street, and also test his guns. What a way to literally 'kill' two birds with one stone!

"Jason, my man," the Fox spoke into the two-way radio, "are you ready? Could you angle the A-frame to the right a bit? I can't seem to see the human silhouette. Just hold it, and I'll call you as I scope so you can arrange it to perfection. Sorry, it may take ten or fifteen minutes to adjust it. I hope that's okay."

"Sure thing, Rusty!" Jason's voice crackled over the radio. "I am here and will move it at your command. Take your time. I have all morning. Nothing to worry about."

On his ballistic computer, the Fox entered the barrel length of his weapon, its twist rate and height of scope above the bore. He then held the weather meter up to capture the barometric pressure, humidity, head and tail wind, wind speeds, and temperature. He keyed the atmospherics and .338 Lapua Magnum ammo, its weight, distance to target, incline of shot angle, and stationary position of the target into his handheld ballistic computer. The computer calculated the precise windage settings and elevation for a hit.

He lay down on the mat and set the elevation knob and parallax knobs on his scope to the recommended settings. All that was technology. Now he had to "true" his shot by doing several test shots so he could figure out exactly how high or low his real shots would compare with what the ballistic computer had predicted. The weight of the bullet, the wind drag that could affect trajectory, and the great distance of the shot planned for—even the curvature of the earth—could cause minute variations for the single shot he would eventually be able to pull off from 55 Water Street.

But he would be prepared with multiple firing solutions just in case he did miss and managed to get one more chance. He was unsure if he would have a chance at a second shot, so he reentered the same data and once again tried to true his shot at a moving target. After the first shot, the subject might duck, and he needed to be prepared.

"You are doing great, Jason. I have several firing solutions now. Another fifteen minutes or so and we can wrap it up." The

Fox did not listen to the crackle of the radio with Jason's response. He moved over and stationed himself beside the TrackingPoint XS1. Fortunately, he did not have to go through all the elaborate arrangements he had had to do on the Arctic Warfare. The TrackingPoint XS1 was a smart gun. It did almost everything on its own, except crosswind information that he had entered earlier when he had set up the gun. He looked through the scope and viewed the target on the heads-up display, ranged it, and pressed the red tag button. In an instant, the computers worked out the atmospherics, and determined the inclination, cant, and shot direction based on launch dynamics and drag coefficient, and a red pip was placed on his target at the precise spot he wished to fire at. The TrackingPoint was ready to fire.

"Okay, Jason," he called out on the radio. "I am done with the human target. Please hold up the prairie dog silhouette. Stand close to the human one and hold it up high."

He saw Jason through the scope of his Arctic Warfare. He took aim, held his breath, saw his target in his crosshairs, and fired a single shot. The .338 Lapua Magnum 8.6 × 700 mm, custom-built center-fire cartridge tore through his weapon at three thousand feet per second, traversing the 1.7 miles in three seconds and tearing Jason's right arm from the shoulder. The prairie dog was still in its clutches as the blood-spurting limb flew into the air. He could see Jason's shocked disbelief and pain but couldn't hear his scream. The Fox took one more shot at his left leg, at the knee joint, and blew off the real estate agent's kneecap. Though he could not hear anything, the Fox could imagine the howling pain. He smiled. He was in his element. He was more interested in the Magneto Speed ballistic chronograph mounted on the barrel and measuring the bullet speed. He was assured he had bettered his standard deviation to ten feet per second. Classic!

The Fox swiftly rolled across the mat to the TrackingPoint XS1 firearm as Jason was hopping, falling over, getting up, and trying to run. But without two limbs, his movement was worse than that of a drunken ostrich trying to do a Rumba. The Fox had already tagged Jason earlier. The tracking scope's built-in laser had illuminated a red dot on Jason's head in his reticle. As Jason kept hobbling in his death dance, the sensors on his gun worked out possible firing solutions fifty-four times a second. Soon the predictive image processing pipeline figured out where Jason would do his ostrich Rumba next, at three miles per hour, and placed a blue reticle on his head three thousand yards away. The foreground and background tracking continuously tracked Jason in his death hobble.

In his jet-fighter-look optics, he could see that wind speed was around 6.5 miles per hour. The tracking algorithm computing the velocity of the bullet to Jason's expected position predicted the next 18.5 milliseconds. The Fox took the shot and held the trigger down. The reticle on Jason's head turned from blue to red. When the reticle and the red tag coincided, Jason's head was blown to a thousand smithereens, brain shards flying all over, blood gushing as from a fountain, and his headless body twitched involuntarily several times, flopped around, and crumpled into the ground. The Fox smiled.

He had decided. He would use the TrackingPoint XS1.338 Lapua Magnum Precision Guided Firearm. This long-range, laser-guided robot rifle with a Linux-powered scope and jet-fighter lock-and-launch technology was the Fox's weapon of choice to kill the American president. Thanks to Jason Goodman.

CHAPTER NINE

Bavaria

Matt, Ashley, and Cynthia arrived at the Cologne airport in Germany and went straight to the Panorama Restaurant in Terminal One. Mitch had agreed to meet them there. Families were on the observation deck watching cargo and military planes taking off or landing. They ordered coffee and had breakfast as they waited for Mitch.

"Welcome to Cologne." Mitch was a tall, heavyset, military-type man in his early forties.

"Great to be here." Matt shot up and grabbed Mitch's outstretched hand.

"Matt Jordan; my daughter, Ashley; and Cynthia," Matt said, waving to his team. All shook hands.

"Mitch O'Donnell. I head up the station here. I'm a good friend of Kareem, so I guess I'm among friends. I know you need to fly out to Bavaria from here. Don't want to hold you up for long. It must have been a long haul overnight from JFK to here, so let me get right to the topic at hand."

"Yep," Matt agreed. "It was a long haul and quite tiring."

"Kareem has warned you enough about not getting involved in any unwarranted investigation, so I will not repeat that and bore you. Enjoy your stay in Bavaria, look around, and see if you can find anything to put your mind at ease without getting yourself or me in trouble. Here's my card. Call me if you run into any trouble. Just in case—not that I think you could really unearth anything of significance—but in case you do, please do not do anything. Call me immediately."

"You seem sure we won't find anything." Cynthia was not pleased.

"Cynthia, I know you lost your boyfriend and must be genuinely upset that nothing came of the investigation. But remember, I'm not part of the local police here. I can only accept the results of their investigation. I do not think they had anything to hide. I am truly very sorry for what happened to Ryan. Trust me, we do not like it when anything happens to an American citizen abroad. We did lean on the German Bundespolizei and went through every piece of their investigation process. They did their best. But there was nothing—no motive, no fingerprints, no known enemies, no leads to follow up—and they closed the case after an extensive and thorough investigation."

"So, it's possible that someone quite powerful could have committed this crime," Cynthia replied. "Someone who had the clout to kill two Americans who worked in one bank within a month of each other and wipe all traces clean."

"That is quite possible," Mitch said. "Trust me, when you have many incidents going on here, it is not easy to connect an accident and a murder as part of one criminal enterprise. One was an operative and the other a civilian. No, Cynthia, the police did not connect it. Now that I hear Ryan did see or hear something, in retrospect it feels that we should have treated both as one case. That's hindsight for you. Remember, we were not privy to the information you have. Whether Amy wanted to follow up the lead she had and report in later, we will never know. But the fact is we did not have a report from her. Even now we have no evidence that Herr Gunther gave the orders to have them killed. It's not easy to walk into the office of the most powerful banker in Bavaria and charge him with murder."

"Mitch, we understand your limitations," Matt said. "That's why we are here. We are not going to step on anyone's toes. We will not do anything illegal. We have lost our loved ones. We just want to snoop around without, of course, raising any suspicions and see if we can augment something that we may just be lucky to turn up. Just a wild chance. Life has not been easy for any of us. It's been a year of pain. Some of us still can't lie down and have a good night's sleep. My daughter has been unable to move on, and Cynthia's case is no different. We are not as powerful as the CIA, FBI, or the Federal Police of Germany. We may unearth nothing, but it will give us great peace of mind if we can simply scout around in our own way. At the very least, it will make us feel better and help calm our troubled minds. If we find nothing, I assure you, we will go back."

Mitch said, "Matt, I can feel your pain. I may not know exactly how you feel, but I do have an idea. I have been in situations where I had to explain to families who had lost loved ones to either terrorist or criminal activities. I have been a Marine and have lost close friends—some whose families I had known for years. Calling them to break the news is not easy. Trust me, sad things do happen even to everyday tourists from America. I completely understand your situation, and that is why when Kareem told me about your plans, I did not discourage it. I am here to *help*."

Mitch was trying his best to sound helpful. "All I am saying is what Kareem also did. Don't overstep and let the German police or even Gunther and his goons catch you in some tricky situation. Be careful. Gunther is no angel. You're right. We do have our suspicions about his activities. That's exactly what Amy was helping uncover. Unfortunately, she didn't make it. I don't want any tragedy to befall you."

"That's good," Ash replied. "We don't hope to do anything that will run afoul of the law. As Dad said, if nothing else, we want to do this at least for our peace of mind. If we find nothing, we will go back. I promise you. We will not do anything that could embarrass you or the local law enforcement agencies. But thanks for your offer of support."

"Any suggestion for a place to stay in Bavaria?" Matt was happy the meeting was going well. "We want to stay in that village … How do you say that? Yes, Schwangau"

"The Waldmann, a small inn with stunning views of the surrounding castles, is a perfect spot. You will love it. I think it's a family-run business. You will enjoy their warm hospitality."

Matt was happy. He knew where the Waldmann was. He had done his homework. It was close to Gunther's chateau.

"I need to get back to my office. Do keep in touch. Enjoy your time in Bavaria and be sure to give me a call before you leave for the US, so I'll know that I don't need to worry about you anymore."

They all laughed at that, and Mitch left. At least Mitch had not put them on the next plane back home. They still had their little enterprise all set up. Mitch had also offered to help. That was good. They spent some more time in the restaurant and then went down and checked in for their flight to Munich.

After landing in Munich, Ashley rented a BMW SUV for their trip. From the Munich airport, they drove to the Augustiner Großgaststätten beer hall in the pedestrian precinct of the city. They got out of the car and stood and looked at the spot where Amy had crossed the street. Matt wanted to stand where she had stood. He looked at Ashley. She too seemed to want to just feel the area where Amy had breathed her last. Matt and Ashley walked across the Marienplatz to the curb from where Amy had most likely stepped off into the path of the oncoming truck. It was not the pain that he felt. It was a closeness. Not because she had died here, but because this was where his Amy's presence was. The Großgaststätten beer hall was where she had come. He could feel her all around him. For him, Amy was alive. He wanted to live her, feel her, and be part of her.

He looked at the Augustiner Großgaststätten beer hall. Steeped in history, it was one of the few buildings from Munich's art nouveau period that still retained its age-old glory of the early thirteenth century, when the foundation stone for the Augustine Abbey was laid. In his mind, Matt could see Amy seated at one of the numerous restaurants or beer halls, reading a book that must have transported her to an age long gone by as time stood still.

Cynthia took them to Amy's favorite part of the beer hall, the Augustiner Arcade Garden. The frescoes on the walls of the indoor courtyard with tables spread out in the open seemed a perfect place to try out one of their famous Bavarian beers. They sat down in the open and ordered the Augustiner Weissbier, a spicy amber wheat beer, matured in their cellars. Matt missed Amy very much. She must have sat here and had this beer. He felt like he could see her. He looked at Ashley, and by the expression on her face, he could tell she too was thinking of her mother. He looked away and drank his beer.

"Cynthia, it's been so long!" Gerhard's voice rang out. "Welcome to Munich!" He hugged Cynthia, kissing her cheeks, and stuck his hand out to Matt and Ashley.

"Matt and Ashley, right? I know we meet under painful circumstances. I wish we had all met last year, when Ryan and Amy were here. We had such good times. Amy was great, and so was Ryan. I wish circumstances were better. But let's figure out how those who made them go away will pay for their sins."

"Thanks, Gerhard," Matt said, acknowledging his condolences, and Ashley gave him a perfunctory hug. She was still thinking of her mother being so close to this place she used to frequent.

"Our federal police and your government agents wrapped up the case pretty rapidly. But I always thought there was more to the case." Gerhard sounded deflated when he said that.

"We want to find out more about the chairman of the G & H Bayerischer Bank, Heinrich Gunther," Matt said. "I hear the German Federal Financial Supervisory Authority and the German public prosecutor's office were investigating him for alleged tax evasion, money laundering, and other financial irregularities. The bank does seem to carry a lot of dirty linen. They must have had something to hide. Both Amy and Ryan walked into that corporate malfeasance, eyes wide open."

"They may have unearthed something and been too late to stop it," Gerhard said. "And someone stopped them before they could pass on that information. I think we need to look up this Heinrich guy. I don't trust him one bit and somehow have a gut feeling that he is connected to this. He is a bloody Nazi son of a bitch."

"Yes, Gerhard," Cynthia said. "That's an angle we should follow up on. Ryan had seen election leaflets of the Alternative für Deutschland party in Gunther's office. He also saw leaflets of the neo-Nazi German Reich party, the National Democratic Party, and the ultra-right-wing, anti-Islamic Patriotic Europeans Against the Islamization of the West, the PEGIDA in Germany, who actually committed violence against Muslims on the streets of Germany. Why would the chairman of a large bank like the G & H be connected to xenophobic and anti-Islamic parties that advocate violence?"

Gerhard's anger at the mere mention of Gunther's name was evident in his tone. "He is an irrational fellow. He picked up a fight with me and fired me on the spot. When I look back now, I don't know if it had anything to do with my friendship with Amy. He probably was already on to Amy and wanted me out of the scene. He thought he would silence an American and hush it up. I agree with you, Cynthia. That crook seems to be up to his eyeballs in this. We need to look him up."

"So many incidents point to his involvement," Cynthia said. "Gunther using a phone with a scrambler device when all he had to do was use his secure videoconferencing facility to liaise with his senior executives."

"Yes," Matt said, "that's the stuff people in the FBI and police forces would use. Why would he need that?"

"Overhearing Gunther's conversation on the scrambler phone about Har … something and that list of names must have sealed my poor Ryan's fate." Cynthia was not crying, but you could not miss the change in her tone as she referred to her boyfriend's slaying.

"He said some names right." Ashley was looking at her notes. "Let me see … Yes, here it is." She flipped through the pages and read out, "Chuck, Christian, Englebert, Aleixandre, and Raymond. That other word was Harmagedon. I looked it up. It's a Hebrew word." She paused, looked at everyone, and added, "It means '*Armageddon.*'"

"What was Gunther referring to?" Gerhard asked. "That Armageddon was on? What kind of cataclysmic event is on? What are he and some friends up to, meeting in a chateau in the village of Schwangau? Fox hunting with a bunch of rich buddies cannot be equated with the final battle by Jesus Christ against Satan."

"Yes," Cynthia said. "That is the puzzling factor. Ryan saw or heard something and connected the dots. He did not live to tell the tale. Amy was also silenced. Someone has something really bad to hide."

"Gerhard, you need to find a way to get us into Gunther's chateau," Matt said.

"That is going to be difficult, but not impossible," Gerhard said. "Leave it to me and I will find a way."

"You two," Matt said, addressing Cynthia and Ashley, "see if you can find more on the Armageddon, the reference to a fox, and those names. Look up old newspapers, talk to people, search the web, whatever, but see what you can come up with. Gerhard here also may be able to help. If we can get something that connects the dots of an Armageddon, a fox, a bunch of friends, and a meeting in a Bavarian chateau, it will help us crack this case." He did not sound very hopeful. They left soon afterward.

Matt drove past the magnificent nineteenth-century Neuschwanstein castle on their way to Schwangau. They drove past tourists on the cantilever iron Marienbrücke Bridge spanning the Pöllat Gorge, viewing the dramatic waterfall above Neuschwanstein. They made their way past the wooded Allgauer Alps down the road to the tiny village of Schwangau, with its age-old inns, restaurants, and souvenir shops, and stopped at the Hotel Waldmann. The hotel surrounded by castles and the Alps was a perfect spot for their enterprise of snooping on Gunther's chateau nearby. They would be among the numerous tourists who thronged the area to view the castles, swim, or go on walks. A perfect cover. Just as Mitch had said, it was a cozy little place.

"Welcome to Schwangau." Gerhard opened the door to help Ashley and Cynthia out of the car.

"It's a shame that Bavarian kings have such a notorious present-day neighbor like Gunther," Ashley said.

"Not for long, Ash," Cynthia said. "Not if we can help it. Let's hope we can find something from his chateau tomorrow and tear his reputation down."

"Let's check in and plan how to get into the chateau tomorrow." Matt and Gerhard grabbed the bags, and they made their way into the hotel.

They checked into their rooms, had some beers and dinner, and ended on the balcony in Matt's room.

"I spent some time at the tourist desk downstairs, appearing to show great interest in the leisure activities around here," Matt said. He had some brochures with him. "Gunther is from here, and we don't want the locals to know we have interests other than the sights and sounds of their town. So, I told them we hope to visit Lake Schwansee, go sailing on Lake Forggensee, and round off with a cable-car ride up Tegelberg Mountain."

"But we will do nothing of the sort," Gerhard said. "We head off to Gunther's chateau tomorrow. We don't have time to lose. He is up to something. I have a feeling that whatever it is, we are sure to find something in that chateau." He looked toward Neuschwanstein Castle, lit up against the night sky. "It's some way up there. We're going to trek up that path tomorrow."

"Yes, I hope we can get something to nail him." Cynthia's anger at the man she was sure was responsible for her boyfriend's gruesome murder was evident in her tone.

"We will, Cynthia." Ashley sounded positive. "Ryan did overhear Gunther planning a meeting here with a group of buddies. Let's hope we can find something."

"Just to be on the safe side, I want all of us to have those tracking devices I gave you before we left—just in case we get separated or lost out there," Matt said. "Sew them onto your jackets, into a pocket—wherever they are hidden from view." Turning to his daughter, he said, "I believe you have that pen camera I gave you. It doubles as a tracking device."

"Yes, Dad." Ash displayed her pen, stuck firmly in the pocket of her shirt. "I need to go to the store in the lobby to pick up a few necessities. Be back soon."

Gerhard settled on the couch in the living room and caught up with the evening news on the TV.

"Always a soldier, I can see." Cynthia was impressed. She took the device Matt proffered her and dropped it into the pocket of her coat." Thanks, Matt." She grabbed a beer from the room refrigerator and walked back out to the balcony.

In a darkened corner, she settled into a chair with her beer. She stared out into the dark, looking at the inky image of the Neuschwanstein. It was an imposing site even in the gathering dusk. But it was not the beauty of the castle she was enamored with. Her mind raced back to the time when she was in Bavaria with Ryan. This was the first time she had been back. It felt weird to be in Germany without him. She was looking toward the castle and the chateau beyond, and thinking of its dark owner, Gunther, who she was certain had ordered Ryan's death.

"I am sorry, Cynthia." Matt stood beside her with a beer. It was almost as if he had read her mind.

"Thanks, Matt." Her voice had lost some of the toughness she exhibited most of the time. "It's hard to be back. Ryan was here. That bastard killed him. I wish to run into him tomorrow and physically strangle his German throat."

"You will, Cynthia." Matt's voice was fatherly. He strode up to the balustrade, leaned against it, and looked at Cynthia. "It's the same for me. This is the first time I have been in Bavaria since Amy's death. You could not have put it better. I can almost see the man who ordered her death seated somewhere in that chateau straight up ahead of us now. Wish I could do the same. But I know it's harder on you. You lived here with Ryan. You saw what they did to him. You must be very angry. I promise you; Ryan will get justice."

For the first time in a year, Cynthia felt vulnerable. She had been strong all this while, having built up a hard exterior since losing Ryan. She had to be strong, so she could find Ryan's killers. She was alone. She had been tough. But suddenly, when Matt said those words, her steely exterior crumbled. She looked up at him and smiled. Her eyes were moist. Matt stepped up to her and patted her shoulder. Instinctively she reached up and placed her hands on his hand, holding it in place. For a moment time seemed to stand still.

Since Amy's death, Matt had not looked at another woman. He'd had no desire to do so. He was so consumed with her loss that he knew he was not being a good father to Ashley. For the first time in a long time, a female hand other than Amy's had touched him. He looked down into Cynthia's eyes. He could see the loss that he felt in his soul. They were two lost souls close to the place where they had lost their loved ones. Their shared loss seemed to be drawing them close, giving them strength.

"I'm back," Ashley called from the door.

Cynthia dropped her hands and shot up. "Did you get what you wanted?" The steely exterior dropped back into place. She was back in her shell.

"Oh yes." Ashley had not seen anything. "I'm off to bed. Do you want to come over or finish your beer?"

"No, I am coming." Cynthia said good night and walked out with Ashley to their rooms.

"See you all tomorrow," Gerhard said, leaving as well.

Matt was still out on the balcony. He just watched Cynthia walking away. He did not know what to think. Amy was all he could think about. But as he looked at Cynthia's retreating figure, he almost felt like asking her to stay back to talk for a while. He turned away and looked at the now completely darkened image of the Neuschwanstein Castle. His lips curled into a grimace as he stared out into the cold face of Gunther Otto

Heinrich, the chairman of G & H Bayerischer Bank, seated somewhere in the recesses of the chateau.

"I am coming for you," Matt said under his breath. His mind went back to Amy's tribulations in Bavaria and what had brought him there. He sipped his beer and thought of all the good days with Amy. He lost track of time and sat there lost in his thoughts for a long while. When he got up to get another beer, he discovered there weren't any more. Despite the long drive, Matt was not sleepy yet. He was so close to his quarry. Amy seemed to beckon from the grave. He decided to go down to the restaurant, hoping to find a quiet corner to sit and think about her. There he found Cynthia seated alone at a far corner table, lost in her thoughts.

"Hello, stranger. May I join you?"

"Ah, Matt. Sure, do sit down." Cynthia waved at the seat across from her. "I couldn't sleep. Kept turning and tossing in my bed. So, I decided to come down."

"Same here, Cynthia."

"We're close to Gunther's chateau ..."

"I know you want to confront him. That's what kept me awake too. Tell me more about yourself, Cynthia." Matt was hoping to change the topic for her sake. This brooding was not helping. "Are you working for any major media houses or freelancing, like Ashley?"

Either she was happy to open up to him or she knew he was trying to wean her away from her painful thoughts. Whatever the case, she was happy to play along. Matt seemed to care. "I freelance for several large media houses," she said. "It's better that way. I am not tied down to one, and I can make my own schedule and choose which stories I pick up. There's always something to work on. All you need is dogged determination, loads of research, and some well-placed informants willing to provide leaks to come up with a good story. Not as easy as it sounds, but generally that's what it takes to make a difference in the community and my bank balance. I have no children, live in a modest apartment, read books, and most of the time am kinda happy with my lot in life."

"I have always admired reporters. I was very happy when Ashley graduated in journalism. In fact, I would have loved to be a Bob Woodward or Carl Bernstein!"

"I think you have done wonderfully well in the military. Ashley showed me your Silver Star and told me the stories of you flying into enemy fire to save your fellow soldiers. That's courage in the face of certain danger. Such selfless service for fellow countrymen is exemplary. To me, you are already a hero, Matt."

"Thanks, Cynthia."

Matt did not wish to dwell on his exploits. He never saw it that way. He did what had to be done. That was that. He was sure his buddies would have done the same for him.

"Did you ever consider remarrying, Matt?"

Cynthia's question took Matt by surprise. They had gone from Gunther to journalism to his personal life. Strangely, he felt at ease with Cynthia and did not mind her asking.

"Twenty-five years of marriage can be a long time, Cynthia. Even if our assignments kept us apart for most of that time, it was still a quarter of a century of being together. It's not easy to let go of Amy. She was so special. We built so many memories together. We hardly had any time together after I returned from active duty and settled down. We had so many plans. We did not get the chance."

"I am sorry," Cynthia said. "What was Amy like to you? I'm just curious. You don't need to answer if you're not comfortable with it." Cynthia was intrigued by a man who loved his wife so deeply. Amy was a lucky woman. She just wanted to know what it felt like from a man's point of view to love someone so deeply.

"Imagine you are standing in a field full of flowers in bloom, millions of flowers," Matt said. He seemed to be in a trance. "You can hear peals of laughter from hundreds of babies. Imagine the riot of color of the flowers and their fragrance and the innocence of babies harkening to heavenly happiness ... and you have Amy."

Cynthia was struck. What a metaphor. Like flowers in bloom and the bliss of newborns. Such devotion. Such love. Amy had passed on. But he spoke of her like she was seated right there. Even after twenty-five years of marriage, he spoke as if he had not had enough time to love her. This man was one in a million. She and Ryan had barely had a few years together. They had not even had the chance to get married. But here was a man who, after a quarter of a century with his wife, still missed her as though he had just met her for the first time. He could smell her like flowers in bloom.

Matt felt comfortable in Cynthia's presence. Ashley and Kareem knew he missed Amy so much that they tried hard to take his mind away from that lonesome world and hardly broached the topic. They wanted to make him happy. They did not want him to suffer. This was the first time someone had asked him so poignantly why he was alone. It had aroused his deepest feelings. Strangely, he did not mind. It was almost as if he wanted to offload his pain.

"We did have our good times in between tours of duty. But our big dream was to retire from active service, take a long vacation, and then settle down. Bavaria was Amy's last assignment. She was to come back home. Finally, we were set to live our life! That bastard Gunther took it all away." Despite his best attempt, the steely soldier's face looked defeated. He did not cry, but he did not need to. His face was ashen.

Cynthia's heart went out to this man. She felt like reaching out and giving him a hug but restrained herself. Her mind went back to her times with Ryan. She wished she had had a chance to spend a quarter of a century with him and feel like a million flowers in bloom. She had a lump rose in her throat. She was normally not emotional. But suddenly she felt vulnerable.

"I'm sorry, Cynthia. I seem to have spoiled the evening for you."

"No, no, it's perfectly okay. We're here because you lost Amy. I can understand you loved her deeply. Sorry, Matt, I honestly am." She was putting on a brave face. For the first time, she knew she did not have the control she normally had over herself.

"I am so sorry I went on about myself there. Here you didn't even have the chance to marry Ryan and raise a family. You must be in a worse place than I am, Cynthia."

Cynthia stifled a sob. She did not know what to say but managed to get out, "I guess I need to get back to my room." She got up. Something had burst the dam of feelings she had kept in check. She knew if she stayed any longer, things would get out of hand. She did not want Matt to see her like that. It would be better if she left.

"Let me help you." Matt shot up, pulled her chair back, and helped her to her feet. They walked in silence up the stairs. She was ahead, and Matt followed. When he got to his door, he stood there, not knowing if he should stop her and wish her good night. He felt guilty. He had gone on about Amy, and it must have aroused her memories of Ryan. She was probably lost in her thoughts and stumbling to her room. The last thing he wanted to do was stop her from the train of thought that kept her going. He quietly opened the door and slipped inside. He shut it gently behind him but just stood there. He kept staring at the door, wondering if it had been wrong not to say good night. He stood there for a long time.

Suddenly the door was thrown open and Cynthia barged in.

"I am so sorry, Matt. I just walked away without saying a word. I should have ..." She nearly walked right up to his face. She had probably not expected him to be standing so close to the door.

She was so close; he could smell her presence. Matt didn't know what he was doing when he took her in his arms and kissed her. It just happened. His strong arms enveloped her, and he cupped the back of her head, bent and kissed her. Cynthia's arms flew around his neck and she closed her eyes, lost in a trance. Time stood still. What had been held back for a year seemed to melt away. The steely exteriors both had cultivated as a barrier against the outside world had dissipated. Two souls lost to the world seemed to unite, melt, and become one.

Matt pulled away and said, "I'm sorry ... I should not have ..."

Cynthia pulled his face down and kissed him. Matt's powerful embrace took her breath away. He led the way to the bed. They did not speak. The lovemaking was not urgent. Nor was it desperate. It was a slow passion, like a dance in the moonlight. He kissed her on the nape of her neck. She let out a gasp. The clothes peeled off and they lay in bed, the moonlight shining through the open window and glistening off their naked bodies. They kissed for a long time and then made slow, passionate love.

They were unhurried and took the time to explore the unknown depths, luxuriating in every moment as if it were a lifetime. They looked into each other's eyes and kissed each other tenderly. Time seemed to stand still as they explored their inner souls, cried, kissed, and coalesced into one. Two souls adrift seemed to find safe haven, a shore, in each other's arms. They went on like that for ages and finally dozed off into a deep slumber.

CHAPTER TEN

The Crusade

"The Fox will assassinate the president tomorrow." Chuck could almost feel the weight of the new position descending upon him, and there was a tone of certitude in his voice. "Gentlemen, next time we meet, it will be at the White House."

"To Robert Chuck Scott Jr., the forty-fifth president of the United States of America!" Christian Hannes said, raising his glass toward Chuck. "To the president!" Volker, Raymond, Gunther, and Aleixandre all raised their glasses and toasted in unison to his success.

"Thanks, all!" Chuck said. "Welcome to the Bohemian's Grove." Being called the president made Chuck feel giddy, and he was positively glowing as he welcomed his buddies to the 2,700-acre private gentlemen's club of the elite of the world in Monte Rio, California. Seated in the Owl's Nest, one of the many sleeping camps ensconced among the giant redwood trees of this exclusive retreat of politicians, artists, and power brokers established in 1878, the members of the cabal felt at home.

It was strange that the Cabal of Christian Crusaders had ended up in an establishment known for its attachment to Babylonian Druidic rituals and a penchant for the occult. Conspiracy theorists held that if one were to rise to the highest office of the land, Christian or not, one had to pass through the doors of this secretive society. The supposed membership would back up that assertion. Presidents William Howard Taft and Herbert Hoover were rumored to have been members, as was General Dwight Eisenhower, who also went on to become president. George H. W. Bush, too, had supposedly passed through the Bohemian Grove. So, Chuck had to be here. It was a masterstroke of his to get the American chapter of the cabal in his homeland to meet at the grove and to monitor the assassination when it happened, all at the same time. He would be declared president in a day. His closest friends in the cabal would be on hand to attend the inauguration. He would also be anointed by the elite at the Bohemian Grove.

He delved into the subject at the top of his mind. "The United Nations, NATO, the Council on Foreign Relations, the Bretton Woods system, the General Agreement on Tariffs and Trade, the European Union, the World Bank, the IMF, the G-20, the World Economic Forum, and many other such groups are all overt attempts at creating a new world order," Chuck observed. "Why then should our attempt be any different?"

"The one difference is that while all of them talk about it, we are the only ones who are prepared to *do something about it*," Father Englebert Volker, the spiritual leader of the cabal, said. As he looked at his flock, Volker thought of how he had ended up as the head of this powerful cabal that would change the world order within the next twenty-four hours. He had been excommunicated from the Roman Catholic Church because of his radical views against dogmatic beliefs. Volker was deeply influenced by the eighteenth-century French writer Voltaire, who had ushered in an age of enlightenment that encouraged religious freedom to question Christian dogma. He was also greatly influenced by another French writer of the same period, Diderot, and had become a deist. He did not give much credence to miracles as a source of revelation of religious knowledge but believed that reason and observation of the natural world were enough proof of God's existence.

At first, these influences of the French Enlightenment had been just beliefs, but when they crept into his sermons and he openly propagated the preeminence of reason over blind dogma, the powers-that-be in the Catholic Church had excommunicated him. It had only goaded him into a further search for enlightenment, and he had become an ardent follower of the Bavarian Illuminati, founded by Adam Weishaupt in 1776 to create one world order under a one-world religion. When he looked back, he was happy that the Society of Jesus, a Catholic order, had chucked him out. He smiled. As the spiritual head of the Cabal of Christian Crusaders, he would ensure one world order and one Christian faith. He would be the spiritual head of the new world order that they were shaping. He would be stronger and more powerful than the current pope.

He stood on a carpet with the image of a pyramid with the letters *D* and *P* on either side, signifying *Deo Proximo*, meaning "God is near." Consumed with religious fervor, Volker was in his element as he went about indoctrinating his colleagues through his lecture. That was his chosen responsibility. His colleagues wanted the religious elixir only Volker could give them. And his friends had gathered here today to let him set the tone for the evening and the shape of the destiny that would befall the world the next day.

Volker had asked each member of the cabal to address the group and detail their plans to unleash Harmagedon so that everyone would know what everyone else was doing in his country. Volker had hoped that the sharing of individual feelings about the cause and their plans would inflame the group further as they continued on their chosen path to Christian glory. But before they spoke, he wanted to rouse his subjects' emotions about the great act at hand.

The future pope of a new world dispensation spoke. "Today we stand at the crossroads of history. The very existence of our civilization is at stake. Radical Islam is taking over not only our Christian lands, but also the minds and lives of our populations." Volker walked as he spoke, looking directly into the eyes of each of them. "ISIS has butchered over eighty thousand Christians, crucified, flayed, or beheaded our brothers and sisters, raped children, and sold women into sexual slavery. Every day around the globe, we hear of terrorist bombings and killings in America, Brussels, France, or the United Kingdom. The Lord calls upon us to act. We are the crusaders for Christ. We must act now, or risk being run over. This is a sign from the heavens. Act now or be annihilated."

Volker was a fiery demagogue and did not mince his words. "We are the capstone of the pyramid you see in our logo—*the chosen elite*, who are entrusted with the sovereign duty of saving this world from profane influences. You are the anointed ones. This pyramid that you see in the logo of our cabal is the same one that was used at the 1782 Congress of Wilhelmsbad, again reflected in the step pyramid at the George Washington Masonic National Memorial and the one at the grave of Charles Taze Russell, the founder of the Jehovah's Witnesses. You are the chosen angels of God! Matthew chapter thirteen, verse forty-nine in the Bible prophesied your role when he said, 'So it will be at the end of the age; the angels will come forth and take out the wicked from among the righteous.'

"Tomorrow is a new dawn for our cabal, when the last obstacle in our path will be removed." Volker was certain that the Fox would kill President Harrison. "Chuck will be inaugurated president, and we will unleash Harmagedon; wipe out the malfeasance of godless Communism and Islam that afflicts our world; fulfill our God-given mandate to 'take the wicked from among the righteous'; purify, cleanse, restore, and renew the world; regain power over this earth; and return it to the mighty Christendom of our grandfathers."

He was every inch a priest as he continued his tirade. "Soon after Chuck unleashes Harmagedon on the world, we will go on to the *second* phase of our plan and engineer a stock market crash. We will do that just as these wars are taking place so the populaces will be dying to put bread on the table rather than worrying about our wars. The culmination of our plans is to rid the Western Hemisphere of Muslims and Communists. I am positive each of you has a plan to help move this process forward. We cannot afford to fail. History awaits us. Unborn generations look to us. A great burden awaits each of you. Let not its weight numb you or distract you from the will of God. You are the servants, the instruments of His will."

His voice rose to a feverish pitch. "As planned, I now command each of you to address the group and detail your plans to the rest of the team. Go through every plan, every major or minor detail, so that all of us are aware of what the others hope to fulfill and are charged with the fervor of our common cause. If one of us is suddenly removed from his position by death or any other cause, it should not be a reason for us to stop our holy enterprise. That is why I repeat that your address should detail your plans so that we can continue in your footsteps should you fall by the wayside. History and future generations are waiting in holy dread for the success of our well-laid plans."

The cabal was immersed in his religious fanaticism and cheered him on.

Volker did not stop to acknowledge the approbation. "Since we met at Gunther's residence a year ago, all of you have had ample time to make your individual plans to rain destruction on the Muslim and Communist hordes in your lands. Now is the time to share it with us. By the end of the day, all your plans will have become the collective plan of the Cabal of Christian Crusaders. They will become one. So now, give us your background, where you come from, how the evil of Islam has afflicted you and your society, and how you hope to vanquish it in the crusade for Christ. This is going to be a long night. I command the rest of you to sit back and give patient ear as your colleagues delve in depth into what made them who they are, why they are here today, and where they hope to be tomorrow. To the new world order, I now welcome Aleixandre to commence with the proceedings of the evening."

Aleixandre Thierry Devereux, chairman of France-Net, stood up. He looked at his colleagues seated on chairs placed under the trees. They were at peace, calm, and eager to listen to him. Eager for the success of the job at hand, they were waiting for the Fox to kill President Harrison and take over the world in less than twenty-four hours. They were the leaders of the free world of tomorrow. He decided to take the tale of his childhood and start from the beginning, so his friends could see where he was coming from.

"When I was a child, my father told me stories about the French Revolution, the Second World War, and the immigration of North Africans—the Algerians, Moroccans, and Tunisians—into France. Most of these ended up in *les banlieues*, the low-income suburbs, and formed ghettoes. France's republican adherence to our founding principles of *liberté*, *égalité*, *fraternité* led our nation to invoke strict *laïcité* laws that separated church from state. I was raised as a conservative Catholic and strongly believed in these principles. There could not be two Frances. Only one. Not a hijab-wearing French woman and then me. As my party leader, Marion Maréchal–Le Pen, granddaughter of National Party leader Jean-Marie Le Pen, said France is 'not a land of Islam' and Muslims can be French only if they follow Christian 'customs and lifestyle.' La petite Le Pen, as Marion is known, is a conservative, practicing Catholic like me and is the leader of the future. I support her wholeheartedly."

"There is no doubt about it, Alex: she will win the elections," Gunther said. "You will have one France!"

"Thanks, Gunther."

Alex looked at his audience. They listened with rapt attention, apparently intrigued by French right-wing politics. "I knew the reason for this was the result of the history lesson my father told me when I was a kid. The immigrants from North Africa had never really assimilated into French culture. They could be never *Français de souche*, of native French stock, as we call it. So, for me, the only way out of this was what we as a cabal are planning—an Armageddon! After that, I will actively pursue the deportation of the entire French Muslim populace back to their countries of origin."

"For *Français de souche*, Alex!" Christian applauded from his chair. The others raised their glasses in Alex's direction.

"Yes, Christian, we are rising again. Marion Maréchal–Le Pen got 45 percent of the votes in the elections and came in a close second in Provence–Alpes–Côte d'Azur. Marine Le Pen, party president, also placed second in the elections in Nord-Pas-de-Calais-Picardie. In 2014 they won twenty-four of the seventy-four French seats in the European parliaments. Yes, we will reclaim France for the *Français de souche*!"

Everyone raised their glasses, toasting to Alex's success.

"When Alfred Dreyfus, a Jewish officer, was arrested for treason in the late nineteenth century, French ethnic nationalism was evoked," Alex said. "My father had been active in the Action Française movement that was born as a direct result of the Dreyfus Affair. As a young man, I joined the Camelots du Roi, the youth wing of the Action Française, and engaged in many street brawls and violent protests. I am willing to do so again. If the Dreyfus Affair, where a Jewish officer allegedly sold state secrets to the Germans, was enough to arouse French nationalism in 1894, then the Islamization of my country, with immigrants killing ethnic French, gives ample reason for another revolution."

Alex went on, "The political fault lines are being drawn again. With the spate of terrorist attacks by homegrown Frenchmen of immigrant descent, France is now a tinderbox of emotions. All I need is a match to light that fire and rouse French nationalism once again. If the terrorists did not do it, *I will.* And put the blame on French Muslims of Algerian descent. Soon after the debilitating stock market meltdown that Raymond has planned for all of us, France will be on its knees—just in time for a series of brutal terrorist attacks that I am planning to execute in the name of Muslims. All I need to do is light that fire. The backlash will drive the Muslims out. Soon after the recent terrorist attacks, Marine Le Pen made a call to 'expel foreigners who preach hatred on our soil' and to strip binational Islamists of French citizenship. Manuel Valls, France's Socialist prime minister, supported her call. Mr. Hollande went on to suggest that citizenship of even French-born terrorists should be revoked. The timing is just right. I just need to kill a few thousand French people in shopping malls, underground trains, schools, and churches. Some have to die if a New France is to be born. I have the financial means and resources to pull off this plan. Only then will there be true *liberté*, *égalité*, *fraternité*. The second French Revolution!"

Aleixandre bowed deeply as his friends applauded his stirring speech.

As Alex returned to his seat, Christian Hannes, his Dutch colleague, took to the lectern and said, "If brutal, senseless cruelty had a name, it would be called Mohammed Bouyeri, a Berber-Moroccan Dutchman. Bouyeri shot Theo van Gogh, our filmmaker, eight times, slit his throat, and stuck two knives deep into his chest, one reaching his spinal cord. What was Van Gogh's crime? He had made a film, *Submission,* based on a script written by a Muslim woman, Ayaan Hirsi Ali, about violence against Muslim women in Islamic societies. You tell a story told by a Muslim, and another Muslim kills you? Where is the logic in that? What a way to die. Van Gogh is dead, and Boyueri is in prison paid for by Dutch taxes. The tragic irony is that Mohammed Bouyeri was collecting unemployment benefits when he murdered Van Gogh. What a way to repay the hand that fed him. I would have decapitated him and torn his body apart, limb by limb."

"Biting the very hand that fed him?" Raymond's anger was palpable. "If he did not like Dutch society and its mores, why didn't he go back to bloody Morocco?"

"That, Ray, is why I am proud of Geert Wilders, leader of the Dutch Party for Freedom," Christian responded. "Instead of fearing for his life, Geert made an equally strong movie, *Fitna*, that exposed Islamic violence and brutality. He once told the Dutch Parliament, 'Islam is the Trojan horse in Europe. If we do not stop Islamization now, Eurabia and Netherabia will just be a matter of time.' Wilders's Party for Freedom, which I belong to, is most popular in polls, and many expect us to win by a wide margin in the 2017 elections. I am also hopeful that the Netherlands would go for a 'Nexit,' just as the British did, and get out of the European Union to keep the throngs of Muslim immigrants out of the Netherlands."

"Nexit it shall be," Gunther prophesied.

"As you all know, I worked hard and built up my business from scratch," Christian said, continuing his diatribe. "Many of these immigrants are on welfare and do not work. I feel like I am working for them. With over a million Muslims, it no longer feels like being in the Netherlands. The crime rate is high in many neighborhoods, and the old way of life is gone. Now there are mosques, women in burkas, Arabic language, and halal meat butcheries. My country welcomed thousands of Muslim immigrants from Morocco, Turkey, Suriname, and Indonesia—giving them welfare and housing benefits, teaching them the Dutch language at state expense, and finding them jobs. More asylum seekers have come from Somalia, Iran, Afghanistan, Pakistan, and Bosnia. The Dutch government has paid for their assimilation into Dutch society, but they don't assimilate."

"Do you have a sharia problem in Holland, like we do in the UK?" It was Ray again.

"Oh yes, Ray, we do have something like your 'Londonistan' sharia problem in Holland as well." Christian seemed happy to expound on the situation. "We have a Muslim Defense League similar to your Anjem Choudhry's Muslim Against Crusades in London suburbs. What the Dutch media refer to as the Sharia Triangle is a Dutch neighborhood of Schilderswijk, where 90 percent of the inhabitants are Muslim immigrants. Some have even named The Hague *Jihad City*. A popular Syrian imam, Fawaz Juneid, had been delivering fiery sermons calling for the deaths of critics of Islam."

"Shoot the bloody imam!" Volker said.

"I agree, Volker," Christian added. "A national poll showed that 63 percent of Dutch citizens feel that Islam is incompatible with modern European life. Something has to be done to stop this. That is why I am part of this cabal and willing to invest a sizable portion of my wealth in saving my country. I am also a follower of the Pro Patria—For the Fatherland—a party that is willing to act against these extremists. I hope to use their large number of young volunteers when the time is right. I have drawn up extensive plans for a major attack against the Schilderswijk neighborhood, the more than four hundred mosques, the imams who preach violence, the Muslim Defense League of Holland, and the local Islamic Partij van de Eenheid. I will annihilate them. I will bomb them all to smithereens."

Like Alex before him, Christian finished off with a flourish, reveling in the amount of death and destruction he hoped to rain on Muslims, much to the delight of his animated audience, who were beginning to enjoy the evening. Death and destruction to their enemies seemed to arouse their basest passions and excite them. "I will bomb universities, schools, the Aalsmeer Flower Auction, and the Royal Palace of Amsterdam, killing large numbers of non-Muslim Dutch citizens and laying blame on the Dutch of Moroccan or Turkish descent, leading to a righteous wrath against Muslims and their eventual mass murder and deportation. That will be better than 'Nexit.' It will be *Mosexit* from the Netherlands."

"Death to the Muslims!" The members of the cabal broke into louder applause this time.

Christian had outdone Aleixandre in pure hatred against Muslims and the amount of violence he planned to unleash. This was their territory. The vitriol against their enemies only aroused them to further action—incensed them into further violence.

Volker smiled. When he'd asked them to present their plans to each other, this was exactly what he'd had in mind: individual tales of murder and mayhem, arousing and inflaming the collective wrath of the cabal into more violence against Muslims and Communists. He sipped his wine, satisfied.

They were ready to take over the world.

CHAPTER ELEVEN

Harmagedon

When Matt woke up the next day, Cynthia was nowhere in sight. He sat up on the bed and thought of what had happened the night before. He did not feel guilty. It had happened. He loved Amy deeply. That, he knew, would never change. Twenty-five years of life with Amy would not be wiped out by one night. Even though what had happened seemed accidental, he had a strange feeling that it had been building up for some time. He looked back at when Ashley had first walked in with Cynthia. He had felt something he hadn't been able to identify. Matt now knew what it was. Cynthia seemed to have something in common with Amy. She had the same human touch, the empathy for those around her. Much as her fight was to get justice for Ryan's killers, Matt had noticed that she had the zeal to get justice for Amy as well. Cynthia had become a part of the family.

Matt had come across many women during the previous year. Some had shown interest. He had not. He was not the one-night-stand type. He was a committed husband and father. He simply could not jump into bed with anyone. So, what had happened the night before was not accidental. From the time they had first met, Cynthia had kind of grown into his psyche without his knowledge. As they had discussed their common loss and pain, they had unknowingly gotten close, their union moving slowly but inexorably into one path. Ashley had been right when she'd said that Cynthia was a lot like her mother. She was a plain woman in some ways, but full of life. That's the way Matt liked it: a country girl, down to earth, yet blunt in her views. He liked the way she spoke back to Mitch when he made light of their chances of unearthing any new evidence. Tough girl. He looked up as if seeking Amy's blessings. He smiled, got out of bed, showered, changed, and went down to the restaurant.

Everyone was there. Ashley gave him a wide smile. Cynthia was having breakfast. She did not look his way. But she did not seem to be in denial either. She was just engrossed in her breakfast, lost in thought. He grabbed some toast and coffee and sat down beside her. She smiled. That was it. She did not seem guilty, nor did she exhibit any overt feelings of joy. She was just her normal self. Matt liked that about Cynthia. It was as if what had happened was natural. She seemed to have accepted it as part of her life and was calmly having breakfast just as a wife would at home. He joined in on the conversation, animatedly chatting away over breakfast about their hiking trip. There was an air of good cheer.

Ashley noticed it. Despite his best attempts at being nonchalant, Ashley detected a slight change in her father's mood. She was a woman and noticed that Cynthia was brighter than usual. Although Cynthia was not normally a chirpy person, she seemed happy today. It was possible that it was because she was close to finding her boyfriend's killers, but she seemed a tad more excited than that. Ashley also noticed her father looking at Cynthia a little more than he normally did. She had seen him suffer since her mother's death, so it made sense that she would notice any change in his demeanor. If it was caused by what she thought it was, Ashley was not complaining. She wanted both her dad and Cynthia to be happy. She smiled to herself and continued with her breakfast.

After breakfast, they took a bus to Neuschwanstein Castle. From there they set off on a hiking trek up the mountains. It took them the better part of an hour to reach Gunther's chateau.

"That's the entrance," Gerhard said, pointing. "Let's see if we can invite ourselves in. If we are stopped, leave it to me to talk our way out of it." The chateau was quite a sight. Clinging to the mountaintop, it seemed inaccessible from way below, but a well-hewn cobblestone path led to the entrance. So far out from civilization, either the caretaker at the chateau was not expecting visitors or no one ever came up here except by prior invitation. There was no one in sight, so they walked right up to the giant doors of the mansion fairly easily. But that was as far as they got. The massive wooden doors were locked. Not that they expected someone to be waiting to show them in, but they tried anyway. They checked some of the windows, but all of them were tightly bolted from within. They spent some more time looking for any entry from the front.

Finally, Gerhard led them to the rear of the house through a wicket gate. They unlatched it, strode in, and tried one of the doors at the back. It too was locked. They checked several doors and windows at the back. The result was the same: all were firmly locked. The owner was probably out, and the caretaker must have locked the place and gone somewhere. At one end, Ashley noticed a set of wrought-iron spiral stairs leading to a balcony. She waved to the others. They trooped up silently and came to a landing. The doors to the balcony were locked. They tried the windows.

They had not come all this way to go back because they could not enter Gunther's house. There was only one way now—to force an entry. If Gunther could get away with murder, Matt did not think a broken window was too much of a criminal act on their part. He took off his jacket, wrapped it around his wrist, stood to one side, and, with the back of his wrists, sharply hit the glass in one window. It cracked. He removed a few of the shards, reached inside, and undid the latch. Matt stepped into the hallway within, came around, opened the door, and let them all in.

Huge gilded chandeliers hung from the high wooden beams of the ceiling, and large paintings and tapestries adorned the walls. The lacquer on wooden paneled walls and large Gothic pillars with intricate carvings around the room shone in the dull early morning light streaming through the tall stained-glass lancet windows. Ornate chairs and plush sofas sat on richly embroidered oriental carpets. It looked like an old castle. Not a soul was in sight. They were in some sort of long passageway on the first level of this massive abode. They trooped down the passage, which led past several doors.

They gently opened the doors, one after the other: bedrooms, a library, a music room, and more bedrooms. No human beings. No one spoke. They did not want to attract unwanted attention. Their job was to hunt for any possible clue. They were not sure they would find anything. They all just had a gut feeling and a deep hope that they would unearth something the law had failed to. Or that Gunther had possibly hidden from the law. Who knows: he was so powerful that maybe no one had even thought of him as a suspect and this site had never been searched? They hoped they might hit upon something to tie this evil man to the brutal murders.

"Here," Cynthia said, holding a door open. The others hastened and entered the room. They instantly knew that they were in the right room. The large-screen television and chairs set around seemed like an ideal place for a gathering. The room itself caused them to feel as though they had stepped back in time. For a few moments, they just stood and took in its sheer opulence. A replica of Da Vinci's fresco of the *Last Supper* was painted on the ceiling, as well as a painting of God reaching out to touch Adam's fingers—a rendering of Michelangelo's *Creation of Adam*—and marble sculptures and busts filled the room. It seemed like a castle out of a medieval era. Clearly this bloke had money beyond the wildest reaches of the common man, to have a chateau this size and have it as well appointed as this one.

They spent an hour going through the room, looking for anything that could give them an idea of what may have transpired in there between some friends. Cynthia noticed a huge sign above the fireplace of what looked like a pyramid inside three red discs. She had no idea what it stood for. Seeing a remote control on a table beside one of the sofas, she picked it up, pointed at the TV, and clicked.

"That's the DVD player you switched on." Gerhard clicked another the remote he'd found on an adjacent table.

Suddenly the room came alive with images of terror around the world on the large television screen. Matt grabbed the remote and cut the volume to the lowest level, and then motioned for them all to sit down. They saw images of the Tunisian Frenchman Mohamed Bouhlel driving a truck through people celebrating Bastille Day; Omar Mateen killing Americans at a gay nightclub in Orlando, Florida; the attacks at *Charlie Hebdo* magazine, the kosher market, and Bataclan theater in Paris; bombings in Brussels; beheadings by Jihadi John; and ISIL butchering innocents the world over. Gruesome murders filled the screens. It was a sickening sight. Matt wondered what this was all about. The only common denominator was terror perpetrated by radical Muslim fanatics on behalf of ISIS or al-Qaeda. They had no idea why Gunther and his friends would be watching this. The answer was not long in coming. The screens suddenly filled with images of Syrian, Afghan, and African refugees streaming in at the borders of France, Greece, and Italy. Reporters of far-right TV stations in France and Germany seemed to connect the terror to the Islamization of Europe.

"No wonder Ryan found those brochures of the extreme far right in Gunther's office," Cynthia said as she paused the video playback. "All those parties are against Muslim immigration and want to ban all Islamic symbols, including burkas, minarets, and their call to prayer! Some even advocate violence against Muslim immigrants. These fellows must be connecting all these instances of terror to migrants from Muslim countries and Islam in general. They sat here and watched this for a reason. I think we are getting somewhere. Let's see the rest."

She clicked on the remote control again.

The screen displayed images of Chinese military jets landing on the artificial islands in the South China Sea, news reports of the Chinese hacking of the Pentagon's email system, Russian soldiers fighting in Ukraine, and the shooting down of Malaysian Airlines Flight 17 from the pro-Russian rebel-held territory in Ukraine.

"Oh, so it's not just Islam they are against," Matt added. "We cannot stop people from watching what they want to watch or even from hating people based on their religious beliefs. But why did a group meet here and see these images? Do they see themselves as some sort of guardians of the Western Hemisphere? Are they planning anything? *That* part worries me."

If they expected more gory images, they were all taken aback by what followed. Biblical verses scrolled on the giant screen, and a baritone voice intoned verses from the book of Revelation:

"'I saw heaven standing open and there before me was a white horse, whose rider is called Faithful and True … He is dressed in a robe dipped in blood, and his name is the Word of God. The armies of heaven were following him, riding on white horses and dressed in fine linen, white and clean. Coming out of his mouth is a sharp sword with which to strike down the nations. Then I saw the beast and the kings of the earth and their armies, gathered together to wage war against the rider on the horse and his army. But the beast was captured, and with it the false prophet who had performed the signs on its behalf. With these signs, he had deluded those who had received the mark of the beast and worshiped its image. The two of them were thrown alive into the fiery lake of burning sulfur.'"

"What in the name of heaven was that?" Cynthia was shocked.

"That is the biblical Armageddon they are referring to!" Gerhard pointed out. "The final battle when Jesus Christ will vanquish Satan at the field of Har Meggido! Radical Islamic terror, Muslim migration, Chinese aggression, and then a reference to a final cataclysmic battle from the Bible? These people who met here and watched all this must have been plotting something big. That's what that Nazi son of a bitch Gunther meant when he said Harmagedon was on! It's Armageddon, Matt! I thought this was about Amy and Ryan. This looks way, way too big. I don't know what we have walked into or how we will stop it."

"Christian fundamentalists, I think," Matt said. "That is where the Bible part is coming from. It sounds like this is a bunch of rich old crazies trying to be some sort of Christian soldiers out to vanquish Islam. I wouldn't worry if they were just your average Joes. You could throw them in jail and forget all about it. If Gunther invited others here, they must be as rich and powerful as he is. *That* is extremely worrying. Money and power can wreak havoc against innocent Muslims. That part where they were watching Russian interference in Ukraine also worries me. Surely, they're not planning to take on the Russian state, are they? That would mean a conspiracy of massive proportions. That would be bloody nuclear! I'm beginning to wonder, like Gerhard said just now, if we have stumbled into something that is way over our heads. But we need to do something about it."

"You are right, Matt," Cynthia said. "These idiots see themselves as some Christian avengers against Muslims. I remember doing an article on a Christian cult in Texas that believed the Judeo-Christian Bible was full of some form of coded warnings about catastrophes. They even claimed 9/11, bin Laden, and al-Qaeda are all referred to in the Bible."

"Bin Laden in the Bible?" It was Gerhard's turn to be surprised. "How could those louts come up with that?"

Cynthia explained, "Well, they believe that the code is based on equidistant random letters of the Hebrew Bible. They use computers to pick up these random words and claim it's a prophecy. Bin Laden? They even claim JFK's assassination was prophesied in the Bible. So, don't write off Gunther's Christian foot soldiers with enormous amounts of resources at their command just yet. Matt is right—they *must* be stopped. God knows they might end up starting a bloody world war if attacking Russia is also in the cards, along with possible genocide against Muslim citizens of the world."

"I think I know what that symbol up there means." Ashley pointed to the image of a pyramid inside three red discs. While the others had been talking, she had been staring at it for a long time. "I once did a piece on Freemasons and other secret societies and came upon Christian fundamentalism. It's deep. Now that these guys are quoting the Book of Revelation and referring to Armageddon, then this sign here is important."

Ashley moved closer, picked up a laser pointer from the table, and shone the green beam on the image. "See this pyramid here?" She ran the light against its sharp contours. "The blue finished pyramid signifies a complete, finished world order, as opposed to the unfinished pyramid on the reverse of the great seal of the American one-dollar bill representing an incomplete American nation. These guys see themselves as the masters assigned with the holy task of reconfiguring world order—say, completing it. Everything here has a Christian significance."

She shone the laser beam on the colors. "The color red symbolizes love, holy zeal, blood, and martyrdom. Red is also a symbol of the Holy Spirit and seraphim, and it's used for All Saints Day, Pentecost, Thanksgiving, and the harvest festival. The color blue signifies heaven, wisdom, and charity and is related to cherubic angels. Blue also symbolizes the Virgin Mary. In Illuminati conspiracy theories, the presence of a pyramid usually represented the top-down command structure of the Illuminati rulers of the universe. This pyramid is like the one at the site of the 1782 Congress of Illuminati, held at Wilhelmsbad, near Hanau in Hessen, Germany."

"Good Lord, Ashley!" Cynthia could not hold her amazement. "It means all that? What are those red discs?"

"They might not be discs," Matt said, looking at them. "Could be letters? Images? I am more convinced than ever now that these guys are some sort of Christian crusaders."

"You are right, Matt." Gerhard was up instantly. "Those could be letters, possibly standing for Christian Crusaders, with the third *C* possibly standing for *Congregation*, *Council*, or *Committee*."

"Reminds me of the Michigan-based CCR, the Colonial Christian Republic, or Hutaree, who were arrested in 2012 for attempting to kill a police officer and bomb a funeral," Ashley said. "They also called themselves Christian Warriors, preparing for the Antichrist."

"This is some form of a Christian fundamentalist group that hopes to eliminate Muslims, Chinese, and Russians in some cataclysmic manner and save the Western world for Christendom," Matt said. "They need to be stopped. But we don't know who the others are, what their plans are, or where, when, or even how they hope to attack. We need to find out more."

"Cynthia, is there anything else on the DVD?" Ashley asked. "Mitch was not sure we would find anything. This will blow him away."

"Oh, I would love to see the expression on his face when I hand it over to him." With that, Cynthia pressed the remote again. What they saw next completely bewildered them. It was a news clip from CSPAN, public service cable TV, showing the annual White House correspondents' dinner. What the clip focused on was perplexing. To the loud accompaniment of the military band, it showed the entrance of Andrew William Harrison, the president of the United States of America, and the camera zooming in on his face.

Everyone looked at one another, more perplexed than before.

Before they could say anything, the disc rolled to its end with some words scrolling past: *Boiler Rooms*, *Pump and Dump*, and *Short Sell.*

"What in the name of hell was that?" Ashley voiced her confusion. "What is their interest in the White House correspondents' dinner?"

"What is the interest in the president?" Matt was concerned. "Note the clip freezes on his face. I think we should inform

Kareem about this. I don't like it. Something tells me there is more to it that we can comprehend right now. KK is good at things like this, and he should be able to check it out. I'll call him as soon as we're out of here. We need to get out of here."

"Those words that we saw scrolling are all stock market terms," Cynthia said. Suddenly her hands went to her mouth in apparent horror. "Unless of course, these men are trying to rip off the stock market. But why would Gunther or his possibly wealthy associates want to rip off the market?"

"How?" Gerhard asked.

"*Boiler rooms*," Matt said slowly, "refer to hundreds of stockbrokers seated in small rooms with rows of telephones, selling bogus stocks to unsuspecting investors. They first pump a stock's value across internet chat rooms and message boards and then dump it to make a quick buck. Most investors lose everything. These are really over-the-counter penny stocks. It's the same with short selling, where they drive down the value of good stocks, buy them, and profit later when prices go up."

"But why would wealthy people want to do what small-time con men do?" Ashley wondered. "What is the connection here? On the one hand, they seem to be Christian soldiers wanting to take revenge on Muslims, and on the other they're mere con men? And then watch a CSPAN video clip of the president at the White House correspondents' dinner? Something does not add up."

"I think there *is* a connection," Matt said in measured tones, "only we are not able to see it now. I am sure Herr Gunther Otto Heinrich, the chairman of G & H Bayerischer Bank, will be able to fill in the blanks."

The door burst open, and a burly German stood facing them. Everyone gasped.

"*Was tun Sie hier*?" he demanded. Gerhard pushed up to him, and the two began arguing in German. From the countless references to Neuschwanstein Castle it was not hard to guess that Gerhard was trying his best to suggest that they had been looking for the famous castle and had decided to stop by Gunther's chateau. The man did not seem to be amused, as he could already see that the TV was on. Fortunately, Cynthia had removed the DVD just before he had barged in.

"He is the caretaker of this place," Gerhard explained to the group. "I told him we were some of Gunther's clients from G & H Bank who had dropped by on our way to Neuschwanstein Castle." Gerhard nodded toward the door, indicating that his friends should move out of the room. "Fortunately, Gunther is in America right now and he cannot call him to double-check. I don't think he buys my story. He insists he'll let us leave only if he can take some pictures of us so that he can confirm with his boss later. I don't think it matters. Let him do whatever he wants. If he calls the authorities, we will be in worse trouble. The police know about Ryan and Amy, and we may not be able to talk our way out of that. Mitch will put us on the next plane out."

The German caretaker used his phone to take several photographs of them. He checked the room again, switched off the TV, and walked them to the door. Gerhard kept up a steady banter in German so that the caretaker did not have much time to digest why Gunther would not have informed him of a visit by his bank's clients to the chateau. And what were they doing in one of the rooms with the TV on? They left before he could figure it all out.

★

"Andrew, it's time you took your pills," Elizabeth reminded her husband. "By the way, that stress ball is not the neck of the Russian president either."

Seated on the couch in his master suite on the second floor of the White House, Andrew William Harrison, the forty-fourth president of the United States, smiled at his wife's joke. She was like that—down to earth, funny, and very forthright. No beating around the bush for Liz. She said it as she saw it.

"Of course, dear," he said. "Though for a moment there, I wish it was that of the Chinese president. If they just wouldn't meddle in the South China Sea, it would make my life easier, especially now as I head to the UN to meet the leaders of Vietnam, Malaysia, and Brunei—who are all livid at these Chinese territorial claims. Diplomacy demands that I somehow walk a tightrope and keep everyone happy but also make our displeasure known."

"So, you squeeze the poor life out of that stress ball, huh?" Elizabeth was her humorous self and wanted to take her husband's mind off the pressures of running the world at least when he was at home and about to get into bed. "Here, take your pills."

He laughed and obliged. But he squeezed the ball anyway. On his way to bed, he dropped the ball twice, picked it up, and continued to squeeze it while he walked.

"You need to stop using that or pretty soon the press is going to want to know whether you have a medical condition that could affect your presidency, create ripples in the American economy, and by extension affect the entire world. We don't want a Cleveland over your harmless little stress ball, do we?" She smiled as she referred to Grover Cleveland, the former president whose cancerous tumor was removed clandestinely while sailing on a yacht. The crew was sworn to secrecy and the public was kept in the dark because of the fear of a possible financial meltdown of the American economy, which was already teetering on the brink of collapse in the depression of 1893.

"Don't worry, dear, those Secret Service guys, especially that sprightly young fellow Jake, know about Bubba, my stress ball. I pass it to Jake as soon as I'm in public. At least squeezing Bubba is a lot better than smoking or downing several shots of bourbon."

He threw his stress ball into the air, hoping to catch it on its way down, but dropped it anyway. He bent to pick it up just as his wife turned and saw him do it. They both had a hearty laugh. She was happy that her husband had not hit the bottle or used tobacco to beat the stress that came with his job. Bubba was okay, she guessed. As long as the scribes didn't see it and write wacky stories about heart ailments and create a ruckus. She smiled at her husband of forty-five years. He was the most powerful man in the world, but to her, he was a good husband and a great friend. He hugged her gently, kissed her good night, and made his way to the large Lincoln Bedroom. She wished him good night and retired to the small dressing room on the southwest corner that served as her bedroom.

CHAPTER TWELVE

The Crusade—Finale

Raymond Webster Coleman took the stage next. "Originally a founding member of the British National Front, I actively fought for the compulsory repatriation of all non-white immigrants, but that has now shifted to the problem of the Islamization of the United Kingdom. From being one of Christianity's pillars, the UK now resembles an Islamic caliphate full of mosques, sharia courts, and Islamic schools."

"Like the Islamic caliphate in Syria?" Gunther asked.

"Yes, Gunther!" Ray added, "Muslims Against Crusades, a group founded by British-born Anjem Choudhary, an Islamist who praised the 9/11 and 7/7 bombers and supported ISIS, plans to turn twelve British cities into a 'Londonistan,' an independent Islamic emirate or Muslim enclaves ruled by Islamic sharia law, and operate outside British jurisprudence. On their website, they name Birmingham, Bradford, Leeds, Leicester, Liverpool, Manchester, and many more that they claim, will be governed only by sharia law."

"We formed our Cabal of Christian Crusaders just in time to counter such evil," Volker said.

"Right you are, Volker," Ray said emphatically. "Muslim hordes have taken over our cities. London has no-go zones for non-Muslims, with loud signs clearly warning 'You Are Entering a Sharia-Controlled Zone' and 'Islamic Rule Enforced.' Other signs warn 'No Alcohol,' 'No Gambling,' 'No Music or Concerts,' 'No Porn or Prostitution,' and 'No Smoking or Drugs.' I have seen self-proclaimed sharia vigilantes, the *Muslim London Patrol,* attacking non-Muslims for violating these rules. In one video these propagators these terrorists say"—Ray fumbled among some papers on the lectern and then continued— "Here, let me read out the exact words so you can hear …

"'We are the Muslim Patrol. We are in north London, south London, east London, and west London. We command good and forbid evil. Islam is here in London. David Cameron, Mr. Police Officer, whether you like it or not, we will command good and forbid evil. You will never get us. You can go to hell! This is not a Christian country. To hell with Christianity. "Isa," in Islam refers to Jesus, a messenger of Allah. Muslim Patrol will never die. Allah is great! Allah is great! We are coming!'"

Livid, Gunther said, "That is blasphemous. They have the bloody audacity to damn Christianity in a Christian nation? They need to be shot, all of them—stood up against a wall and shot, I say. They are taking over England. I see you now have a Muslim mayor in London!"

"Yes, Gunther. I could not agree with you more. At this rate it will not be long before we have a Muslim prime minister, and sharia law may replace British Common Law and the principles of the Magna Carta that have stood the test of time. You can now see why Trevor Phillips, the former chairman of the Equality and Human Rights Commission of the UK, warned that British Muslims are becoming *a nation within a nation*. Former British Prime Minister Tony Blair said in an interview, 'Many millions of Muslims hold a viewpoint that is fundamentally incompatible with the modern world. They came to the United Kingdom, settled and raised Muslim families, but never became British.' They remained isolated and became enemies of the English stock. The London bombings that killed fifty-two people and injured over seven hundred while using the public transport on 7/7 was carried out by British-born Muslims. A British soldier, Lee Rigby, was murdered by an Islamic madman. In June 2012, five terrorists tried to bomb the English Defense League. In 2015 Ali, a terrorist, purchased enough ricin to kill over fourteen hundred people but was nabbed. On the anniversary of the 7/7 bombings in 2015, Mohammed Rehman and Sana Ahmed Khan were arrested before they could bomb a shopping center or the London Underground. I could reel off endless instances like that. Recently, many Muslims traveled to Syria to fight alongside ISIS. It is rumored that many have come back and are plotting more attacks against the homeland."

"You do have a sizable Muslim population, Ray," Volker said. "That is worrisome.

"*Worrisome* is an understatement, Volker," Ray said. "Our Muslim population in the UK is growing by leaps and bounds. A 2011 census shows that one in ten people in the UK under twenty-five years old is Muslim. One in twelve schoolchildren in England and Wales is now Muslim. With over three million Muslims there now, Islam will be the dominant religion in the United Kingdom in ten years. This explosion of Islam in the Christian kingdom cannot be allowed to happen. The UK managed to make the first giant step by getting out of the European Union so as to arrest unchecked immigration."

"These vermin need to be wiped out, Ray." Chuck did not comprehend the depth of the Muslim problem in the UK. It was not that bad in the United States. "They cannot be allowed to breed like cockroaches and take over the United Kingdom!"

Ray was happy his tirade was influencing his colleagues. "Oh yes, Chuck, they need to be. This is the Islam, my friends, that I want to join with you in rooting out of the Western world. It is my job to ensure that its threat is neutralized within the United Kingdom. It will be an uphill task because of the British sense of justice and fair play. But I have devised a plan with the *British National Party* and the *English Defense League* loyalists who are willing to help create a climate that will make it untenable for the British parliamentarians not to adopt legislation to stem immigration and deport vast numbers of Pakistanis and other Muslims to their countries of origin. The ones that British law fails to capture in its deportation net, I and my supporters will wipe out as mercilessly as they kill us.

"And here is my plan to root them out." Ray looked at his colleague and repeated, "I *do* have a very clear plan to put a stop to this Londistan and sharia takeover of my land. I have two Royal Air Force officers whose families have been victims of Islamic terror to support my cause. They fully well comprehend the enterprise they have agreed to. They will most certainly be court-martialed, and lose their commissions, pensions, and respect in society. For all intents and purposes, they could even be shot out of the skies before they return from their missions. But they have faced loss. One lost his wife and three young children in the 7/7 London bombing. The other lost his son to the brutal knife of British Islamic terrorist Mohammed Emwazi, aka Jihadi John, after being captured when his plane went down in Syria. He had watched that scene on TV. Britain did nothing to bring him back, and let that British Muslim, slit his throat.

He had children. They are willing to pay the ultimate sacrifice to rid British society of this evil."

Ray's face was a mask of hatred as he concluded, "They will fly their Typhoon FGR4 aircraft from the Royal Air Force Lossiemouth military airfield in Moray, Scotland, and deliver rocket-propelled, radar-guided Brimstone bombs on the so-called caliphate, the bloody no-go zones, the Muslim enclaves, and the Islamic emirates in London and incinerate them to kingdom come. The bastards will be annihilated. There will be no more Muslim problem in England. No more Muslim population explosion or British terrorists killing our own children. No, instead of an Islamic caliphate we will have a Christian Britain. We will finally have a Britain under Her Majesty, the Queen, and the archbishop of Canterbury as our spiritual head, a British way of life that we have known for thousands of years before and will know for thousands of years to come."

That was a hit. Christian and Alex stood up to applaud Ray's impassioned presentation and his plans to kill thousands. The others raised their glasses toward him.

Volker said, "That was a masterstroke, Ray! Rocket-propelled Brimstone weapons for wiping out the Muslim scum in their evil enclaves! Take out their nest, Ray. Kill them all!" Volker clapped his hands enthusiastically. He then looked at Chuck, who rose to his feet to address the crowd, and added, "Let's welcome the president of the United States of America, Robert Chuck Scott Jr.!" Everyone cheered for Chuck as he came up to the lectern.

Chuck smiled and raised his hands in acknowledgment. Looking at the group, he said "I can see that the United Kingdom does have a serious problem with its Muslim populations. In fact, all of Europe is afflicted. I like that word Christian used—*Eurabia*. It is my affirmed belief that Christianity and Islam cannot coexist. In fourteen hundred years, Muslims have butchered over three hundred million people, razed their cultures, and violently imposed their religion on others. We have over 6.67 million Muslims in the US. Now under the Resettlement Accountability National Security Act of 2015, our leaders want to allow more refugees into America! We are caving in to demands made by a small margin of the politically correct establishment that does not seem to see the fact that Islam and America will never coalesce into one. They will only destroy us from within."

Chuck could see his compatriots listening to him as he built the case that would end in Armageddon and result in a new world order. They had chosen him to pull the first trigger. He went on, "Whether it was bin Laden, who killed three thousand Americans at the World Trade Center, or a Muslim American military psychiatrist who shot dead thirteen of his compatriots at Fort Hood in Texas, the jihadist who killed sixteen innocents in San Bernardino, the Orlando nightclub shootings, or the Somali immigrant who stabbed Americans in the Minnesota mall, these deranged followers of the Muslim faith know nothing but murder, mayhem, and evil. Post 9/11, the United States went to war in Iraq and Afghanistan, resulting in the deaths of 6,800 US service personnel and more than 6,900 contracted personnel. As a result of battle injuries, many service members have undergone amputations, lost limbs, and suffered from post-traumatic stress disorder. We have known nothing but pain and death in our dealing with this accursed Islamic terror. I believe that they should all be rounded up and shot like Brigadier General Jack Pershing did in the Philippines in 1911, executing Muslim terrorists with bullets dipped in pigs' blood and burying them in a grave filled with their entrails!"

"Yeah," Gunther said, raising his glass. "I like the part that says Pershing killed forty-nine of those animals and let the fiftieth go free so he could spread the message. We hear there were no terrorist attacks anywhere else in the world for the next forty-two years! Chuck, we need to unleash Harmagedon so that we can rid the world of this scourge for the next thousand years!"

"Oh, yes, Gunther, we will." Chuck's words were having an effect. "The twisted logic of Islamic terror and the knuckleheads like Kim Jong Un of North Korea wanting to send missiles America's way, the Chinese wishing to appropriate sea routes in the South China seas, Russia annexing Crimea, ISIS butchering Christians, Muslims attacking all of you in Europe, and large hordes of Muslim immigrants migrating into Europe—all must, and will be, arrested.

"America has the military wherewithal to attack all these targets." Chuck's tone took on the authority that came with his high office, and he declared sternly, "As soon as I take the oath of office, I will sign executive orders to nuke the artificial islands in the South China Sea, annihilate the Iranian and North Korean nuclear sites, and bomb the Russian Black Sea navy fleet in Sevastopol. In Volker's words, we will 'unleash Harmagedon; wipe out the malfeasance of godless Communism and Islam that afflicts our world; fulfill our God-given mandate to "take the wicked from among the righteous"; purify, cleanse, restore, and renew the world; regain power over this earth; and return it to a mighty Christendom of our grandfathers!'"

Mention of Harmagedon and butchering Muslims and Communist populaces resulted in loud cheers. The Owls' Nest at the Bohemian Grove was coming alive with the members of the cabal reveling in tales of mass genocide and the extermination of large numbers of their Muslim populations. Just as Volker had imagined, individual tales of vengeful attacks only heightened the resolve of the others to one-up each other. His plan was unfolding precisely as he had wanted it to. The more the members learned that their individual motivations were part of the cabal and listened to others' plans to murder millions of Muslims, the more it heightened their collective resolve to do the same.

"To the president!" Everyone toasted Chuck, on whose success in ascending to the presidency all their plans depended. Chuck bowed and returned his seat.

Everyone turned to look at Gunther, the last person to address them that evening. Gunther was also the main patron of the cabal, the driving force, and its chief financier. Germany had seen a lot of attacks by Muslim terrorists, so his colleagues were assured that he would make a powerful statement. He was also quite an orator.

Gunther's opening statement did not disappoint. "We have had over six million of these bearded radical Muslims from Turkey, Iran, and the Middle East in our Deutschland for some time now. Just like what they're doing in all your countries, these Salafist Muslims in Germany have been trying to turn parts of our country into some sort of a medieval Islamic caliphate. In Wuppertal, these Muslims, in orange vests with the words *Sharia Police*, tried to enforce Islamic law at nightclubs, warning young partygoers that they were violating Islamic law by drinking and smoking. In Hamburg, some of these hooligans attempted to impose Islamic rules and values in schools. Germany has more than seven thousand radical Muslims, who are opposed to our German way of life. Many have joined ISIS, received training in Syria and Iraq, and are now living in German cities and waiting to attack us. Just as Christian said, even in our case, many of these would-be Jihadists are also collecting welfare benefits."

"What about your government, Gunther?" Chuck asked. "What are they doing to stop such brazen instances of Islamic terror?"

Gunther raged on, "Instead of stopping such attempts to change the German way of life and its democratic traditions, our local officials are caving in to the demands of the immigrant societies. In Berlin, officials have allowed Muslim women to wear veils and headscarves in public places. In Bremen, Muslims have been allowed to build mosques and insist on halal food, and their Muslim holidays have been acknowledged. In Bavaria, here, Muslim children do not have to do the mandatory visit to former concentration camps as part of an education program on the Holocaust. Though 61 percent of Germans said they believe that Islam is not part of Germany in a recent poll, Angela Merkel has gone ahead and opened the floodgates to more than a million refugees from Syria in one year alone! The vast majority of them are Muslims. What did she expect? Over a thousand of these drunken North African Muslim men raped or molested more than five hundred German girls at Hauptbahnhof, Cologne's central railway station, on New Year's Eve in January 2016!"

Alex said, "We saw it on TV. Where do these savages come from? They attacked young girls in large groups." Disgust was evident on his face.

Gunther went on, "Yes, Alex, groups like the PEGIDA and *Hogesa*—hooligans against Salafists—hit the streets along with a flash mob of close to two thousand at the Hauptbahnhof, demonstrating against the immigrants with slogans like 'RAPEfugees not welcome.' Some held images of Merkel wearing an Islamic headscarf, showing their disdain for the German chancellor's decision to allow the immigrants to run amok in Germany. I actively funded many of the street protests, especially the violent ones."

"Way to go, Gunther!" Chuck said. "You also need to win the country's elections and change the laws to send these vermin back to the caves they came from!"

"Very soon we will, Chuck," Gunther said. "My party, the Alternative for Germany, is now in third place with 15 percent of the votes, behind Andrea Nahles's center-left Social Democrats at 20 percent. In Berlin, we have routed Merkel's party and won 14 percent of the votes. So, we now have opposition seats in ten of Germany's sixteen states! At its 2016 congress, I actively campaigned from behind the scenes for the adoption of the AfD policy banning Islamic symbols, including burkas, minarets, and the call to prayer, based on the slogan 'Islam is not a part of Germany.'"

Alex raised his glass toward Gunther and proposed a toast. "To the AfD! Merkel must be stopped. A million RAPEfugees? Send them back!"

"To the AfD!" five other voices echoed in unison.

That encouraged Gunther to spew more hatred. "Oh, yes, friends, we will send them packing—including Merkel. She is selling out Deutschland! Merkel has said that there is no 'legal limit' to the number of refugees she will take in. Scenes of hundreds of thousands of refugees streaming across the borders of Macedonia, Serbia, Hungary, Bulgaria, and Romania fill our television screens every day. I can see Muslim immigrants flood into my homeland from Afghanistan, Iraq, Syria, Iran, Algeria, and Morocco. The Germany that I was used to will be no more. The number of rapes and other violent crimes, sharia laws, and no-go zones has quadrupled. Mosques, minarets, and the muezzin's call to prayer have already replaced churches and the German democratic way of life. Every day one hears of some crazed Islamic radical killing Germans. Bavaria has just experienced a terrible week. A seventeen-year-old Muslim immigrant stabbed four Germans on a train in Wurzburg. An eighteen-year-old German immigrant of Iranian extraction shot and killed nine people in Munich. And a Syrian asylum seeker exploded a suicide bomb outside a music festival in Ansbach."

Gunther's anticlimax was chilling: "And a million more Muslims are waiting to enter Germany."

By now his colleagues seemed to be in a state of bloodlust. Tales of radical Islamic terror had been unfolding all afternoon. It was evening now. If a Muslim had passed by just then, one of them would have torn him limb from limb. Such was the mood that was created from hours of anti-Muslim rhetoric. Gunther looked at Volker, who smiled in return. It was a knowing smile that affirmed to Gunther that the diatribe was meant to arouse and inflame. They had a new world waiting.

Gunther did not fail his spiritual master. "This will not be tolerated! Not on my watch. As soon as Chuck wages his war around the world and the Deutsche Börse Group crashes, I will personally pour a sizable portion of my wealth, including the spoils of the boiler-room scams, into the most violent base of the AfD, the neo-Nazi National Party, the PEGIDA, and the Hogesa to bomb refugee shelters, Muslim enclaves, mosques, Islamic schools, halal butcheries, and wherever they come across large gatherings of Muslims. Street protests and demonstrations will make Germany, already reeling from economic ruin, grind to a halt. More iconic German landmarks such as the thousand-year-old Dome Cathedral in Cologne will be torched in the name of Muslim extremists, giving rise to more anger against the Muslim population."

Gunther rounded off his speech with a dire prediction: "I will bankroll the AfD into obtaining more seats in the Bundestag and try to push for reforms to the laws to deport Muslims as well as curtail their free movement within Germany. Veils, headscarves, and mosques will be banned, making it difficult for these radical Islamists to live in Germany. Many will run from Germany to Muslim lands. I will ensure Muslims are killed in the millions, burned at the stake, and crucified like their ISIS brethren do in Raqqa and Mosul. Muslims will be evicted from homes, forbidden to congregate, and hunted like wild animals. I will ensure that Germans are once again the Aryan race of the world."

The applause went on for a long time. Volker stood up and cheered along with the crowd. This was his moment. His flock had been invigorated with religious fervor. His Christian soldiers were ready for the battle of the ages—to kill in the name of Christ. Just like Pope Urban II had ordered Holy Crusades to stop the westward-marching Turks, he would order his cabal to arrest the westward-marching Muslim migrants.

"Thank you, everyone." Volker was proud of his disciples. "I am positive now you are all charged up and raring to go. The Cabal of Christian Crusaders is ready. All of you are angels of God, chosen for this noble task to save mankind from the scourge of Islamic influence. Each of you I can see has detailed plans to wipe out the threat of Islam, cleanse your societies, and raise a Christian kingdom. The last crusade is well underway."

Volker concluded the session at the Bohemian Grove by reminding everyone of the plan: "All we have to do now is await the death of the American president! That will be the *trigger* that will set Harmagedon in motion. Until that happens, we do not do anything, since that one act will ensure that our man is in the White House. As soon as Chuck unleashes nuclear Armageddon, we will commence attacks across Europe. As Gunther aptly described it, we will cleanse our planet from the scourge of radical Islamic terror, Russian imperialism, Chinese aggression, North Korean saber rattling, and Iranian nuclear ambitions—*the sum of all evils*!"

"We will vanquish the sum of all evils," Alex said, raising his glass to more applause, "but tonight, we wait for the Fox and our new dawn. Let us now party into the night as we await the glorious dawn of a new Christian millennium!"

As he walked back to his seat, Gunther's phone rang. "Yes?" he intoned. It was the caretaker at his chateau in Schwangau.

"A bunch of clients from your bank strolled into the chateau today," the gruff voice of the caretaker said. "I found them in your meeting room. They said they were passing through on their way to the Neuschwanstein Castle. They said you had permitted them. I did not quite trust their words, so I took their pictures. Have already sent them to you. Please check."

I didn't send anyone to the chateau, Gunther thought. He could feel anger and a sense of foreboding in the pit of his stomach. He looked at his phone and saw pictures of a group of four people. Gunther froze when he recognized two of them—Gerhard, a former employee whom he had sent packing, and Cynthia, girlfriend of the American Ryan, the IT consultant who had seen too much and had had to be silenced.

Cynthia had also been a close friend of the other American, Amy, who had worked for him. Amy had begun to track his cash transfers to the cabal, especially the five-million-dollar down payment for the Fox that he had transferred to Chuck. She had been asking too many questions. He had not known who she worked for, but he was not one to take chances and had arranged for a convenient truck accident. A hit-and-run. That was a year ago. Gunther had assumed that those things had settled down. But now, seeing the pictures of the two Americans, an older man and a younger woman in Cynthia's company, he knew that they had to be related to Amy. The problems had not gone away. They were coming back to haunt him. This was bad. Something had to be done, and quickly. He made several calls to Germany. After about twenty minutes, he was at ease. He turned to see his colleagues already drinking and making merry. Tomorrow a great dawn awaited the cabal.

CHAPTER THIRTEEN

Assassination!

The Fox lay prone on a table with his TrackingPoint XS1 .338 facing Downtown Manhattan Heliport. He peered through the scope and saw armed US Coast Guard patrol boats sweeping the harbor of the East River, bomb-sniffing dogs, and explosives experts checking every vehicle as hawk-eyed Secret Service counterassault teams took up their positions on rooftops.

He had bored a hole in the thick glass of the window, and the muzzle of his gun covered the small circle so perfectly that from the outside it looked like nothing more than a black dot on the glass. No portion of the metal muzzle stuck outside, so there was no chance that any deflection of light would give away his position to the Secret Service. The Fox looked at the presidential motorcade close to the Heliport offices with Cadillac One, the Beast, parked up front. He moved his weapon to measure the distance to the nearest landing pad. Of course, they would not have the president walk too far from where he got off Marine One helicopter on his ride. That would pose a significant threat, because he would be out in the open. He zoomed to a spot where he imagined POTUS would have to step out and make the short distance to his car on foot. A Secret Service agent stood at the spot he chose. Probably he was right, and the agent was also marking the territory he would have to be in when Marine One touched down.

This agent would be the perfect dummy target for his boss. He looked through the scope and saw the hairs of his crew-cut head, his dark glasses, and his handheld radio. He ranged the agent's head and pressed the red tag button on the side of the trigger guard. Sensors and gyroscopes measured the ballistics, and a red tag was placed on the head of the agent. The target had been marked.

Now all he wanted was the real target, the president of the United States, to step into the red tag where the agent now stood. He took a deep breath and decided to wait. It was going to be a long wait, but he was used to that.

★

Marine One took off from the south lawn of the White House in Washington with its celebrated occupant, President Harrison, and flew across the Potomac to Andrews Air Force Base. Secret Service agents based at Andrews, who had tracked his trip all the way from the White House, were ready to receive their commander in chief. Air Force One was waiting, engines running. Marine One landed. President Harrison came up the stairway and boarded the plane, the doors closed, and Air Force One was airborne. A seamless transfer. Harrison went to his mini Oval Office in the sky and settled down for the forty-five-minute flight to John F. Kennedy Airport in Queens.

On the plane, Harrison spent time going through the speech he planned to deliver at the UN that day. It was the usual stuff, but he still went through the minefield of telling the truth while not getting his wires crossed with world leaders. The press would have a field day. But Harrison still said it like it was. He squeezed the stress ball again. He looked at it and smiled. Liz would be mad if she knew he was carrying Bubba to the UN.

While he was in the air on Air Force One, Marine One, his aircraft for the next stage of his trip, and the security operation around it, were already being readied with the utmost precision on the ground at Queens. It had to be a seamless operation again. Once he landed, the next and last leg of the president's journey would take him on a ten-minute ride across the East River, past the Brooklyn Bridge, and to the narrow strip of concrete, the Downtown Manhattan Heliport. Then it was a five-mile ride in the Beast to the UN for a General Assembly session.

A presidential airlift was on. And his security apparatus was in full swing. Security personnel had cordoned off an area of the busy JFK airport for the next ninety-six hours, turning it into a high-security military base. This was the president of the United States, the most powerful man on earth, on the move. Every eventuality was foreseen and planned for. The military was at hand for rapid response.

Colonel Ramon "Rambo" Ramirez, commanding officer HMX-1 and its primary pilot, was seated in Marine One as Sergeant Ted Thomas, crew chief, stood in his spotless uniform outside to handle the hatches, safety, and ceremony of a presidential airlift. Rambo and Ted were Marine Helicopter Squadron One, "Nighthawks" crew members. To make it here they had trained hard and had category one Yankee White clearance to fly their commander in chief. They were the best of the best. The VH 3D Sikorsky Sea King Helicopter Marine One helicopters, also known as presidential Whitetops, had sophisticated defenses to protect their most important passenger. As

Rambo and Ted waited for their commander in chief, Air Force One was on its way from Andrews Air Force Base to JFK in Manhattan.

Soon Air Force One landed, and President Harrison came down the aircraft steps. He shook hands with a few people and strode toward Marine One. He seemed to drop something, bent, and picked it up. Secret Service agents rushed to his side to assist. He smiled and walked toward Marine One. Sergeant Ted Thomas had dropped the hatch as his right palm sliced the air in a crisp salute. Harrison walked past Ted, saluted him, and strode up the narrow steps. He looked at the pilot and greeted him: "Good morning, Rambo. How's the family?" Harrison was a family man and always made it a point to ask people about their families.

"They are well. Thank you for asking, sir." Colonel Ramon was quick in his response and deeply grateful that the most powerful man on earth should take the time to inquire about his family. Then he asked, "Did you drop something, sir?"

"Ah, Rambo, nothing." Harrison laughed. "Just my stress ball, Bubba. Don't tell Elizabeth. She'll be mad, especially since she told me not to bring it along. I'm always dropping this little fella. Next thing I know, the press will have a field day saying I'm suffering from some vile condition."

Colonel Ramon laughed at the president's sense of humor. Sergeant Ted had pulled the hatch up, so Colonel Ramon started the engines, and soon they were airborne. Two troop carrier helicopters had already taken off with the press and support staff, who would land first. As a security measure, three more identical Whitetops also took off along with Colonel Ramon's Marine One. Serving as decoys, the four Whitetops shifted in formation upon taking off to obscure the location of the president. Known as the presidential shell game, this aerial dance of deception was a security tactic, a smokescreen to provide more security for the president. Soon they were approaching the East River, and Colonel Ramon could see the majestic Brooklyn Bridge and the Manhattan skyline from a distance. It was always an impressive sight.

On the ground at Downtown Manhattan Heliport, Secret Service agents and assault teams had virtually locked down the landing zone. The Presidential Protective Division was the president's shield that covered the intimate area around the president. The Secret Service called it the kill zone. They would take a bullet for him. "Mustang will land in four minutes," Secret Service radio crackled to everyone within the zone. That was the Secret Service code name for President Harrison. For the moment, it was a Mustang, probably in tune with his love of thoroughbred horses. When the press picked it up, they changed it.

Coast Guard patrol boats were sweeping through the East River. Secret Service agents were on the rooftops, scouring the landscape and the waterways through powerful scopes for any sign of the untoward. FBI Special Agent Kareem was stationed on FDR Drive, keeping an eye on all the buildings that fronted the helipad.

The first two troop carriers landed, churning up the water in the powerful gust created by the rotors of the helicopters. Press and support teams exited and made their way to the passenger lounges. Then the Whitetops appeared on the skyline, dancing in the skies, performing the shell game as it came down. Still no one knew which one had the president. One landed. No one disembarked. Then the second one landed. This bisected the first one and Cadillac One. The rotors came to a stop. Sergeant Ted dropped the hatch, went down the steps, and stood beside it, his right hand angled in a perfect salute. President

Harrison came down, saluted Ted, and walked out. He waved to the assembled staff and made his way to his limousine. Secret Service agent Jake was holding the door of the car open. Harrison put his hand into his pocket to retrieve Bubba and give it to him.

From between the rotor blades of Marine One and the open door of the car, the Fox saw his quarry. The tracking scope's built-in laser illuminated a red tag on Harrison's head in his reticle. Harrison was still moving toward the open door. In seconds, he would enter the car. The Fox knew he could pull off only one shot. There would be no time to take a second one. The distance to the limousine was very short. The Fox was calm. The sensors on his gun worked out possible firing solutions fifty-four times a second based on his target's changing conditions. The predictive image-processing pipeline figured out where Harrison would move next and placed a blue reticle on his image. The foreground and background tracking continuously tracked Harrison as he ambled up to the Beast. In his jet-fighter optics, the Fox noticed that the wind speed was around five miles per hour. The tracking algorithm computed the velocity of the bullet to Harrison's expected position predicted in the next 18.5 milliseconds. The Fox took the shot and held the trigger down.

The reticle on Harrison's head turned from blue to red. When the reticle and the red tag coincided, the gun fired the 338 Lapua Magnum ammunition at President Harrison's head. In that instant, Harrison dropped Bubba and bent to pick it up, and the bullet traveling three thousand feet per second smashed into Agent Jake's head, blowing it to a thousand pieces. Blood and gore flew in every direction, including the president's chest, as Jake's limp body crumpled onto the concrete. In an instant, the entire helipad came alive with hundreds of Secret Service men throwing themselves onto the president and dragging him away to the cover of the waiting Marine One.

The Fox could not believe it. *He had missed.* Impossible. It had never happened in three decades. Why did the damn president suddenly duck? This was too big a contract to fail. Against his better judgment, he pulled off four more shots. Bullets thudded into more bodies and more agents fell, defending their commander in chief. But POTUS was safe aboard Marine One, and it had taken off with the Whitetops doing their shell game and disappeared into the horizon. Secret Service agents were shooting toward the general direction from which the assassin's shots had come.

"Twelve o'clock," Kareem was screaming into his radio as he pointed in the general direction from where he thought the shots had come. "Fifty-five Water. Seems to be some way up." Helicopters flew straight toward 55 Water Street as agents, police officers, and military personnel rushed toward the building. Security personnel from the beachhead at JFK took off in helicopters, headed to Manhattan. Sirens screaming, police cars blocked the FDR freeway, and roadblocks were set up in a ten-mile radius on all sides. State police officers were stopping all cars and checking for anyone or anything suspicious. The chase was on. Kareem had only one moment to look back. He saw Special Agents Garcia and Samantha covered in blood on the concrete pad of the heliport. He remembered meeting them at their offices when Gwen introduced them. They were too young to die. He gritted his teeth and ran toward the 55 Water Street office building.

He had failed! For the first time in a career that spanned thirty years, the Fox had failed in a mission. He had emptied the four rounds in the magazine in rapid succession. But the Secret Service had crowded the president. They had moved the president out of the crosshairs and replaced him. The last four bullets had thudded into them. He had placed the red tag on Harrison's head, and the predictive image-processing pipeline on the TrackingPoint XS1 had figured out where Harrison would be next and placed a blue reticle on his head. When the red tag and the blue reticle coincided, Harrison's head was supposed to have been blown off. But the damn president had ducked before they could coincide, and the Secret Service agents, moving faster than a fifty-fourth of a second, had come into the firing frame. The bullet had gone straight to the agent! The president's servant had died defending him. The Fox had failed. Well, that was done. But he had one more chance. He had a Plan B in place. He would get Harrison the second time around. This time he would not fail.

He had lost precious time taking four more shots. He had planned for only one. He did not have time to pack up. Not that it worried him. He had been extra careful, worn gloves, and not left prints anywhere. He rushed to the bathroom, threw the gloves he wore into the toilet, and flushed them down. No one could trace him from the gun at the window. It would take the FBI ages to figure out the connection between the dead Jason, if they ever found his body, and the lease in this twentieth-floor office. Working office to office, covering twenty floors before the investigators reached this office, would be time-consuming. He would be far away by then. He had practiced his getaway several times. It was perfect.

Even before he could catch his breath, he was out of the office and down the elevator. He stepped off at the third level of 55 Water to the "elevated acre" between the towers, a full acre of landscaped park with trees, plants, and flowers, and a breathtaking view of the Brooklyn Bridge, the city, and the East River. The Fox pulled a baseball cap down his head, slipped on dark glasses, thrust his hands into his pockets, and strolled down the boardwalk among the lunch crowd to settle down on one of the many seats. He drew a small brown paper bag from his pocket, pulled out a sandwich, took a bite, and sat back, calmly munching away and enjoying the sight of the East River.

The crowd, disturbed by the sirens of the police cars, the helicopters buzzing above, and armed men storming the building from all sides, began to move toward the entrance of the building. The Fox moved with the crowd, still munching on his sandwich and looking around as though he were just as disturbed as any normal stranger suddenly woken from a reverie or afternoon lunch would be. Many employees were also streaming out of their offices, and there was quite a crowd down the escalators to street level. The Fox stepped into the first available cab and disappeared into the afternoon crowd.

Meanwhile, Kareem had stormed into the lobby of 55 Water Street. Someone had shot from one of the windows of this building. That someone had to be a tenant. Most probably a *recent* tenant. So, the investigation had to start here.

Kareem called Gwen Sanders, special agent in charge of the New York field office of the Secret Service. He knew she would be blaming herself. This security bubble had been set up after months of intense planning. How had they missed a vantage point like this? When she came on the line, Gwen was inconsolable. "I bungled this one, Kareem. I am sorry."

"No, Gwen, it's not your fault. You did your best. Don't blame yourself. No one would have imagined a shot from over a mile and a half away. You guys did your best."

"I lost Garcia and Sam. I am sorry. The investigation is now yours. Promise me one thing, Kareem: get the son of a bitch, whoever did this. To fail the commander in chief is devastating. Garcia and Sam have children, Kareem. Young kids, really. What am I going to tell their families?"

"I promise you one thing, Gwen. I am going to catch this bastard, whoever it is. They will pay for this. Trust me."

His next call was to report to his FBI director. They spoke at length as Kareem brought him up to speed on the situation. He'd made it a conference call, with the director of the CIA also in attendance. The two agencies did not need to work together; one worked outside the United States and the other inside. They had different terms of reference. Instances of intense rivalry were not just legendary but also painful, especially because of the contention that intelligence sharing might possibly have prevented the 9/11 terrorist attacks. That helped change the scene post-9/11 with the creation of the Interagency Terrorist Threat Integration Center. Now intelligence sharing between the agencies was the norm.

The president of the United States of America had been attacked, which was an attack on the USA. At that point, it was not clear whether the suspect was homegrown or international. If the criminal was domestic and had fled abroad or was a foreign citizen and had to be apprehended in another country, then the CIA would assist the FBI in apprehending him or her. But only the FBI could make a case that could stand in an American court of law, since the crime had been committed on American soil. Kareem's director had teamed him up with the Secret Service for just this eventuality. The assassin had to be brought in, charged, tried, and prosecuted in an American court of law. So, the best bet was for Kareem to be the face of the investigation, whether it was in the homeland or abroad, where a local CIA agent would assist him, but he'd still be able to bring the culprit to face justice in America.

They asked Kareem to head up Operation Brimstone, and he agreed. Next he chose a small but highly efficient team, Special Agents Tanya, Bob, and Huey. They were already on their way to 55 Water. His colleagues had set up a temporary command center in one of the conference rooms. Within an hour or two, the place was teeming with staff, and office and other equipment. Phones, copiers, computers, and other machines were set up. Coveralls, boot covers, latex gloves, fingerprint kits, biohazard bags, forceps, evidence collection bags, containers for firearms and ammunition, and a camera with a tripod were arrayed on the tables, along with every kind of crime scene investigation kit.

More agents and office staff were roped in, and the conference room was a beehive of activity. Tanya, Bob, and Huey had arrived and had a brief meeting with Kareem. He asked them to form teams and commence the investigation. One group scoured the recent leases, another group interviewed employees of 55 Water, others viewed the CCTV footage, and yet another team questioned the general crowd, looking for anyone who may have seen or heard anything untoward. Agents made copious copies of all documents, recorded information, and took thousands of pictures and video footage of the scene from every possible angle. Sometimes criminals stick around as part of the crowd to view the aftermath. A sharp-eyed agent might pick out a face or run a face through the bureau's database and spot someone worth following up on. So, the cameras clicked and rolled.

Kareem knew this was not going to be an easy task. There was no way they could shut down 55 Water as a crime scene. Nor could they interview several thousand staff and visitors. For all intents and purposes, whoever had pulled this off had already left the scene. They had the list of tenants and employees of various companies and organizations. They also had CCTV footage. They would have to pore over it for weeks, possibly months, unless they got lucky and chanced upon a lead. Or someone who had seen or heard something volunteered to come forward. The only chance they really had was to gather evidence meticulously.

Agents were recording witness statements on all sorts of things imagined or seen. Had anyone seen a suspicious person? Had anyone seen somebody carrying arms or what looked like weapons? Was there a gym that employees frequented? A cafeteria in the building? Exits were checked and cameras at such points were noted for further investigation. Even the restrooms, trash cans, and dumpsters were not spared. Agents went over the 55 Water Street building floor by floor. This was an attack on the president of the United States, the man, the office, and the symbol. This was an attack on America.

Kareem was still lost in his thoughts when Alpha One, the team poring over the leases, got lucky.

"Guys, we have something!" It was Tanya. Everyone stopped what they were doing.

"Look at this lease," Tanya said. "Drawn up just a month ago as a bird-watcher's studio on the twentieth floor. The strange thing is that the lease is signed for by the real estate agent, Jason Goodman, and not the tenant."

"Who is the tenant?" Bob asked.

"Someone by the name of Rusty Newman."

"Well, those things can happen," Kareem said. "People can get agents to do their jobs. Does anything strike you as strange, Tanya?"

"There are peregrine falcons on the fourteenth floor, so that ties in with the story of a bird-watcher setting up offices here," Tanya went on. "But I called the manager. He tells me that Jason, the real estate agent, has not been seen since then. His girlfriend, Chloe, has come here looking for him for two weeks now. She says Jason sent her a message from Hunters' Lodge, somewhere in Santa Clara, that his client on the twentieth floor, Rusty Newman, was offering to buy the lodge. Jason was excited because he'd make a fifty-grand commission on the sale. That's the last she's heard from him."

"That is good work, Tanya," Kareem said. "Bob, can you figure out who owns that property in Santa Clara? As of now Jason is a person of interest. Let's get his girlfriend, Chloe, here. We need to talk to her. We are going to investigate Rusty Newman's birder's office on the twentieth floor. From my vantage point at the FDR, I thought the bullet came from roughly the tenth floor or above. It could just as well have been from the twentieth floor. Let's go, guys."

They went to the twentieth floor and donned white coveralls, boot covers, and gloves before they opened the office. There would be fingerprints on the door handles. They did not want to destroy evidence. At first, they saw a typical bird-watcher's studio with paints, easels, brushes, canvases, frames, and paintings of birds. Suddenly everyone froze. A table at the window held a long-range gun still in place. *They had struck gold.* Kareem created four teams. The crime scene search team would divide the room into zones and lift latent fingerprints, shoe prints, fluids, and fibers. The sketches, photographs, and videotape team would make scale drawings and photograph evidence. The evidence-control team would code, package, and transfer evidence to the FBI Property Room, and, most importantly, the firearms team would record the serial number, make, model, and caliber of the weapon, and information about the bullets, casings, gunshot residue, fingerprints, and fluids.

Huge studio lights with six-hundred-watt bulbs illuminated the bird-watcher's office. The four teams set about swabbing and attempting to lifting fingerprints off glasses, doors, bathrooms, and faucets, and transferring evidence into bags, coding and naming them, and taking extreme close-up shots of the weapon, window, bullet casings, and even the location of the furniture to triangulate the exact position of the evidence. After it had been dusted for fingerprints, they cut and packaged the entire piece of window glass, which had a hole bored into it. They checked suspect fluids with luminol that, when applied, reacted with blood, resulting in luminescence. But they did not find any. The agents were meticulous in their military-style approach of stepping into their own footprints as they scoured the crime scene so they did not contaminate any footprints that might belong to the suspect.

Kareem looked at his teams and read the scene. Years of experience on the job had given him a sense of a crime scene at one glance. Whoever had occupied this room had been careful. There wasn't going to be an enormous amount of evidence. Whoever had been in this room had possibly worn gloves the whole time. It seemed that the culprit had planned to pull off the assassination, wipe the room clean, and take the gun, ammunition, and casings with him after he was sure nothing would point back at him. But having missed his target, he had tried more than once to complete his multimillion-dollar contract, thereby losing precious getaway time. He must have also noticed the cavalry of the FBI and the Secret Service making a beeline for 55 Water; his survival instincts had no doubt taken over and he had simply bolted.

Probably he was certain he would not be traced. Likely, there existed no records on such a person. He must be at the top of his trade to have been chosen for this job. Top assassins seldom had records. But it was also possible that he had left some trace. The eminent criminologist Edmond Locard's theory held that "Every contact leaves its trace." That is what Kareem counted on: a criminal's one slipup. Bureau detectives were trained to pick up evidence that the average person would miss, although sometimes luck did play a part. Tanya's sharp eyes had picked up a clue. Six hours after the assassination attempt, they had a possible suspect, Rusty Newman; a missing Jason Goodman; and Jason's girlfriend, Chloe, who could throw some light on this investigation. Kareem was getting *somewhere.*

"Chloe will be at our office tomorrow," Bob said. "Hunters' Lodge is a six-hundred-acre camp in the Adirondack forestland in Franklin County, near Santa Clara, New York. It's a family weekend retreat for hunting black bear, turkey, duck, and grouse. It's owned by Robert Chuck Scott Jr."

"What?" It was Kareem's turn to be surprised. "The vice president?"

"Yes."

"Well, I'll be damned." Kareem called Tanya over and addressed both of them. "Tanya and Bob, after meeting with Chloe tomorrow. I want both of you to visit Hunters' Lodge and see what you can find. I don't like where this is going. But we are going to get to the bottom of it."

CHAPTER FOURTEEN

"Every Contact Leaves Its Trace"

Kareem was preparing to leave 55 Water when his phone rang. It was Matt, calling from Germany. For the next twenty minutes, he listened. He could not believe what he was hearing. A group of men had met at the chateau of the chairman of G & H Bank in Germany. Matt described the recorded images they had seen on TV screens. The scenes of terror attacks by Islamic fundamentalists in Europe and America, scores of Muslim refugees crossing into Europe, end-time prophecies from the Book of Revelation, a pyramid symbolizing Christian fundamentalism, a clip of President Harrison at an official dinner, references to stock market pump-and-dump schemes, and finally, the last word: that Harmagedon was on.

Kareem updated Matt on what had happened at the Manhattan heliport. It was Matt's turn to be surprised. Kareem was happy Matt had the DVD of the images they had seen at the chateau. Both Matt and Kareem could see a connection between what had happened in America that day and what Matt and his team had stumbled onto in distant Bavaria. President Harrison was in that clip. Harmagedon was mentioned. Someone had taken a potshot at Harrison. It was two names in the group of people who had met at the chateau that made the hair on the nape of Kareem's neck stand on end.

"MJ, can you repeat exactly what Cynthia told you that Ryan overheard Gunther say on the phone?" Kareem had heard the name when Matt had related the conversation during the barbecue at their home. Something in Cynthia's story that he had heard at Matt's place had been nagging at the back of his mind. He had not been able to put his finger on it then. Just now Matt had said something that struck him. He wanted to be sure he had heard right. "I know she told me that part of the conversation when I met her last time. But at that time those names did not make much sense. But now in the light of what has happened here in New York, those names *do* mean something. Please repeat Ryan's words exactly as Cynthia said it that day."

"KK, let me give the phone to Cynthia. She can help." Matt handed the phone to Cynthia.

"Hi, Mr. Khan," Cynthia said. "Ryan surprised Gunther when he walked in and saw him on a scrambler phone. If I remember correctly, the words were something to the effect of, 'Yes, Chuck, we will meet at my chateau. Christian, Englebert, Aleixandre, and Raymond will join us. Harmagedon is on! The timing will depend on you getting the Fox … I know it may take a few months. Sure, I'll await your word. Agreed, will inform others only when I have a confirmation from you. Thanks, Chuck … Bye for now.' That was it, Mr. Khan."

Kareem nearly dropped his phone. He had heard right. Those two names on the list sent a chill down his spine. It could not be true. Jason Goodman, who had rented the 55 Water Street offices for Rusty Newman, the supposed assassin, who had taken a shot at President Harrison, had met at Hunters' Lodge in Santa Clara. Jason had not been seen since then. Hunters' Lodge was owned by Robert Chuck Scott Jr., the vice president of the United States. Among those who had met at Gunther's chateau and watched the image of President Harrison was a Chuck. This was bigger than he had thought.

The other name… *the Fox*! Something had been worrying him about that part of the conversation that Cynthia had just told him. "The timing will depend on you getting the Fox." *That was it! The Fox!* That was the nom de guerre of the assassin, who had been a shadow to the intelligence world for over thirty years. He had assassinated countless high-value targets the world over. There was no record of him in any police database worldwide. Everyone knew he existed because of the trail of dead people he left behind. But the trail had always gone cold. It never led anywhere. There were no fingerprints. No pictures. He was long gone by the time the authorities arrived at the scene of the crime.

He was a professional and left the scene completely sterile, with nary a fingerprint or any form of evidence. No hair samples, no fluids, no fibers or footprints. Nothing. A ghost. Until now. If this was the Fox, as Kareem felt deep down in his bones it was, then the world's most shadowy criminal may have finally made his first slipup in a career spanning thirty years across several continents. Locard was damn right: "Every contact leaves its trace." He had bolted from 55 Water, and fortunately, Tanya had linked him to the bird-watcher's office, Jason Goodman the real estate agent, Rusty Newman the tenant, and Hunters' Lodge in Santa Clara. A first slipup. There was a connection between him and a group of wealthy businessmen who had met at a chateau in Bavaria. The name of the vice president of the United States was somehow tied in.

"Are you there?"

"Yes, MJ, I'm here. This is way, way bigger than I thought. Be *very careful*, buddy. I am going to call Mitch right now to arrange to move you guys to a safe house. Hand over the DVD to him. Move out of the hotel right now and hide if you must, until Mitch contacts you. Do not have the slightest doubt about what I am saying to you. Your lives are in *great* danger. You may have gone to check on Amy and Ryan's death, but I think you have stumbled onto something way bigger. Way, way over your head. You have no idea about the kind of people you are dealing with or the sheer scope of the conspiracy. I am on the next flight out to Bavaria!"

He called and updated his director on the situation. Next, he called Gwen and told her about the Fox. He was on the loose, and she should ensure that the Washington office beefed up security for the president. The assassin had missed once. He would try another shot. His reputation in the shadowy world depended on it. The people who hired him would want him to. There was a lot riding on this contract for the people who had hired him. She agreed to talk to Washington and ensure the president's security bubble was tightened. She wished him luck in finding the Fox.

He called for a quick meeting with his team. "Guys, this is where we stand. Rusty Newman rented this office a month ago. All the paperwork was done by Jason Goodman. So, no one at 55 Water Street has seen Rusty Newman. I have information that six extremely wealthy and powerful people from several countries met in Bavaria and watched images of attacks by Muslims on people of other faiths worldwide, plus North Korean, Chinese, and Iranian leaders and President Harrison. One of the six was a Chuck."

Kareem saw everyone's eyes widen at the tale, especially at the last name he had just said. "Yes, guys, I know that it sounds preposterous and frightening, but it happens to be true. My information from Bavaria is from a very reliable source. I am personally going to Bavaria to check it out. Now, back here we know that Jason disappeared at a lodge owned by Robert Chuck Scott Jr., the vice president. I am not saying it's the same Chuck, but the coincidences seem darn strong. Yet another important fact is that the people who met in Germany also referred to a fox."

"The elusive assassin?" Tanya asked.

Kareem looked at his close-knit team. They were good. They had already made good ground within a day. But he knew it was not going to be easy to nab the Fox, let alone prosecute him. "Too early to say if the Fox referred to in the conversation and the shadowy assassin are the same, but it's definitely a lead I hope to follow up on. Jason went to meet Rusty, or the Fox—whoever—at Hunters' Lodge. He has not been seen since then. Was he silenced by the Fox, aka Rusty, so the trail could not lead back to him? And Jason may have signed his own death warrant when he met him at the lodge in Santa Clara. That is what Tanya and Bob will need to find out after they meet with Chloe tomorrow. Turn Hunters' Lodge inside out and see what you guys can rake up there. Get email and telephone records of Chuck Scott, the VP. Let's confirm or rule it out. Right now, it looks too strong to pass up."

★

"Jason was just an average guy." Chloe held back her tears. "But he always called. There is no way he would just disappear like that. I don't like this."

"Sorry, Chloe," Tanya said. "There must be a perfectly good reason for Jason's disappearance. I am sure he will call you."

"He always called. Or sent texts. Like this one he sent saying Rusty was going to buy Hunters' Lodge and he hoped to rake in fifty grand in commission. He was so excited. I wish I had called him back. We were engaged to be married. We had made all the plans. I think Jason was hoping to surprise me by making a down payment on a house as a wedding gift. He was such a sweet man. I really wish I had called him back." She sniffed more and wiped her tears.

"I am sorry, Chloe," Bob said. "Is that the only text he sent?"

"There was one more, and I did not give it much thought at that time," she said. "But now that he is missing, you better see this." She clicked on the message and passed her phone to Bob.

Bob read the message. "'This Rusty guy's a funny chap. He's testing the telescopic sights on his long-range weapons. These prairie dog and other animal silhouette targets are so darn small that I dunno how he will see them from two miles out, where he's got me holding 'em up for him! But he's got the greenbacks, so who cares? Will call you soon, after he's through with scoping his targets. Love you, babes.'"

Strange. Scoping targets with Jason holding silhouettes two miles out. Who shoots prairie dogs from that distance? Or was it a dry run for the 55 Water Street assassination attempt on POTUS? Tanya could not help seeing the coincidences. She knew they had something here. But Jason was already missing, and no one had any idea who Rusty was.

"That was it?" Tanya asked. "No calls or messages after that, right?"

Chloe just shook her head. She probably feared the worst and did not want to dwell on it. Her mind was on the man in her life and the quandary she was in right now. She did not know if she should grieve or hope for a miracle. But she was no baby. She feared the worst. As Chloe left, Tanya also felt something had happened at Hunters' Lodge when Jason went there to meet Rusty Newman, whoever he was. That target practice seemed crucial. What had happened there? There was only one way to know. She had to go to Hunters' Lodge.

Tanya asked Bob to check on the vice president's email and telephone records while she drove to Santa Clara. She did not want to arouse the vice president's suspicions, so she decided she would tell the local police she was just conducting a routine follow-up on a missing person, one Jason Goodman, last seen at Hunters' Lodge. She made it to Santa Clara by nightfall and checked into a local hotel. She could not sleep, thinking of all that had transpired. She had been lucky in connecting the twentieth-floor birder's office and Chloe, and now she had two names: Jason and Rusty. She was excited that she was in Franklin County, where she hoped to connect all the dots. This was the biggest case she had ever worked on. Try as she might, Tanya could not fall asleep for a long time.

The next day she paid a visit to the Franklin County Sheriff's Department. Small-town officers were not often very happy to see big-city G-men raking up things in their backyard. She was used to it. Tanya assured them it was merely a case of someone missing and she would just be doing a cursory check before she went elsewhere to track him. The missing man had sent a message from the lodge, and that is what had brought her there. It was possible he was here on a private vacation, had had an accident on the lodge grounds, or was hurt, sick, or somehow incapacitated. She just needed to find out. The officers were unsure, but they bought her story. Two police officers and their canine support teams accompanied her to Hunters' Lodge.

They spent the better part of the morning scouring the lodge and its environs for any trace of Jason Goodman. They got nothing. Tanya remembered that the last message Jason had sent was about holding up animal silhouette targets two miles away from Rusty Newman. She got the officers to take the dogs two miles downhill past hardwood and conifer forest to the wetlands. As they came up to Jennings Brook, the dogs began to sniff around in earnest. Soon the dogs, straining at their leashes, led the officers to a small hillock in a clearing.

Tanya walked up and squatted on the ground. She saw what looked like holes driven into the dirt. Bolts or stakes of some sort had been used to drive something into the hard surface. A target, possibly. For the next half hour, they scoured the area carefully. It took them well over two hours before they got their first clue: an empty casing of 338 Lapua Magnum ammunition. As Tanya lifted it off the ground with forceps and laid it on her gloved palm, she espied a dark ruddy color on one side of the bullet. It could have been from the reddish earth they'd found it dug in. Could it also be dried blood? She dropped it into her evidence bag, marked it, and put it away. She took several photographs of the site.

The dogs were now barking madly at the edge of Jennings Brook. Using some long sticks, one of the officers was poking into the water. It took them an hour but at the end they hit pay dirt. They found something weighed down by a large boulder and dragged it out.

It was a gruesome sight: a headless body with some limbs ripped off. The flesh was peeling off from prolonged immersion in the brook. The stench was unbearable. Tanya stared at the body for a long moment. She knew who this could be, although a part of her did not want it to be him. Chloe was so looking forward to her marriage and her wedding gift of a new house with a fifty-thousand-dollar down payment. *Not this*, Tanya thought. Kareem was right. If this was the handiwork of the Fox, then Jason had signed his death warrant by coming here. The Fox had killed him, hoping to erase all links to him.

They searched the grounds for a long time but found nothing else. The body was bagged, and the deputies took it to the county coroner. Tanya drove straight back from the hillock. After about two miles, she saw another clearing. Again, the dogs did their work and it did not take them long to sniff and bark, suggesting there had been a human presence at this spot. Tanya looked at the spot the dogs were most enthusiastic about. So, this was from where the Fox had fired the shot that killed Jason. She was a professional agent and knew she had to wait for forensics to confirm that it truly was Jason. But she could not help this nagging feeling deep down in her gut that this had to be him. He had sent Chloe that message from her. Now she had found a body that, for all intents and purposes, had to be Jason's. The poor guy had trusted a man who had blown his head off.

The deputies were careful not to disturb the area. Tanya found some dried shoe prints in the muddy ground. She photographed them and used her kit to raise the print. It was almost evening when she left. She asked the sheriff's department to keep the find under wraps until she had informed the next of kin. She did not want to tip off Chuck just yet. They were tired from hanging around with her the entire day and did not care as long as this FBI agent would handle this case related to someone missing in some other state. Not their cup of tea.

She called Kareem, who was at the airport, waiting to fly to Munich, and updated him. Kareem was not surprised. This was what he had feared. He was glad she had the bullet and had fished the body out of the brook. That would incriminate Chuck. Their case was getting stronger. She promised to get the ballistics on the bullet and the forensics on the body done. Kareem thanked her.

She drove back to New York City in silence, thinking of Jason, Chloe, Chuck, the mutilated body she had seen, and the bullet casing. Someone had been brutally killed at Hunters'

Lodge. The autopsy report and DNA matching would identify the dead body. Though she knew it had to be Jason, she was still a professional agent. She would wait for the identification. The bullet with its reddish marks would also have tales to tell.

She drove straight home. It was pretty late when she got there. She took a long shower, made herself a sandwich, and thought of everything that had happened that day as she ate in stony silence. Lying in bed, later on, she thought of the body they had found in the brook, Chloe's tearstained face, Vice President Chuck Scott, shadowy powerful men in Bavaria, and a faceless assassin.

"Oh yes, Chuck Scott, the vice president, is involved in this all right," Bob said grimly at the office next day, confirming her worst fears. "Here are two emails from a John Smith, most likely another assumed name of the Fox, to a Joshua Taylor, a pseudonym for Chuck Scott, asking him to get someone to rent an office at 55 Water Street for a Rusty Newman. He asks Joshua to get someone who cannot be connected to him to draw up the lease. John Smith promises to 'dispense with' that person! In a second mail, Joshua Taylor confirms that the rental of the twentieth-floor office at 55 Water was done by Jason Goodman and that Jason will meet Rusty Newman at Hunters' Lodge the next day! From what you tell me, Jason the real estate agent did go to Hunters' Lodge and was effectively 'dispensed with.'

Tanya read the emails, her heart beating faster at the thought of how high up this conspiracy reached.

"'Rent an office on the twentieth floor of 55 Water Street in New York. I have already checked the property. There are several vacant offices available on that floor. It should be one that faces the Downtown Manhattan Heliport. Furnish it as a birder's studio. It should look like that of a professional birdwatcher, not an ornithologist, who studies birds for scientific reasons. The office will be used by one Rusty Newman, who enjoys bird-watching and sketching birds. Have loads of bird pictures set up: kestrels, bald eagles, merlins, northern harriers, and especially many of peregrine falcons. Since 1999 a pair of peregrine falcons has been nesting on the fourteenth floor of 55 Water. Rusty will like watching the falcon pair named Jack and Jill and their offspring.'"

She read on.

"'Fill it with paints, easels, brushes, canvases, frames, paintings, and the furniture to go with it. They should be exclusive and done tastefully. Get it done within a fortnight. The person who draws up the rental agreement should be someone who cannot be traced back to you. And it should be someone we can dispense with. After he has signed the lease, send him to Hunters' Lodge in Santa Clara next weekend. Tell him it's up for sale and that a prospective buyer wishes to check it out. I will ensure all loose ends are tied up.'"

That was a chilling death warrant for Jason Goodman. Tanya read and reread the message several times. So, Chuck Scott, the vice president, was an *accessory* to murder most foul. According to what Kareem had told them, Chuck was also involved in some dangerous liaisons with men in foreign countries to carry out even greater evil plans. This was getting more dangerous by the minute.

She turned her attention to the second email. It was even more damning. Chuck Scott, the vice president, had implicated himself badly in this one. This was enough to put him away.

"Jason Goodman, the real estate agent I hired to rent your office at 55 Water will meet Rusty Newman tomorrow at Hunters' Lodge."

So, Chuck had sent Jason to his death. What a fall from grace for the high office of the vice president of the country, an accomplice to murder.

"This is enough to lock him up for the rest of his life," Tanya said. "He sent Jason to a sure death. We need to bring this man down."

"Oh, the old man will go to the slammer for several lifetimes, Tanya, for high treason. See his phone records?" Bob was holding a sheaf of papers. "There are scores of calls between the VP and Jason that were made from just before the lease was signed until when Jason went to Hunters' Lodge. Soon we should have confirmation from the coroner that the body you found is that of Jason. Who else would it be? Anyway, let's wait that one out. Ballistics have shown that the bullet you retrieved from Hunters' Lodge was fired from the same gun that we found at the offices at 55 Water. So, for all intents and purposes, the gun that shot at President Harrison was the same gun that killed Jason. Well, I presume Jason. That connects not only Rusty Newman, aka the Fox, to the act, but also Vice President Chuck Scott. Oh yes, Tanya, we have enough to lock up the vice president for high treason and an accessory to murder. Lock him up and throw away the key!"

She had been unable to reach Kareem, because he was still on his way to Bavaria. She sent him a long email. Kareem would be happy that they could tie up the loose ends on this side. She wished her boss would be able to figure out the greater international conspiracy he had gone to check up on. And its connection to the assassination attempt in America.

"I had no idea this was so big, Bob. Kareem tells me there is some group of wealthy and powerful men from different countries in Europe who are planning something they call Harmagedon. What have we stumbled upon here? This is a massive plot that spans several nations—an attempted assassination of the president of the United States with the involvement of the vice president!"

"Kareem's visit to Bavaria should unlock the rest of this conspiracy. It's quite a Gordian knot the boss has to unravel. Wish him luck. We need to nail these bastards." Bob was angry.

What agent wouldn't have felt that way after discovering that the leaders they had held in high esteem were actually worse than dirt? That's a sucker punch to a person's self-esteem. If you can't trust and respect the vice president, who's a heartbeat away from the presidency, then whom can you respect?

"Yes, Bob, we need to get these bastards. I'm sure Kareem is right now in the middle of something explosive. I can't wait to hear from him."

CHAPTER FIFTEEN

Captured!

Kareem *was* indeed in the middle of something explosive but sadly not the type of investigative break that Tanya had visualized. Kareem had landed in Munich and walked straight into trouble. Mitch, the CIA station head, was to meet him but was helping move Matt and Cynthia from the Hotel Waldmann to a CIA safe house. So, Ashley and Gerhard had offered to pick up Kareem and meet Mitch at the Augustiner Großgaststätten beer hall. They planned to drive from there to the safe house.

But things had not gone as planned. Kareem arrived in the evening and got into the BMW with Gerhard and Ashley, who was behind the wheel. They had barely left the airport when several large black cars drove up and tried to force them off the road. At first, Ashley thought the drivers were drunk revelers, and she cut her speed to let them pass. An SUV came alongside the car. Windows rolled down, and she saw the ugly snout of a submachine gun pointed at her head. Gerhard moved forward and tapped Ashley's shoulder, pointing to her right and screaming at her to get away. She saw another gun bearing down on her from the car on the right and a burly German gesticulating to her to pull over.

She remembered Mitch telling them earlier that they were in great danger. Kareem had said the same thing to her when he got off the plane. The gun said it all. From the corner of her eye, she checked out what she was up against: one SUV on her right, another on her left, and two sports cars behind her. One of the sports cars was trying to come up front so the four of them could box her in. She floored the pedal and gunned the BMW onto the autobahn before the formation could close her in. The four cars shot after her.

Ashley was no Formula One driver, but was no rookie either. She knew the danger she was in. She had heard of the assassination attempt against President Harrison and some connection to what was happening in Bavaria. The perceived danger was such that they were being moved to a safe house. So, she knew that whoever was in the cars, weren't ordinary people. They meant business. She had come to Bavaria seeking her mother's killers. Suddenly she was caught up in something bigger, something involving an assassination attempt on the American president and some dangerous plans known only as Harmagedon. She got off the main road at the first exit and hit the back routes. She temporarily left her pursuers far behind and zoomed past terrified drivers on the road. She hoped some traffic cop would stop them, but was not lucky on that count.

Kareem shouted, "Gerhard, call Matt."

"No chance, Kareem," Gerhard said. "Mitch had asked Matt and Cynthia to switch off their phones while at the safe house to keep anyone from tracking them."

"There's a way I can reach Mitch on a private line. The cabal guys don't have our numbers," Kareem said. "But we need to get out of here fast. Ashley, turn in there!"

Kareem pointed to a basement parking garage and told her to duck into it. Ashley hit the gas and brake simultaneously, turned sharply, and shot into the basement. The smell of burning tires hit their nostrils as the car screeched into the narrow space with seconds to spare. One minute they were on the road, the next minute inside. The cars following them did not see them enter the parking lot and thundered straight past. Ashley cut the engine and came to a stop, breathing heavily.

"Kareem, who are these people?" she asked.

"I don't know, Ash. Right now, we have no time to figure out what's what. Move over and let me drive. MJ will kill me if I let them capture his baby."

Ashley and Kareem had barely had time to switch seats when four cars roared into the basement, brakes screeching as they powered straight at them. They had obviously retraced their steps and caught up with them. Kareem hit the gas and roared out of the garage, which gave them a few minutes' edge, since their pursuers had to reverse to come after them. Kareem floored the pedal, and the BMW's monster 381 bhp tri-turbo-powered engine swallowed the road as it torched its way down the darkened side roads of Munich. They jumped across concrete road islands and zoomed at breakneck speed. When they seemed to have lost their pursuers, they cut their speed, pulled over, and parked. Kareem wiggled around in the seat and fished out his phone from one of his pockets. He needed to call Mitch and get the cavalry here.

The power of the crash was so strong that their SUV almost jumped the parking curb and airbags opened up into their faces. Their bodies were hurled against the seat belts. The phone flew from Kareem's hands, and Ashley almost blacked out from the force. Their pursuers had arrived and crashed into them. The big SUV had hit his side of the car, and Gerhard had not been wearing his seat belt. Ashley remembered earlier that he had moved forward in his seat to warn her of the car on her right. He may have removed his seat belt at that time and in the rush, never put it back on. The sheer force of the crash had thrown his body to the roof of the car and snapped his neck. He lay against his seat, eyeballs hanging out of their sockets. He was dead. Ashley screamed in terror.

Balaclava-clad men wielding semi-automatic guns threw open their doors, yanked them out of their seats, tied their hands behind them, stuffed some cloth into their mouths, dumped them into the trunks of two sports cars, and sped off. The entire action had not taken more than a few minutes. The cars sped off into the gathering dusk at great speed. Lying bent double in the trunk of a car, Kareem felt like an idiot for walking straight into trouble. Worse still, he had put Ashley's life in danger. Gerhard was dead. He cursed himself and hoped that Ashley was safe. But for Special Agent Kareem Khan, head of Operation Brimstone, this was a shocking failure. Kareem was hard on himself. He wished Mitch had come.

Bumping along in the trunk of the other car, Ashley shared Kareem's sense of anger at having been captured. She cried at the thought of Gerhard lying dead in the car. All wanted to do was help. Now he was dead. Ashley felt terrible. She had to do something. She was not going to wallow in self-pity. She had been in bad situations before and had not buckled under pressure. Although this one scared her, a part of her had always switched on in adverse conditions. She was in great danger, but she was a fighter. You either took life head-on or you were dead anyway, she told herself. So instead of panicking, she calmed down and took stock of her situation. Luckily, the tracking device was still in her shirt pocket. It had a tight clip, and during the crash and subsequent rough hustle into the trunk, the pen had not fallen out. She was grateful for her dad's foresight. Now there was a chance they would be rescued.

Rescued if their captors did not have any other plans for them, that is. But she would play for enough time for her father and friends to reach her. The car sped along for more than an hour. She had no idea where they were being taken. To be shot? She doubted that. They could have done that the moment they crashed into them. They could even have poured gasoline into the car and burned them alive. She had read stories of people eliminating their enemies. There was no point in stuffing cloths into their mouths and tying up their hands. Someone wanted to see them. Gunther and his friends? She did not know.

A part of her dreaded such a meeting, but another part was curious about unmasking this animal. She wanted to see the face of the man who must have ordered her mother's killing. She would love to gouge his eyes out with her bare hands. But she knew she would not be able to do that. She was not like him. Her mother would not have approved of it. Still, she longed to confront him, tear away his veneer of sophistication, and treat him as the animal he was. She was angry, and that kept her fear at bay. She was going to fight this out. Or die trying. The car sped on into the night. After what seemed ages, it came to a stop. She waited as she heard the doors open and slam shut. No one came for her. Were they going to leave her all tied up in some remote location in the trunk of a car to die? That would be a horrible way to die. It was uncomfortable enough with the cloth in her mouth and her knees bent double as she lay on her side in the darkened trunk. Again, her calm mind told her their captors could have killed them with a single bullet each and wouldn't have had to tie them up. Someone wanted to see them. She waited, ready to face a bullet or her captors.

Suddenly the lid of the trunk popped open. Balaclava-clad men stood against the night sky, looking into the car. They reached in and pulled her out. She had guessed right. They were outside Gunther's chateau. They untied her hands, removed the cloth from her mouth, and pushed her toward the mansion. They were so far out from civilization that no one would have heard them even if she had screamed. She would not have made ten paces if she had tried to run. Her captors knew that when they had freed her. She could see Kareem ahead of her being frog-marched. Their captors searched them for weapons and found only phones. They removed the batteries, threw them away, and returned the phones.

One of them removed the pen from Ashley's top pocket. Her heart missed a beat. Would he throw it away or crush it? He returned it to her. She fixed it in place, managing to switch the camera on as she did so. They were brought to the same meeting room they had been in just a week earlier. Only this time it was not empty. All the seats were taken. She counted five men. As they sat her down, she recognized Gunther from the images she had seen online. She recoiled at the sight as if she had seen a venomous reptile.

"Welcome to my chateau," Gunther said. Guards stood behind both her and Kareem but did not tie them up. "Though I can see this is your second visit to my house, lady." Ashley still could not bring herself to look at the face of the man who had had her mother killed. She hoped to God that the camera pen was recording. If anything was going to be said here, she wanted to have a record. If she made it out of this place alive, she would ensure these criminals were brought to justice. She did not want to respond to Gunther's caustic reference to her earlier visit to the chateau. She controlled herself. She needed to buy time to help her dad and Mitch rescue them. Attacking Gunther with her bare hands and getting shot would not help. So, though her anger was boiling over and every tendon in her body wanted to strike him, she did what she did best under difficult conditions and calmed down. First, she would study her situation and plan her course of action. She exhaled deeply and looked around at the other members of this nefarious cabal.

"Kidnapping us is a grave error of judgment," Kareem said. "Add murder to that. Your goons killed Gerhard."

"Entering my house and snooping around was an even greater error of judgment on your part," Gunther replied. "Gerhard, that ex-employee deserved exactly that. I only wish I had knocked him off much earlier. That way he would not have given you so many leads."

"Special Agent Kareem Khan, welcome to Bavaria." Ashley and Kareem looked over in horror as Vice President Chuck Scott Jr. walked through the door. "I know you oversaw the assassination attempt on President Harrison. In my position, it's not difficult for me to know these things. But of course, you know that. Though I must say, I didn't expect you in Bavaria. Who do we have here? Ashley Jordan! Your mother, Amy, worked for Gunther. But she too poked her nose into Gunther's financial transactions, especially a large amount sent to me. Now, that was way too sensitive a transaction for us. We could not let her follow up on that one. So, Gunther had to—what shall I say? —arrange for her speedy dispatch? I can see that you are following in your mother's footsteps. Not to worry, though, for we'll arrange for you to join her soon enough."

Chuck went on, "Fortunately for us, the caretaker took some pictures of you when you trespassed here last time, so it wasn't hard for us to identify you. We have sent a team to pick up your father, Matt. Sorry, but we can't afford to have you bungle our carefully laid plans. None of you will leave here alive tonight. We stand at the cusp of history, and a new world order beckons. Our first plan to assassinate the president failed, but we have a Plan B that will take Harrison out. I will yet be the president of the United States of America!"

The words *speedy dispatch* hit Ashley like a sledgehammer. Just like that. These animals had ordered her mother's death. Chuck had just confirmed it in ruthless language. She recoiled at the thought. It had never been a hit-and-run accident. It was as she and her dad had always suspected—a cold, calculated murder. That truck had waited for her mother to cross the street and then deliberately run her over, and Gunther had ordered it. She could imagine that huge truck smashing into her poor mother's frail body. Ashley's eyes were bloodshot with anger, but she controlled her rage and said in coldly measured words, "You animals, you will pay for this. You will all pay."

Chuck smiled and said, "The five-million-dollar payment for an assassin to kill President Harrison was not part of your mother's investment banking portfolio to follow up on, my dear. If we had let her live, it would have brought our entire plan crashing down. Sorry, but she had to go, along with her friend, that other American, who overheard part of Gunther's discussion with me. Well, these things should not bother you. You'll die tonight."

"You are a traitor, sir!" Kareem said scornfully to the vice president. "You will face charges of high treason for collaborating with foreign agents against the United States."

Matt was right—they had killed Amy, and Ryan too. *The bastards*, he thought. He looked at Ashley. The poor girl had to hear about her mother's death. She must be seething with rage. But he could also see that she was controlling herself. She must have some plan. Perhaps she was playing for time for someone to come save them. He knew Ashley. She was a calm one. She took after her father. Kareem looked around at Gunther's friends seated at the tables. There were several guns in front of them, but Kareem knew he'd be shot before he could grab one. There were far too many armed guards around.

"It's Muslims like you who are the traitors," Gunther interjected. "You are killing Christians throughout the entire Western Hemisphere! Flying planes into the Twin Towers on 9/11, the London bombings of 7/7, driving a truck into people in France, shootings in Orlando, Florida, the terror attacks at *Charlie Hebdo*, killings in San Bernardino, beheadings by Jihadi John, ISIS—all are *Muslims like you* butchering us Christians!"

"I did all that?" Kareem asked.

"You are all the same. You come into our lands and create sharia zones. Where we once had churches and a Christian way of life, we now have mosques, women in burkas, the Arabic language, and halal meat butcheries. Millions of refugees are pouring into the West from Afghanistan, Pakistan, Iraq, Syria, Iran, Algeria, and Morocco. Guess how you repay our kindness? Enjoy our unemployment benefits, rape our women in Germany, or kill a filmmaker in Holland. Our way of life, civilization, culture, values, and very existence as a race are threatened. We *cannot* let you do that!"

Kareem said, "You are generalizing what some criminal characters may have done. Painting all of us with one brush is fundamentally incorrect. Agreed, some misguided elements have given us a bad name, but that does not mean that Muslims hate all other faiths. Islam means peace." He was unsure if his words had any effect on this crazed, fanatic group.

Gunther waved toward the assembled friends, who until now had been listening quietly. "Come on, soldier. Haven't we heard that spiel about Islam meaning peace before? We have had enough. We are going to rid this world of Muslims. You will die tonight, so it doesn't matter if you hear of our plans. Meet the Cabal of Christian Crusaders—Chuck, myself, Christian Hannes, Father

Englebert Volker, Aleixandre Thierry, and Raymond Webster Coleman. With our considerable resources, we will rid the world of the Islamic menace. Consider that the second crusade of sorts."

Ashley could not believe what she was hearing. So that was what *CCC* stood for—the Cabal of Christian Crusaders. She hoped to God, again, that the hidden camera in her pen was recording all this. "What? Christian crusaders? A second crusade? Are you morons for real?"

"You have a worse mouth than your mother. If you don't shut up now, I'll ask someone to gag you," Gunther said, angry at being interrupted. He was in a fanatic delirium. He ignored Ashley's comments and addressed Kareem, the Muslim enemy in the room.

"You will not live to see the new world. But I want you to die knowing what awaits your Muslim flock. We have more than six million of your radicals from Turkey, Iran, and the Middle East in Germany. I have set aside enough resources to bomb refugee shelters, Muslim enclaves, mosques, Islamic schools, halal butcheries, and Muslim homes. We will massacre the hordes of Muslim immigrants now flooding Germany from Afghanistan, Sudan, Iraq, Syria, Iran, and North Africa. We will destroy German landmarks and lay the blame on the Muslims, giving rise to local anger against the immigrants."

"How could you?" Kareem was shocked. "What have those innocent people—Muslims and people of other faiths who will be affected by your crazed schemes—done to you? Will any of those mass murders give you anything in return, except a misguided sense of vengeance for the acts of a few criminals?"

Gunther raged on, "Slaughtering innocent journalists at *Charlie Hebdo* or shoppers at Hypercacher kosher market and throwing grenades in the Bataclan theater in Paris was not misguided?"

Aleixandre said, "Just like Gunther, I have plans in place to kill a few thousand French people in shopping malls, underground trains, schools, and churches, and I'll blame it all on the Algerian Muslim immigrants in France. French citizens already at their tipping point will massacre your Islamic brothers and sisters in the thousands."

Kareem could only stare in wonder. This was truly madness on an epic scale. These fanatics were worse than any he had ever come across. He didn't think his words were having any effect on their demented brains. He knew he couldn't change them. So, he was desperately trying to buy time until Mitch and the team arrived. He was sure Mitch would come—or would he?

"Two wrongs will not make a right, sir," Kareem said. "That will be murder, pure and simple."

"Forcing an eighty-four-year-old priest to kneel at the altar of his church and slitting his throat is not murder?" Alex shot back at Kareem.

"These guys will always find some excuse not to accept responsibility," Christian said. "You can defend all you want, Mr. Special Agent, but this time around, Islamic terror against peace-loving people has reached a tipping point. We have looked the other way for far too long. Everything has a limit. This time you have crossed that line in the sand."

"Christian is from Holland," Volker said, pointing to the Dutch tycoon, "and he has experienced terror by your ilk, Muslim man. Dutchmen of Moroccan origin in Amsterdam are involved in violent gangland crime, muggings, armed robberies, drug trafficking, and extortion. Enough is enough. We need to take action. That's why Christian, like the others in this room, also has specific plans to eliminate members of your religion."

"Yes, Mr. Khan, I do have plans. No more of this. I am tired of The Hague being called *Jihad City* and listening to the imams calling for death to Christians. I plan to bomb the Dutch neighborhood, the 'Sharia Triangle' teeming with your kind, torch more than four hundred mosques, and kill the Imams who preach violence. Like my colleagues here, I have plans to kill Dutchmen by the thousands and lay the blame on Muslims. Trust me, government agent, your lot will be burned alive by an enraged Dutch populace. We will wipe Islam out of the Netherlands. It will be a bloody *Mosexit*, Muslim man!"

"You can kill me if you want, but will it give you peace of mind?" Kareem was horrified by what he was hearing. "The mass atrocities that you speak about so callously will not bring you peace of mind or any imaginary civilization you dream of. The world has moved on from those polarized days when we were known by our religion or ethnicity. Today's world is one large village, and we are all dependent on each other. Mass murder, mayhem, and violence will not solve anything. Muslims don't hate Christians, nor are they ganging up against Western civilization. A few misguided people who have twisted the teachings of Islam to suit their devious ends do not speak for all people of the great faith of Islam. Why else would you have so many Muslim nations fighting against ISIS?"

"Whatever atrocities are unleashed by Muslims, none of your religious leaders stand up to vilify the perpetrators," Ray said. "The sound of their silence is deafening. That shows complicity. You are saying all this, but deep down you like it. You are also a Muslim, and it's simple—you want an Islamic caliphate in the world with no other religion. 'Not every Muslim is a terrorist' is something we have all heard. But you will agree with me, Muslim government agent, that *all terrorists are Muslims*. Everyone knows that. No, my friend, that is not on the table anymore. No Islam. No more terrorism. Two RAF officers in Typhoon aircraft will bomb the Muslim enclaves of London and kill your kind by the hundreds of thousands. No more terror, Mr. FBI Agent. No more."

"You are all raving mad xenophobic outcasts from some distant past." Ashley had heard enough. They had blatantly attacked Kareem as if he were a spokesperson for his religion. "You are the ones who fail to assimilate people who are not like you, and when they find places where they are accepted, you brand them as enclaves. You don't like Muslim women in hijabs and see them as and a symbol of Islamist threat? Have Muslims attacked Christian nuns who wear attire that reflects *their* religion? People like you profile Muslims—you don't hire them, and you target them in hate crimes. Just because a few disgruntled elements of a religion—Christian, Muslim, or any other religion—carry out atrocities, does not automatically mean that everyone in that religion is to blame."

Chuck said, in a voice of authority, "But they killed us, created ISIS, bomb hotels and public places, drive trucks through crowds, and kill and maim innocent people. This has gone on far too long, past the breaking point for many of us. This is not just about Muslims. We also plan to rid this world of the scourge of Communists. All of us assembled here are men of considerable wealth and influence over the destiny of men and events of this world. Our plans to rid the world of Muslims and Communists are at an advanced stage. There is no turning back. It's too late.

"We will yet assassinate the president," Chuck continued, "and I will ascend to the presidency of the United States and unleash Harmagedon on millions of people across the Atlantic. Within my first one hundred days in office, I hope to nuke North Korea and Iran back to the Stone Age, bomb the artificial islands the Chinese have built in the South China Sea, wipe out ISIS in Syria and Iraq, stop Muslim migration, and have Muslims deported to their countries of origin. So, Kareem Khan, in one fell swoop, we will do what a hundred leaders and their politically correct stances have failed to. We will *redraw the map of the world*."

"Did you say that you will use nuclear weapons?" Ashley was mortified. "You hope to ascend to the highest office of the land and unleash the worst weapon known to mankind? Do you have any idea of the devastation such a bomb can cause? Hundreds of millions of people could die, and millions of tons of smoke will block sunlight and create a nuclear winter colder than the Ice Age! The world will be a bloody wasteland for eons, you numbskull! The domino effect of a retaliatory strike by North Korea, Iran, Russia, and China against your ill-advised idea could easily consume our planet in a fireball!"

Volker, the excommunicated priest, did not want his disciples to dwell on the dark image that Ashley was creating. So, he resorted to religious fervor to arouse the cabal to the project at hand, completely ignoring her comments. "We will unleash Harmagedon; wipe out the malfeasance of godless Communism and Islam that afflicts our world; fulfill our God-given mandate to 'take the wicked from among the righteous'; purify, cleanse, restore, and renew the world; regain power over this earth; and return it to the mighty Christendom of our grandfathers!"

It worked. They thumped their tables in appreciation. Volker always knew how to push his flock's buttons.

"Once we have pummeled the world into submission with our weapons," Gunther said, "we will bring financial ruin of unimaginable proportions in the Western world, so that the spirits of our subjects will be so crushed that it will be easy to rule them. We will bring the Western world to its knees."

"You will destroy the financial order of the world?" Kareem was praying that Mitch and the team would come soon. These men had described their version of Armageddon in its entirety to him and Ashley, so now there was no chance that the two of them would live to tell the tale. Yet a part of Kareem wanted to glean from them as much information about their evil plans as possible. If by chance he did manage to escape, he could help stop their manic schemes, so he played for more time.

"Ah, soldier boy, that's fairly easy for us in the trade," said Raymond, the real estate broker. "Of course, you have heard of pump-and-dump schemes, short and distort, and the like. You don't look that wet behind the ears. Only we will do it on a scale that your puny brain cannot comprehend, and we'll crash stock markets across the continents. Don't worry if you do not understand it. It does not matter anymore for a dead man like you."

"Pump-and-dump schemes!" Kareem remembered seeing those words on the TV screens in this very room. "You will wipe out the livelihoods of not just Muslims but thousands of average people of every faith!"

"That's the general idea, Mr. Federal Agent. We need to crush the spirits of the populace. Then they'll be concerned only about putting food on the table and not be bothered by our plans of exterminating Muslims or setting up of a Christian administration. A populace reeling under financial ruin will not have the time or the inclination to object, when we destroy their very souls. It's called total domination."

"Pump and dump, Mr. Khan, is merely the start," Aleixandre Thierry said. "We will hit the large institutional brokerages, the mega-corporations, banks, pension funds and hedge funds, and wipe them out with similar schemes. It will be an apocalyptic collapse of the financial world across both sides of the Atlantic!"

"You are all animals." Ashley could not believe the xenophobic diatribe and the plans to destroy the financial world. "It's not Muslims who are the enemy, but raving mad, megalomaniac, racist bigots like you. Are you meatheads sane? Take over the world? Nuke other countries? Engineer a stock market crash and destroy the wealth and livelihoods of millions? Go get your heads examined. You will never succeed in this."

"Really, young lady?" Chuck was sarcastic. "Watch this space then. The moment the Fox assassinates President Harrison and I ascend to his office, we will unleash Harmagedon. Muslims and Communists will burn and roast in hellfires."

"I am an American." Kareem wanted to turn the tide of hatred. "I was born and raised in Kansas. I grew up in a country where people of all faiths, proudly American, are free to live and exercise their faiths. It's a value that Ashley, her father, and millions of Americans strongly believe in. It is also the ethos on which European societies were built. The countless millions of citizens of the free world accept all faiths, and the world will go on like that. My religion stands for peace. Those who kill innocent people in the name of Islam are not true adherents of my religion. We detest them more than you do. You may find this hard to believe, but Iranian president Hassan Rouhani referred to the Paris attacks as a 'crime against humanity,' and the leader of the world's most populous Muslim nation, Indonesian president Joko Widodo, said that his nation 'condemns the violence that took place in Paris.'"

"Politically correct noises." Gunther was not ready to change his mind. "I don't believe a single word these Muslim leaders say. Bloody liars, all of them!"

"Oh really, you German pig?" Ashley said. "Then you are the one who is bloody wrong. I am a journalist and covered the 9/11 attacks." Hatred for her mother's killer enraging her, she went on. "Countless Muslims and Muslim organizations around the world condemned the 9/11 attacks and spoke up vehemently against them. Abdulaziz bin Abdallah, the chief mufti of Saudi Arabia, called what happened on 9/11 'a form of injustice that cannot be tolerated by Islam, which views them as gross crimes and sinful acts.' The Muslim Brotherhood of Egypt said that they condemn such activities that are 'against all human and Islamic morals.' The Islamic Conference, chair of the American Muslim Alliance, and scores of Islamic organizations around the world condemned it. I could quote hundreds of voices of reason from the Muslim community, who kept saying that Islam, like Judaism or any religion, is meant to bring people closer to God. A few morally bankrupt people have used the name of Islam to wreak wanton acts of terror, but the vast majority of Muslims are peace loving and do not wish to kill and maim, as you plan to do."

"You are a bloody Muslim pig as well." Gunther was livid.

Kareem confronted him. "So suddenly a Christian girl is a pig because she does not conform to your bigotry? Is that it? Or is it because deep down, you know that she's speaking the truth? Want to hear more? Are you people aware that the Los Angeles County sheriff testified before Congress in 2011, saying that seven of the past ten al-Qaeda plots in the United States were foiled by tips from the American Muslim community? Or that it was three Syrian immigrants who went to the police station in Berlin and got them to nab the Syrian immigrant who wanted to cause terror? It's only when we work together that we can root out these criminal elements. More violent attacks, such as what you plan, will only stoke more recruiting grounds for such groups. We need to stick together, not face off and kill each other."

"Team up with Muslims?" Christian said in apparent disgust. "Over my dead body."

"No sir, no." Kareem was pleading, trying to hammer some sense into their heads, not that he believed it would change them. They were past redemption, but he had to try. "Exclusion is not the way to solve this problem. We need to be inclusive in this battle. We are with you in the fight. We need to eradicate the evil of terrorism and make our society as peaceful and egalitarian as it was for hundreds of years.

"Instead of listening only to voices of hate, have you ever tried to hear the voices of reason from both Muslim and Christian leaders fighting the evil of terrorism? More than a hundred Sunni and Shiite imams in England produced a video denouncing the Islamic State. The Organization of Islamic Cooperation, representing 1.4 billion Muslims in fifty-seven countries, condemned the persecution of Christians and minorities in Iraq by ISIS. When Pope Francis met Muslims and members of other faiths in Sri Lanka, he said, 'Men and women do not have to forsake their identity, whether ethnic or religious, in order to live in harmony with their brothers and sisters.' The archbishop of Canterbury denounced the attacks on mosques and said, 'Diversity is a gift, not a threat; it is a hope, not a danger. Listen to peace, not war. As Christians, have you forgotten the Sermon on the Mount, where Jesus exhorts us to show the other cheek instead of seeking revenge?'"

"You throw the Bible at us, Muslim man?" Volker said to Kareem, his eyes blazing like hot coals. "Oh yes, we do follow Jesus Christ. And like Christ appearing from the clouds and riding on chariots of fire, we will descend upon our Muslim and Communist enemies and annihilate them. Our battle of the ages to institute a new world order, our Harmagedon, is now."

Ashley knew that these men were beyond repair, and that reason did not appeal to them. They had not caught the import of Kareem's reference to forgiveness in Christ's teachings, but instead reveled in the prospect of cataclysmic, end-of-the-world battles. They were crazed fanatics, too far gone, and they had to be stopped. But she needed to buy time. She desperately hoped someone would come save them before these idiots resorted to violence.

"Are you guys for real?" she said. "Carpet-bomb your way through history and turn the clock back to some medieval Christian world? Armies and weapons are for deterrence, you morons, not to settle petty scores. Nations sit across tables, not on the fields of war. Are you animals even sane? Muslim immigrants are average everyday people escaping from war-torn areas to seek a better life, not enemy combatants for you to wipe out. Just because a few unhinged terrorists have attacked and killed others, you do not go after an entire religion!"

"That is exactly why Islam grew," Gunther said, "because Christians like us sat back and allowed them to. You're right. Nations no longer go to war. That's why we failed. We were passive, and the bloody Muslim hordes invaded our lands. Christians have welcomed Muslims into our lands, opened our hearts and societies for them to settle in. And how did they thank us? By killing us! Today it's the Muslims who are persecuting the Christians. So yes, you're right, we are going to wage a war—a holy war. Consider this a Christian jihad."

Ashley asked, "Have Christians not persecuted people of other faiths? I'm a Christian, and I'm not proud of many things that my religion has done to other people. Over the centuries, Christianity has destroyed pagan temples, prohibited other religious beliefs, burned Jewish books, and banned Talmudic studies. Close to two hundred thousand Bosnian Muslims were killed and fifty thousand Muslim women were raped. Muslims in Serbian concentration camps were subjected to torture, gang raped, with their throats slit, and left to die. Are the Muslims of this world or the Jews coming after you now for all those atrocities? Have you asked yourself that?"

"That's ancient history, lady," Gunther said. "We're talking about what's happening to Christians now. We are being slaughtered by Muslims across the Western world, and we cannot watch in silence anymore. So, don't throw history lessons at us."

"Oh, you want recent history?" Ashley was in her element. "What about Scott Roeder, the violent, right-wing, Christian anti-abortionist who shot and killed Dr. George Tiller in 2009? Or Robert Doggart, the former congressional candidate from Tennessee, a right-wing Christian fundamentalist, who in 2015 planned to firebomb Muslim enclaves in New York? Or Eric Rudolph, who killed a spectator and wounded a hundred and eleven people in Atlanta during the 1996 Summer Olympics? Or when Timothy McVeigh drove a truck filled with forty-eight hundred pounds of explosives into a federal building in Oklahoma City in 1995, killing 168 people and wounding more than 680? According to studies, 56 percent of domestic terrorist attacks and plots in the US since 1995 have been perpetrated by *right-wing extremists*. Attacks by Islamic extremists accounted for only *12 percent*. Hard to believe? It's bloody true, and you are raving-mad, right-wing fanatics."

Volker was tired of hearing this diatribe against the cabal's views. The new world order was within touching distance, and he would be the spiritual head of a new Christian empire that would dominate the world for several millennia. This woman was fishing in troubled waters, and she had to be silenced.

He walked up to Ashley and literally screamed, inches from her face, "We are not right-wing fanatics, woman. We are the new world order. Whether you like it or not, we will wipe out Muslims and Communists—the bloody sum of all evils in this world—and usher in glorious Christendom for a hundred thousand years!"

Unfazed, Ashley shot back at Volker, "It's not the Muslims, Chinese, Koreans, or Iranians who are a danger to the world.

It's you, the bigoted, xenophobic bastards, who are the real sum of all evils!"

Incensed, his eyes bloodshot with religious fervor, Volker slapped Ashley with a violent backhand, sending her careening to the ground. Kareem jumped up to hit Volker, but his German captors held him down in his chair and then hauled Ashley back up.

"Restrain both of them as we wait for their friends to arrive. Tie them up, if need be," Gunther ordered his men. Then turning to his friends, he said, "This has been a needless diversion. We have plans to make. The Fox missed his first shot, but he's already in place to execute Plan B. Chuck has to leave for Washington now."

Kareem and Ashley heard that last bit and wondered what Plan B was. This evil cabal had to be stopped before they destroyed the free world. Mitch and his team still hadn't arrived, and Ashley feared that these crazed men might kill them before that happened. It was not her life that mattered—she wanted to escape so that with Kareem's help, they could stop Harmagedon. She had to create more diversion to buy time, so she decided to take on Gunther. She had enough anger against him for what he had done to her mom, and she had saved it for last. If her gamble failed and she got killed, then so be it. She would have avenged her mother's death in some small measure by facing up to her killer. This was a life-and-death moment. She had controlled herself, but now it was time to act.

"You German animal, you killed my mother, Ryan, and Gerhard," she exclaimed. "Now you want to kill millions. You are evil incarnate. You're no Christian soldier. You are bloody vermin, and I curse your unholy cabal of sinners and rogues." She knew she would get hit or possibly even be killed.

Gunther was livid. He saw himself as the pillar of German society and the driving force behind the cabal. He was above mere men, and this woman had torn his character asunder. She had trashed the cabal, insulted, abused, and belittled them. His eyes were raging embers of wrath. Holy ire coursed through his veins, and his blood boiled as he walked toward her and viciously snarled, “For you, I don’t need a truck. I will kill you with my bare hands.”

He grabbed her neck with one hand and choked her as he repeatedly slapped her back and forth with his other hand. Ashley’s eyes and mouth were wide open as she gasped for breath. Kareem was straining against his captors, trying to rush to her assistance while screaming for Gunther to stop. But Gunther’s rage was uncontrollable, and he kept hitting Ashley violently. Blood gushed from her lips, and her scream rang through the empty bowels of the mansion.

CHAPTER SIXTEEN

Counterattack!

Seated at the El Obrero, a restaurant in the La Boca neighborhood of Buenos Aires, Argentina, Tanya looked at the *bife de chorizo* and chimichurri sauce that the waiter had served her and read up on the history of the place from a cheap brochure. La Boca, it said, was named after the mouth of the river where it was located. It was the most colorful neighborhood in Buenos Aires simply because of the eclectic splash of brightly colored ramshackle buildings in an otherwise poor district. Home of the world-famous soccer club Boca Juniors, La Boca was a great tourist attraction because of its photogenic colors, but the waiter told her that the people of the district painted it like that with whatever leftover paint was available. Tanya looked at the walls decorated with football paraphernalia and the antique furniture around her.

She dropped the brochure and looked at her meal. The steak grilled over the *parilla* at the El Obrero—in Argentina, the land of beef—had a unique, succulent taste, but her mind was far away. She bit into the beef empanada, sipped on Malbec wine, and thought of what had transpired since she'd left New York.

Bob and Huey had managed to lift footprints from the 55 Water Street offices and later compared them to the footprints she had raised from the Hunters' Lodge scene. They were a *perfect* match. The 338 Lapua Magnum shell casings found at 55 Water and Hunters' Lodge had been fired from the same Tracking Point weapon that they had found at the 55 Water office rented by the Fox. The body they had pulled out of Jennings Brook was that of Jason Goodman, the real estate agent. The reddish color she had seen on the bullet casing she had found at Hunters' Lodge was Jason's blood. But the most vital piece of evidence was the one fingerprint they had lifted off the toilet flush valve. The Fox had been very careful, possibly wearing gloves all the time, and he had sanitized the offices at 55 Water every time he had visited. On the last day, when he took the shot at the president, he had touched nothing and lain on the table.

But the Fox had touched the toilet flush valve with his bare hands, possibly to flush his gloves. In an assassination attempt, shooters plan for only one shot. They are generally good at their trade and don't miss. But because President Harrison had done something out of the ordinary, suddenly bending to retrieve the stress ball he had dropped, the bullet had missed the target. That had been a huge contract, so the Fox had emptied the magazine, hoping to get a shot at his target, but it had cost him valuable extra time. So, he had thrown the gloves into the toilet and flushed them away—with his bare hands! In that rush, he had made one cardinal mistake and left a fingerprint.

Running the fingerprint through every known database, they found nothing. Then they checked with the databases of other countries. Hundreds of agents in several countries tried databases of driver's licenses, birth certificates, social service numbers, identification cards, and passport registers. Finally, they hit gold. The Fox *was unmasked.* Gabriel Marquez Lopez was a native of La Boca, in Buenos Aires. After three decades, the world's most enigmatic and elusive assassin of all time was unmasked—by one fingerprint on a toilet flush valve. After thirty years, a man who never left a calling card had finally left a trace. There were no known pictures of him, and then suddenly from one fingerprint, the FBI unearthed a picture and a passport number in Argentina.

But though the FBI had gone through all airport entry points in the United States, there was no record of a Gabriel Marquez Lopez having entered the country. How had he managed to evade US Customs and Border Protection, which welcomes nearly a million visitors on a typical day? That is what had brought Tanya to Buenos Aires—to get more information on Gabriel Marquez Lopez and figure out how he had left the country. The address given in the passport was in a barrio in La Boca. She had visited it in the company of Argentinean Customs authorities, only to be shocked that a Gabriel Marquez Lopez had died more than twenty years ago and was buried in a local church. The Fox had stolen the identity of a dead man. So even though she had a picture and fingerprints, the Fox was an enigma, a shadow unto a shadow. What nationality did he truly belong to? Was this just one of his passports? Did he use some other passport to exit Argentina? Did he have more identities of owners long interred six feet under? Tanya had no idea.

She signaled to one of the waiters to get her some more Malbec and dug into the steak. How to trace him now? Where was he? He had taken one shot at the president. He would certainly try again. Assassins like him normally took huge down payments with the explicit understanding that they will not fail.

Failure meant loss of reputation and future contracts. In their trade, such news traveled the grapevine faster than in the normal world. No one would touch him. It was not necessarily the loss of monetary gain that would hurt him. He would have tons of money by now. Loss of reputation was akin to death. Tanya knew the Fox would strike again. But from where? She drank the wine and ate her grilled meat. She was still upset.

Her phone rang. It was Huey. He had good news. They had figured out how the Fox had entered the United States! Huey said once it struck them, it was easy, and the mode stared them in the face. The Fox was an Argentine citizen, which meant that he would have required a visa to enter the United States. No such visa application was ever made or granted. How had he come in then? The only way he could have slipped in would have been inside someone's boat from Canada under the Pleasure Boats and Flyers program of the US Customs and Border Protection Agency. The moment Huey said *pleasure boats*, Tanya knew the method he must have used.

"Let me guess: the I-68 from Canada?" she asked Huey. The Fox had either worked with someone or forced someone to use the Canadian border landing permit, the I-68 that allowed boaters from Canada to enter the United States for recreational purposes. They had these permits for the entire boating season and were required to report their arrival only by telephoning in.

"But how did you know whose boat he used? Unless the vessel master called in, you would not have known."

"Stroke of luck," Huey said. "Once we thought of the I-68 angle, we checked the nearest point, the northern New York State arrival. We checked every boat that had come in during the last three months. It was an arduous task. We then checked all the boats that had reported and compared that list against all the boats at the pier. It took time. We found three. Two were down for repairs and had not moved for over a month. The third one was from a regular boater the Customs guys knew very well. He always called in with the name, date of birth, citizenship, and passport numbers of everyone on board, and other details. So, it was strange that he had not called in.

"We inspected the boat. We found a dead captain stuffed in the freezer. We dusted for fingerprints and were able to get one of the Fox on the grillwork, which he must have held on to as he got off the boat. He must have forced the boater to ship him in and then disposed of him. He had no place to dump the body, so he stuffed him in the freezer. He obviously does not plan to use this route on his way out."

"Excellent work, Huey. Kareem will be happy!"

★

Matt was tense. His baby was missing. So were Kareem and Gerhard. It was not good. He knew something had gone wrong—horribly wrong. He had checked the tracking device and his fears were confirmed. It showed her at Gunther's chateau.

"I am so sorry, Matt," Cynthia said. "I wish I had gone instead, or at least gone with her."

"Then you would have gone missing too. No, Cynthia, I'm glad you're safe. I can't afford to lose you too." He walked up to her and gave her a hug. She nearly cried at the thought that Matt still had the grace to think of her at a time like this.

"Ash is a tough girl, and I'm happy that Kareem and Gerhard are with her. Mitch and his team are on their way here. Let me go to the chateau with them. We'll sort this out."

Cynthia looked at the man whose daughter had been kidnapped by extremely dangerous men. In the face of such danger, most men would feel helpless and crumble. If his mind was in turmoil, Matt did not show it. He had the calm demeanor of someone in control. He did not seek pity. He merely thought and acted. He did not wallow in doubt and despair. He was a soldier, strong and resolute. Cynthia looked at a father who was crushed from the inside but stood there calmly. Gunther had no idea of the stature of the enemy he had taken on when he had kidnapped Ashley.

"Be careful, Matt," Cynthia said.

"I'll be careful, Cynthia. Something tells me Ash is safe. We brought her up to be a tough girl. As a reporter, she has taken on some tricky assignments. She has even received threats, but she's not the type to buckle easily. Trust me, if she comes face-to-face with Gunther, I would feel sorry for him."

"You are right about that part of Ash. I worked with her. I don't think the likes of Gunther will frighten her. Yes, if he gets her upset, Gunther may be in for a rude shock. But all the same, I am worried about her safety. These are dangerous men. Did they learn Kareem was coming, panicked, and while trying to kidnap him, grabbed Ashley and Gerhard as well?"

"You may have a point there. It's quite possible that Chuck, in his position as the vice president, knew that Kareem was investigating the attempted assassination, feared their so-called 'Harmagedon' plans were at stake and their goons may have gotten jumpy and kidnapped him. Ash and Gerhard were in the way and had to go along."

They heard a car drive up and park. Mitch walked in. "Matt, let's go! Cynthia, stay here. Hang on to this phone. It's safe."

They drove to a command center not far from the safe house. Waiting for them was a group of Grenzschutzgruppe 9, a counterterrorism unit of the German Bundespolizei. Dressed in black, wearing bulletproof vests, masks pulled over their faces, tactical shoes, and helmets, and carrying Heckler &

Koch submachine guns, the GSG-9 looked quite a menacing lot. Matt was beginning to feel better already. The cavalry was here, along with personnel from the Bureau of Diplomatic Security of the American embassy. The DS special agents were the regional security officers, or RSOs, primarily charged with providing security for US diplomatic missions, their personnel, and families. They were also called in to assist in emergency situations such as hostage taking.

"Matt, I have some bad news for you," Mitch said. "We found Ashley's car. Gerhard is dead. Someone crashed into the car. He was killed, and the assailants made away with Kareem and your daughter. I am sorry."

Matt felt very bad. Their battle to find Amy and Ryan's killers was getting personal. Gerhard was dead. Ashley and Kareem had been kidnapped. He remembered Kareem's words before he left that they were dealing with dangerous people. After the assassination attempt, Kareem had been clear that this was much bigger than they'd thought. He had saved them by sending them to a safe house. But he had gotten caught, and so had Ashley. Gerhard was dead. That was painful. Gerhard had been such a good sport, and a huge help. Matt was now angry at Gunther and his group.

"That's sad, Mitch," Matt said. "Gerhard was so helpful. Poor guy. Thanks for not telling me back there. It would have really hurt Cynthia to hear that. She knew him a lot better than I did. I will break it to her slowly."

Mitch agreed to permit Matt to tag along, but on strict conditions. He did not give him any weapons.

"Matt, I know your daughter and best friend are in the chateau. I know I cannot stop you from coming. If my daughter was in there, I'd go, too, with or without permission. But you know the rules. I cannot let you be part of the assault team. But you are a decorated soldier, and I am assured that you know the ground rules. I also know you can take care of yourself. Kareem would have wanted me to let you come. So, come but stay at a safe distance."

Matt was grateful. He knew he could not get into a firefight on foreign soil. He was not even an official agent. Having his daughter in the mix made it even worse. Even if he had been an officer, they would not have taken him along because of his proximity to one of the prisoners. His personal hatred of the kidnappers would be a liability. This was not a personal vendetta. This was a raid to stop an assassination plot against the president of the United States and prevent murder and mayhem of epic proportions in several countries. So Matt was grateful that Mitch had agreed to let him tag along.

Mitch addressed the team. "We are picking up signals from Ashley's tracking device at the chateau. We are positive they have been kidnapped and are inside that house. She had gone to pick up Special Agent Kareem at the airport when they disappeared, so we can safely assume Kareem is there, too. This chateau belongs to Herr Gunther Otto Heinrich, chairman of the G & H Bayerischer Bank. As of now, he is a suspect. Time is of the essence. We go in with three teams. We enter the chateau from three sides: the front, the rear, and the balcony. Helicopter teams will hover above the chateau to eliminate any attempt by those inside to flee by air. Any questions?"

"Do we take prisoners?"

"We save Special Agent Kareem and Ashley." Mitch was very calm. "Their safety is paramount. We do not know how many are in the house. Arrest and prosecution are good. But if you are shot at, take them out. I am not at liberty to disclose what is at stake. But I can warn you that these are extremely powerful men who have plotted to kill and maim hundreds of thousands in numerous countries. If we are unable to apprehend them, we cannot afford to let them escape to unleash death and destruction. Prosecution would be ideal, but it isn't necessary. So, if you need to, it's okay to use deadly force.

He paused briefly and looked at the assembled attack force. Stony faces looked back at him. The room was deathly quiet. All were raring to go.

Mitch waved his forefinger in a circular motion in the air and barked, Let's rock and roll, gentlemen."

They all stormed down the hallway to the waiting Bearcat armored counterattack vehicles outside.

It took them three-quarters of an hour to reach the chateau in Schwangau. At the gate, two teams of agents fanned out across the grounds of the massive estate. Trained in urban warfare, the GSG-9 disabled the armed guards in rapid succession. Like cats in the dark, they cleared the grounds with surgical precision. Drivers in Bearcat armored vehicles switched off their lights, drove quietly up the driveway, and stationed themselves behind the building. The fifteen-foot-perimeter mobile ramp rose from the Bearcat to the balcony. GSG-9 agents rushed up and jumped onto the balcony. They used their tools to breach the windows and entered the chateau in under three minutes flat.

The American RSOs stuck thru-wall stereo microphones on the doors and walls, to detect any conversations close by the door. They heard no sounds in the living room. They slid an under-door camera under the door and toggled its four lenses left, right, forward, and upward in every possible angle. Again, no guards were in sight. The chateau's inhabitants likely thought the numerous guards on the estate were enough to keep intruders at bay. Or they did not expect any assault teams of this caliber to attempt an entry here. With no sign of any guards in the living room, the agents signaled to the teams behind it that it was all clear to breach the door. They blasted the door open with battering rams and entered the chateau.

The teams of agents slid inside in quick formations, assault weapons at the ready, deftly maneuvering cat like from room to room, until they reached the first-floor study. They stopped. They could hear voices beyond the door. Teams that had entered from the balcony had already spread out to other rooms on the sides to check for any possible signs of activity. All teams met outside the door, where they could hear the conversation emanating from inside the room. Agents held battering rams at the ready, waiting for the signal. When it was clear they were ready to enter, the teams signaled each other.

Mitch looked one last time at all the officers, raised his clenched right fist into the air, and commenced a countdown by thrusting three fingers out in quick succession. Bloodcurdling screams came from within just as Mitch sliced his outstretched palm toward the door. Mitch's signal and Ashley's screams were enough for the commandos to tear down the door and storm into the room, shouting warnings to the occupants to hit the floor or be shot.

Christian and Raymond grabbed the guns from the table in front of them and made as if to shoot the agents. But the older businessmen were no match for the lightning-fast reflexes of the German commandos. Before the two cabal members could raise their guns, the German officers had felled them in a hail of gunfire. Gunther's hands were still wrapped around Ashley's neck. Hearing the sounds, he turned to look at the intruders, dropped his grip, and fled from the room with Aleixandre in tow. Kareem rushed to Ashley, who had collapsed into a crumpled heap on the floor. She was holding her neck and gasping, trying to catch her breath. Kareem helped her up. Matt picked Ashley up and ran out with her. Volker did not offer much resistance, and was captured, handcuffed, and taken away.

Kareem and Mitch ran after Gunther and Aleixandre. They came to a passageway that led down a long corridor with several doors on either side. The officers opened each one, rushed in and out in quick succession, and raced down the corridor, where stone steps led to a basement. An army of agents stormed down the spiral way and reached a hallway with several doors. Mitch signaled the teams to a station outside the first door. At his signal, the teams shot out the lock and forced the door open. They found Gunther and Aleixandre cowering in a corner with their hands over their heads. Kareem and Mitch yanked them to their feet and frog-marched them back to the meeting room.

"So, you want to kill millions and change the world order, huh?" It was Kareem's turn to mock Gunther, who had lashed out at him earlier. "You are lucky we are apprehending you. Unlike you, we believe in the rule of law, and you will have your day in court."

Back in the room, he looked at the dead Raymond and Christian. He remembered the boasting he had heard just a short while ago about the scores of people they would kill.

"We will *still* kill you, Muslim pig!" Gunther was seething with rage. "Harmagedon is still on! We will change the face of this world once and for all. We will set the clock right to a Christian order of things. This is for Christendom. When it dawns tomorrow, President Harrison will be dead, and we will be in control of the world!"

As he hurled abuses at Kareem, Gunther inched closer to the dead bodies of Christian and Raymond. Both were lying hunched over the weapons they had attempted to shoot with earlier. Gunther caught Aleixandre's eyes, and his eyes rolled over to the weapons under the bodies.

"Mitch, where is Chuck Scott?" Kareem felt a sick sensation in his stomach. "He's missing. Search the chateau. He is on to some Plan B to kill the president. He must be found and stopped."

"Go look for him," Mitch ordered the RSOs, who stormed out with the commandos in tow.

"Chuck is gone, you dogs," Gunther screamed. "Our assassin is still in place. It's too late to stop Project Harmagedon. *Die*, you scum."

Gunther and Aleixandre fell sharply sideways, reached below the dead bodies of their colleagues, and grabbed the weapons. Aleixandre shot at Kareem. The bullet grazed Kareem's shoulder, and he hit the ground. Three bullets from Mitch's weapon thudded into Aleixandre's chest, killing him instantly. Gunther shot wildly at everybody, hitting two agents and felling them. A bullet hit Mitch's forearm. His weapon flew from his hands as he grabbed his arm to stem the flow of blood and crashed to the floor. Gunther raised the submachine gun and aimed it at Mitch, his finger on the trigger.

Grabbing an MP 7 submachine gun from a fallen German agent, Matt shot Gunther. Exiting the muzzle of his gun at 2,461 feet per second, the high-velocity ammo thudded repeatedly into Gunther's chest. The copper-plated, solid steel DM11 ammunition, designed to go through twenty layers of Kevlar-covered 1.6-mm titanium plate, tore open Gunther's chest and threw his body like a rag doll across the room. Matt walked up to him and said, "That was for Amy, Ryan, and Gerhard, you scum!"

As he looked at the body of the man responsible for snatching away his family's happiness, the man who had ordered his Amy killed, Matt felt the weight of the anger he had nursed for a year slowly dissipate. He could count the hours, the minutes, the seconds of the past year as if they were an eternity unto themselves. The twenty-five years that he had lived with her.

Then the pain of suddenly losing her and the dark abyss he had sunk into. The nights he had sat up and cried. The way he had hung between life and death in some sort of purgatory where he had agonized and ached for answers. He had vacillated between knowing and not knowing. As he looked at Gunther's body at his feet, he felt he had finally purged his demons.

The pain of not knowing was over. Now he could go back to the land of the living. Matt wondered what would have happened to him if he had not been able to avenge Amy's death. He might never have recovered from his vegetative state and sunk deeper into despair and depression. He would not have survived that kind of life for long. But fate had been kind. Although he had killed Gunther to save Mitch's life, Matt knew deep down that fate had contrived for him to be on hand to mete out justice for Amy. He could bury Amy in his mind now. He was at peace. He knew Amy would be at peace now, too. For the first time in a long time, he smiled.

"Thanks for saving my life," Mitch said.

"Poetic justice that you should have killed him." Kareem could see that his friend's troubled heart was finally at peace. He could see it in his eyes. "Back there he confessed to having ordered Amy and Ryan killed. So, I guess you had your chance to settle scores, buddy. He deserved it. If you had heard all that I was forced to hear, you would have killed him with your bare hands. You just saved millions of lives by killing him."

"Amy, Ryan, and Gerhard can now rest in peace." Matt was grateful to both of his friends. "Thanks, guys." Matt sounded a lot better now. Military paramedics were already bandaging Mitch and Kareem.

"We have one of the crazies in our custody, a priest," Mitch said. "The GSG-9 agents are already interrogating him. We need to find out what the so-called Plan B is."

"Get that priest to tell you the command structure of the staff working for Raymond, Christian, Gunther, and Alex," Kareem said. "They have surrogates waiting to unleash untold suffering and mass-scale murders across England, France, Germany, and Holland. I heard the trigger to unleash their version of Armageddon is the assassination of President Harrison, so they will do nothing until that happens. It is vital that we get Volker to tell us where and how they plan to kill the president tomorrow. That will not just save the president, but also millions of innocent people on both sides of the Atlantic!"

"Chuck is already on his way back to America," Mitch said. "He may try to contact his buddies, and most of them are dead."

"We need to be careful not to let Chuck know that his team is dead or that we have Volker," Kareem warned. "He has committed high treason. I already have enough on him to put him away for the murder of Jason Goodman and to implicate him in the assassination attempt. We need to catch him plotting before the day is out tomorrow. Take the phones of his dead colleagues and destroy them. Volker is in custody and cannot reach him. You are right, Mitch. Chuck may try to call his friends. We cannot let him know what transpired here. We need to keep the illusion that all is okay with the cabal just for tonight. If he knows the truth, the Fox will disappear for good. We need this to go on as planned so we can nab the Fox before he can do anything."

"When I told Matt and the team not to get into trouble, I did not expect the day to end like this. I owe you an apology, Matt." Mitch was smiling. "Hey, but guess what? With your help, we got the cabal and saved the world. Well, almost saved the world. We have one more cabal member and a slippery assassin on the loose. Okay, guys, we have a videoconference scheduled with the White House. POTUS, the Joint Chiefs of Staff, and the military brass will be in the Situation Room shortly. Come on, guys, let's go."

As they rode back to Mitch's office, Kareem called Gwen with an update. She was happy to hear that most of the people responsible for the deaths of Garcia and Samantha had been killed. Kareem told her the danger was not yet past, because the assassin was still on the loose with a Plan B. He told her about Chuck but said the plan was not to alert him for fear of losing sight of the assassin. But as of now, the presidential security bubble needed to be ramped up. She thanked Kareem and agreed to bring the Washington office up to speed on the situation.

On the way to the airport, Matt called Cynthia. She was elated to hear of the success of the operation and that most of the cabal members were dead.

"Now Ryan can rest in peace." Cynthia's voice had a tinge of sadness. "Thank you, Matt. You promised justice for Ryan, and you followed through with exactly that. I don't know how to thank you."

"Then don't," Matt said lightly. "Without your help, we would not have made it this far, Cynthia. So, thanks are due to you! Let's meet at Mitch's office. Ash is on her way to the safe house with some of the RSOs from the consulate to pick you up. We have a videoconference with the White House, and I want you to be there!" With that, Matt got off the line. Cynthia was touched by Matt's insistence on having her beside him during the conference call to the White House. He was a good man. One in a million.

Cynthia thought of the events that had brought her to Bavaria and how the day had ended. Matt had killed Gunther. Finally, there was justice for Amy and Ryan. She felt an immense sense of relief. Like Matt she too had agonized for a year, unable to move on in life. She had seen Ryan's body riddled with bullets. She was angry, and like anyone else, had wanted to hunt down the killers. But on her own, she had been unable to do anything. Powerless, she had often cried herself to sleep during the past year. Then Ashley had come looking for her. She had met Matt and Kareem. Suddenly life had new meaning. There was hope for retribution for Ryan's death. She had come to Bavaria, and now Gunther, the animal who had ordered Ryan's killing, was dead.

She liked the fact that Matt had killed Gunther. Now Ryan could rest in peace. She felt an immense sense of peace, too. She also had a family in Matt and Ashley. Kareem had proved to be a good friend. Suddenly Cynthia's world was brighter. She looked to the heavens, and it seemed Ryan was smiling down at her. Cynthia smiled right back at him.

CHAPTER SEVENTEEN

Operation Brimstone

President Harrison stood with the sergeant at arms at the door to the chamber of the US House of Representatives, prepared to give his State of the Union address. Inside the chamber sat members of Congress, paired with colleagues from across the political aisle in the so-called "date night" seating arrangement designed to ease partisan tension. The Supreme Court justices, the Joint Chiefs of Staff, and the president's cabinet were seated at the front. The sergeant at arms nodded, and the Speaker of the House said, "Members of Congress, I have the high privilege and distinct honor of presenting the president of the United States."

As he handed both Vice President Chuck Scott and the House Speaker envelopes with printed copies of his speech and shook their hands, President Harrison felt a surge of pride in his country. The United States of America had come a long way. In his five years in office, he had seen a lot, including a bloody war in Afghanistan and Iraq that had brought home many Americans in body bags. It wasn't something he was proud of, but it was the result of one of many difficult decisions he had to make as president. It had reduced the number of terror attacks in the homeland. Al-Qaeda was all but vanquished, but ISIS had grown. That pained him, but he had decided enough was enough; he would not put any more American boots on the ground. He wanted the countries in the Middle East to fight their own wars. He would support them with training, but there would be no more body bags for American sons and daughters. He knew he had to fight and win other battles on the domestic front.

"Mr. Speaker, Mr. Vice President, members of Congress, and my fellow Americans," President Harrison began. His words came straight from his heart. "I wish to spend my last term in office helping to build an equitable society that does not differentiate citizens based on color, religious beliefs, or sexual orientation. Xenophobia does not make us. We are a land—a melting pot, as we are sometimes referred to—of people who have migrated here from many lands. Hatred against peoples of other faiths and political persuasions, immigrants, and the LGBT community demeans the high ideals our founding fathers instilled in us. We are the most powerful nation on earth not just because of our military might but because we are the land of the free and the home of the brave!"

Members of Congress rose to deliver a standing ovation.

Harrison continued, "Terror haunts us and is a blemish on the collective conscience of humanity. Laying blame on a religion or group is an easy but an erroneous panacea that only takes our eye away from its real causes. We need to pull down the barriers that divide us and build a just and equitable society. Islam is a religion of peace that does not condone terror. According to its holy tenets, the killing of one is tantamount to killing all humanity. Let us vow not to hate religions or differences in our faiths, but to welcome the diversity, that melting pot of cultures and beliefs that make us the United States of America, the most powerful nation on the face of the earth. Let us vow to take up cudgels against the perpetrators of evil as they ought to be dealt with simply as criminals and vanquish them with the full force of the law—like we did with Osama bin Laden."

That brought the members to their feet again. If there had been one rallying moment in recent American history that had brought people together across the aisles and the divides, it was when the perpetrator of 9/11 was brought to book. Mention of that evoked a sense of patriotism hitherto unknown. In the House, the applause went on for a long time.

Chuck Scott, seated behind the president with the Speaker of the House, was uneasy at the endless standing ovations, which was the norm during such occasions. He kept shifting in his seat and looked up toward the gallery of the House of Representatives. He had reason to be uneasy. Early in the day, he had helped a visitor up to the gallery. Someone crucial to Project Harmagedon. Having failed in his original endeavor to assassinate President Harrison from 55 Water Street, the Fox's Plan B was to kill the president while he was delivering his annual State of the Union address.

That posed a serious risk, because this was one of the most highly guarded locations in the United States right now, with people from all three branches of the federal government—the legislative, the executive, and the judicial—as well as the military and representatives of foreign governments, all under one roof. On an occasion like this, the House of Representatives was guarded by the elite United States Capitol Police and the Secret Service. The secretary of the Department of Homeland Security had designated this evening's event a National Security Special Event, and the entire Capitol Hill area was under lockdown.

The Federal Aviation Administration had also tightened airspace activity around Washington, restricting aircraft and drones. Several blocks around Capitol Hill were blocked off from traffic. No one could sneak in here. But Chuck had managed to sneak the Fox inside long before the elaborate security blanket was in place.

Though he too was forced to stand and applaud the president, Chuck was still thinking of the job at hand. The Fox was already in the visitors' gallery. He had sneaked the weapon inside months earlier, hiding it in the ceiling of one of the washrooms serving the gallery of the House. This was Plan B. This was his last chance to become president. So, he had managed the impossible: sneaking the world's most wanted assassin and a weapon into the US House of Representatives. It was a brazen attempt. It was the Fox's only chance. It was the only chance at Christendom and a new world order. It was the only chance for Harmagedon. The last and only route left by which to banish Muslims from the Western world.

All plans hinged on the assassination of the president. Even the stock market crash and massacre that would cleanse the world of the sum of all evils *hinged on this one act.* Chuck knew it. The Fox's reputation depended on it. If he did not complete this mission, the Fox was finished. He was no simple hired gun. He was the world's most trusted assassin—someone who had not failed in any mission in three decades. Death was better than failure in this case. He was confident about the success of his plan. He had assured Chuck that he would shoot President Harrison dead and also escape. Chuck believed him.

But by the time he was seated behind the president, Chuck was understandably fidgety. Things had not gone as planned. Phones were going unanswered, so he had had no news from Bavaria. Perhaps they had switched phones off as a security measure so close to the final act. No news could be good news—but it could also be bad news. What if the Fox missed his shot and was unable to escape? What if he was captured alive and confessed? Such thoughts worried Chuck as he looked up at the gallery.

Harrison looked at the faces of the members of Congress and continued, "I want us to discuss and agree on, across the aisle, guaranteeing equal pay for equal work for men and women. We have come a long way in these two hundred and forty years, but unborn centuries look to us and will judge us unfavorably for saying 'all men are created equal' and yet standing by silently as women earned less. I hope to live to see the day my little granddaughter can look back and say this great House and its fine men and women voted to make a difference."

Elizabeth Harrison stood up in the gallery and began the applause that resonated across the House in a thunderous standing ovation. It had been his signature election promise, but his opposition had shot it down every time it had come to the House. If he could not get that legislation passed, he would at least leave it there in the collective mind of the members and the American people who were tuned in. A movement once started would have its day someday.

I doubt if you will live for another hour, the Fox thought as he looked down at his quarry. He had missed him once. He was not going to miss him again. He left his seat and went to the restroom. He entered and looked around. He was alone. Good. He walked into the last stall and locked it behind him. Inside, he stood on the toilet seat, raised a panel on the ceiling, reached inside, and pulled out an Uzi submachine gun and two L83 smoke grenades from their hiding place. He sat down on the toilet seat and checked the weapon. The 9 × 9-mm caliber, 32-round magazine was already loaded. He folded the metallic buttstock and slid it inside his jacket.

He pulled the tape on the smoke bombs from its cylindrical cover and put them in the left pocket of his jacket. He flushed the toilet, left the stall, and opened the door. The entire operation had taken only five minutes. No one was in sight. No one wanted to miss the State of the Union address. He went back to the gallery and sat down on a seat closest to the edge.

Since the failure at 55 Water Street, the Fox had trained for this shot. All he had to do was raise his weapon and shoot straight. At that fairly short distance his chance of failure was minimal. He was a crack shot. He would throw a smoke grenade into the audience, shoot some of the seated guests, and disappear in the ensuing melee. He had done this before. The sight of a gun, blood from several dead people, and smoke was enough to create a moment of chaos. A moment was all the Fox needed to escape. He was certain he would escape. The only problem would be that his cover would be blown. But he knew that after the first try, the FBI would have done their homework, and at some stage, they were bound to get to his identity. It was only a matter of time. He would alter his face. A plastic surgeon and another identity would do the job. After all, there were so many dead men in so many countries whose identities he could easily assume.

He looked down at the president as he spoke about Medicare for all. He reached inside his coat and extended the buttstock of the Uzi. He removed the safety and had his finger on the trigger. He inserted his index finger into the wire pull rings attached to the pins of both the smoke grenades and held it in place. He waited for his quarry. He *would not miss* him this time.

Harrison was passionate when he said, "We have only one planet, and unless we strive to preserve it for our children and grandchildren, there will be no world to gift them. We must cut our greenhouse gas emissions by half. But more importantly, we must stop our insatiable dependence on fossil fuels and learn instead to harvest the boundless, clean, and sustainable energy sources of wind and solar-generated alternatives."

President Harrison was punching the air, emphasizing his point. The standing ovation and cheers went on for close to three minutes. The first lady cheered her husband. But she was tense. He seemed to sense her concern at that moment and looked up at her and smiled. He had to calm her down. He knew the danger he faced. He could be killed at any time. Most likely he was in the crosshairs of an assassin's gun at that very moment. He paused to take a drink and turned to glance at the vice president seated behind him. He braved a smile, though he could have strangled Chuck with his bare hands. He had been a soldier and was trained in unarmed combat. Harrison's mind raced back through the events of the night before. It was probably only a minute's distraction, but it seemed like an eternity.

"No!" President Harrison had been every inch the commander in chief when he spoke up in the Situation Room of the White House the night before the address. He was responding to Mitch; whose image was up on the large television. "I will not call off the State of the Union."

Interrogation of Father Volker by German police had revealed that the Fox would attempt to shoot President Harrison on the floor of the House of Representatives during his annual State of the Union address. Mitch had set up the call to inform the president the previous night. The chairman of the Joint Chief of Staffs, secretary of state, attorney general, Speaker of the House, secretary of defense, secretary of homeland security, and directors of the FBI and the CIA were seated around the table in the Situation Room, in the basement of the West Wing of the White House. They stared in surprise as their commander in chief refused to stay out of the line of fire and insisted on delivering his scheduled address to the nation, despite Special Agent Kareem Khan and CIA officer Mitch O'Donnell describing Project Harmagedon in detail, including the Fox's plan to assassinate Harrison in the House the next evening.

"But Mr. President, what if this assassin takes a shot at you?" asked General David Reed, chairman of the Joint Chiefs of Staff and the highest-ranking military officer in the room. Though he did not have operational command authority, since the chain of command went from the president to the secretary of defense and the commanders of the Combatant Commands, Reed spoke from the heart. He had known Harrison ever since they served together in Vietnam, and he didn't want any harm to come to his friend.

"Quite simply, David, what may or may not happen tomorrow in the House will have ramifications for the lives of millions of people on both sides of the Atlantic," Harrison said emphatically. "From what Mitch and Kareem reported just now, my death is the trigger to set Project Harmagedon in motion, killing millions of people and bringing the stock markets of the Western Hemisphere to ruin. I am grateful that Mitch and his team have managed to neutralize most of the members of this nefarious cabal, but my less than illustrious vice president, Chuck, the traitor, is still alive and can yet set this project in motion. We can safely assume Chuck has not tried to reach his colleagues and doesn't know that one has been captured and the others killed."

Harrison continued, "But we don't know if Chuck still hopes to pull off the genocide of large populations with the assistance of others in the organization, even if his buddies are dead. We cannot take a chance of warning him of any change in plans. If I cancel the State of the Union address, he *will* suspect something is afoot. He will try to reach his friends and fail. He may try to reach their surrogates and may or may not try to trigger a third world war. The raving megalomaniac plans to use nuclear weapons, David, and I owe it to the world to stop him tomorrow."

"But how do you hope to stop him, sir?" asked Dustin Walker, the secretary of homeland security.

"Your teams will, Dustin," Harrison said. "I want Special Agent Kareem Khan to oversee my security, working in tandem with the Secret Service. I will speak to the heads of state of Germany, France, the Netherlands, and the United Kingdom and share the information we have gathered from that priest Volker. The plans are to wait until your team is in place tomorrow, capture or neutralize the assassin in the House, and arrest Chuck. Simultaneously our European friends will swoop down on the surrogates of the cabal and dismantle Project Harmagedon."

"I still feel you are putting your life at risk," David Reed said. "This assassin is supposed to be the best in the trade. He missed his first shot, and he'll try his best to salvage his image. We don't want to lose you, sir. What does the first lady say about this proposal?"

"I will speak to Liz shortly." Harrison seemed tired. "Of course, she'll be worried. What wife wouldn't be? But what choice do I have? The Fox, or whatever you call this hireling, already made one attempt on my life. If he's on the loose, he will do it again. One day he may succeed. For three decades, you say, this man has lived like a shadow, and for all you know, he'll disappear again. Tomorrow is your only chance to corner him. If he succeeds in killing me, at least you will have found and either neutralized or prosecuted him. Most importantly, it will stop this crazy Armageddon scheme and the genocide of millions of innocent people—including, from what Special Agent Kareem reports, nuclear holocaust. In the face of such danger to humankind, David, I am willing to make the ultimate sacrifice and stand in the House tomorrow. I have great faith in you gentlemen to guard me."

"You do have a point," said Sam Thompson, the secretary of defense. "But it's your life that's in the balance. For the people of the United States to see their president in the line of fire tomorrow will be unimaginable. When they eventually learn that we allowed you to do this, they may judge all of us in this room harshly. The press will have a field day postulating a million ways in which the Fox could have been killed without endangering your life. That doesn't worry any of us in this room. It's your life that matters and concerns us now."

Harrison stood up, looked the secretary of defense in the eye, and said, "You are not making that decision, Sam. *I am.*" Looking every inch a president, he added, "If my life can stop a genocide and prevent a religious divide from which we may never recover—wanton murder of Russians, Chinese, and North Koreans; economic ruin across nations; and nuclear Armageddon—then my life was worth living. The most important job will be to see that Chuck is tried for high treason. How could he be part of this? Whichever way this goes, whether I am dead or alive after tomorrow, you have enough on him. I want him arrested on the floor of the House tomorrow and unmasked before the whole world. Can you put the team in Germany back on the screen?"

As the faces of Mitch, Kareem, and Matt came on the screen, Harrison turned toward them and said, "Lieutenant Colonel Matt Jordan, my sincere condolences for your loss. Jesse, my CIA director, tells me that Amy was an excellent operative who served this country with great valor and dedication. She gave her life to save others around the world. Your exposure of the cabal and their evil designs, initiated by Amy's investigation, has saved millions of people in this country and across Europe. Please accept my condolences on behalf of a grateful nation and convey my condolences to Cynthia and Ashley as well. I thank you and all the officers who have sacrificed so much for the United States and our allies in Europe."

"Thank you, Mr. President," Matt said.

"Agent Kareem Khan, I want you to get on an air force plane right now and be here tomorrow. I want you to oversee the operation in the chamber of the House tomorrow and nab this foxy creature. You have done an admirable job until now of chasing and unmasking a shadowy figure. If I make it through this in one piece, Mr. Khan, you are going to be in charge of my personal security detail. Now get on that plane right now!"

"Thank you, Mr. President. I will defend your life with my own, sir!" Kareem saluted his commander in chief.

As the TV screens were switched off, the president turned to the secretary of state and said, "Megan, get me the German chancellor, the prime ministers of the United Kingdom and the Netherlands, and the president of France, in that order. We need a plan to tear down the massive schemes these evil men have set up in these countries. But first let me spend a few minutes with Elizabeth, which is not going to be easy." Harrison smiled at Megan Hill, secretary of state, trying to figure out how he was going to explain to his wife of forty-five years that he planned to stand in the line of fire of the world's deadliest assassin. Handling the people in the Situation Room was easier.

GSG-9 helicopters had flown Kareem and his team into Ramstein Air Base in Rhineland-Palatinate, Germany, from where its host Eighty-Sixth Airlift Wing flew to Washington, DC, aboard a special USAF plane. As the team was landing after their nine-hour flight to Joint Base Andrews, the American capital was being effectively placed under lockdown. Dustin Walker, secretary of homeland security, set in motion a massive operation to blanket the House of Representatives on Capitol Hill, using all the resources of the Secret Service—the Airspace Security Branch, Counter-Sniper, Emergency Response, Counter-Surveillance, Counter-Assault, Hazardous Agent Mitigation, and Medical Emergency Response teams. At 1700 hours, the UH-60 Black Hawk with Kareem and agents had flown to the grounds of Capitol Hill. In three hours', time, the president would commence his State of the Union address. There was no time to lose.

The National Guard had encircled the Capitol Hill buildings. Police officers and Secret Service agents packed the hallways and stood guard at all entrances and exits of the House chamber. Everyone had pictures of the Fox with them. Dogs sniffed for weapons and any chemical or hazardous material. The tiered platforms of the House chamber were filled with members of Congress.

The president was halfway through his address. "Our youngsters deserve free college tuition, so that the attainment of skills and education is not the preserve of a privileged few or one that is attained under a burden of debt." Harrison was in his element. "A tuition-free university education should be the birthright of every American, so that we can build a strong workforce that can compete with the best in the world."

Kareem was in the visitors' gallery for two reasons. He could not be on the floor of the chamber because Chuck would recognize him. The only way an outsider could attempt a brazen attempt at a shot at the president had to be from the visitors' gallery on the upper level. Kareem wanted to nab the Fox himself. Not just because he was the most wanted criminal in the world, but also because the president had personally asked him to head the operation and safeguard him. Kareem would lay down his life for his commander in chief.

There was no time to lose. Kareem scanned the gallery. An assassin was seated somewhere in this crowd. Any minute he would take a shot. Kareem had planned with his team to flush the Fox out into the open. There was no time to go through the vast number of faces and check every single person in the assembled crowd. There was a chance the Fox would see them. Yes, there was the chance that he would take hostages in a bid to escape but saving the president's life was paramount.

So, if the Fox saw the team and broke cover, they would rush him, shoot him, or manage a hostage situation. All possibilities led to taking the Fox's attention *away* from POTUS. Kareem raised his wrist and spoke into the hidden microphone to his team waiting below for his command. He looked down at POTUS behind the lectern, his address still in full flow. Knowing the Fox might act at any second, Kareem looked around and made his decision. On the count of three from Kareem, the teams burst into the gallery and the floor of the chamber. On the floor of the chamber, two teams of Secret Service agents and the Capitol Hill police reached the presidential rostrum, pulled Harrison down, and dragged him away . Members of Congress panicked and screamed at the sight of heavily armed men and women and began to rush the doors.

In the gallery, Kareem's team, holding their weapons at the ready, fanned out among the crowd and ordered everyone to remain seated. Just as Kareem had hoped, the Fox stood up, threw smoke bombs at the armed men rushing him, whisked his gun out, and shot down at the departing image of the president. The rat-a-tat of the Fox's Uzi submachine gun filled the air as fire grenades exploded, releasing a dense cloud of gray-white smoke that partially hid his location. Two agents shielding the president were hit by bullets from the Fox's Uzi, but the rest of the team got POTUS out to safety. Kareem's plan had worked.

Having surprised the Fox, he made it impossible for the assassin to get a perfect shot. The Fox got off only a few wild shots as the Secret Service agents converged on him from all sides.

Instead of crouching below his chair for safety as the Speaker had done, Chuck got up in sheer terror and attempted to bolt. He tripped over the Speaker and fell forward. The Fox knew he had failed twice. He would never ply his trade again if he did not succeed. Rage overtook his otherwise normal, calm demeanor, and he emptied his magazine, aiming wildly at the receding image of the president just as Chuck's body slumped forward. Stray bullets from the Fox's Uzi tore across Chuck's body, and the sheer force of more than twenty rounds of the 9 × 9–mm caliber ammo punctured his frame and momentarily threw his face up into the air before he flopped like a rag doll across his own table. Chuck had been killed by the very man he had hired to kill someone else. *Poetic justice*, Kareem thought as he saw the drama unfold.

Secret Service agents and the Capitol Hill police were flying over the seats through the smoke, firing at the same time. Visitors and members of the press seated in the gallery screamed and hit the floor between the seats, and some were hit by the rapid fire from Fox's Uzi. But the specialized 5.7-mm caliber ammo from the far superior FN P 90 submachine guns of the Secret Service agents found their mark and fragmented inside the Fox's body. Their guns illuminated the Fox's position through the smoke and reduced the chance of hitting nearby visitors. More shots from Kareem and Secret Service agents from several vantage points felled the assassin. The Fox was on the ground between the seats, but he kept trying to shoot.

Kareem vaulted over the seats and rushed to where the Fox lay on the ground. He looked into the eyes of the most wanted man on the face of the earth. The Fox's cold eyes were devoid of any feeling, not even anger or regret. They were just as empty as his soul. As the Fox raised his Uzi to shoot, Kareem shot him point-blank, killing him instantly. The Fox's body bucked up and down from the sheer force of the 5.7-mm caliber ammo from Kareem's submachine gun.

Kareem still looked down at the face of the man whom security agencies around the world had hunted for three decades. Gabriel Marquez Lopez was the name on his documents, but Tanya had said that was the stolen identity of a man dead more than twenty years earlier. So, who was the Fox in real life? Kareem felt that no one would ever know the identity of this man who had lived in the shadows. In life and in death, he remained a mystery. This time it was Kareem's turn to smile. Operation Brimstone had come to a successful close.

And so, had Project Harmagedon. Father Englebert Volker was helpful with information on the boiler-room operations that had been set up in Holland, France, England, America, and Germany. President Harrison's calls to the heads of government helped dismantle the schemes related to Project Harmagedon. Numerous associates of the cabal members in Europe were arrested and plans to bomb or kill Muslims in large numbers were averted. The RAF officers in England who had hoped to fly planes into Muslim populations were apprehended, and large caches of arms and explosives were recovered from several sites on both sides of the Atlantic.

After their debriefing by the FBI, Ashley and Cynthia had sent the video they had captured of the cabal discussing Harmagedon on the pen camera at the chateau to all the news channels. Major TV channels broadcast the image of six wealthy men planning to kill thousands in the name of religious hatred. Americans were shocked to see the involvement of their vice president in this nefarious cabal, but happy to watch on CSPAN as he fell in a hail of bullets from his own assassin. Later, President Harrison addressed the nation about Project Harmagedon and how the intelligence community, both the FBI and the CIA, had averted a nuclear holocaust. Major newspapers carried Ashley's glowing account of President Harrison's heroic insistence on standing in the line of fire to help flush out the Fox, and Harrison became a hero for millions of Americans and Europeans alike.

★

Matt laid flowers on Amy's grave. He looked at the Intelligence Star that the Central Intelligence Agency had awarded her "for voluntary acts of courage performed under hazardous conditions and for outstanding achievements or services rendered with distinction under conditions of grave risk."

"Thanks, Mom, for helping destroy the Cabal of Christian Crusaders—the real sum of all evils," Ashley said as she too laid flowers on her mothers grave. She felt she had buried her mother now, and she was at peace. Her mother had been a hero. For the first time in a year, Ashley felt like a burden of pain had lifted. Her mother's death was avenged.

"That night in Munich a year ago, when she crossed that street and was run over by a killer's truck, Amy's sacrifice saved the world from certain apocalypse," Kareem grimly added.

"Yes, Kareem, Amy made a huge sacrifice, and so did you," Matt said. "Mitch, the German commandos, and the FBI agents are all heroes for uncovering the Fox and saving the day. I know that many people have given their lives in protecting the president, and I salute their sacrifice. A stock market crash across Europe and America would have devastated a world already reeling from their genocidal plans. It would have split this world of ours down a religious and ideological divide that we can ill afford. For people who professed to live by the Bible, the Cabal of the Christian Crusaders did not know the old biblical adage that those who live by the sword shall die by the sword. Thank you, Special Agent Kareem Khan."

"Oh yes, now they knew," Kareem said. "That's why most of them are dead."

They all laughed.

"It was a masterstroke to flush out the Fox in the gallery of the House," Matt said, "and help derail his planned shot. Once a sharpshooter fails at an assassination attempt, he's bound to take a second shot. Brilliant, Kareem! And guess what? Though you didn't plan it, I give you credit for the Fox's stray shot that killed the crooked vice president. You the man, Kareem." Matt high-fived Kareem.

"That's why Kareem was awarded the FBI Shield of Bravery, Dad," Ashley said. "He has been moved from the bureau to head the Presidential Protective Division. Kareem is the chief agent in charge of the presidential security detail. Apparently President Harrison insisted on it."

"Congrats, KK," Matt complimented his friend. "You deserve it. Amy would have been proud of you today."

"I actually told POTUS that it was his Bubba—not me—who saved the day," Kareem said, laughing. "Our president outfoxed the world's deadliest sharpshooter assassin by bending to pick up his stress ball. Because of that, we were able to successfully investigate and close this case. Of course, POTUS said that although the first lady has permitted him to carry Bubba around, she too was insistent that it did not fit the job description of the Secret Service."

"That's the first time a stress ball has saved a president's life," Cynthia said with a broad smile. "Made for a striking heading to my piece, which has been published widely: 'Bubba Saves the World from Armageddon.' Americans love Harrison, and I'm sure all the legislation he spoke about in his last State of the Union, under the shadow of a gun, will pass. Congress owes it to him. The man stood there and defined his causes while in the crosshairs of a deadly assassin's gun. A true American hero!"

"Thanks, Cynthia," Matt said. "If not for Ryan's sacrifice, I would've never known about Amy's murder. Ryan is a hero. Thanks, Cynthia, for joining our team, going to Bavaria, and helping bring down the evil cabal and their nefarious schemes. I'm sorry we lost Gerhard, though. He was a good guy, and he shares in the credit for today's success."

"Poor Gerhard. You're right, he was truly a good man," Cynthia said. "But thanks, Matt, Kareem, and Ashley. Thanks to you all, Ryan can rest in peace. Thanks for helping me find his killers and avenge his death. Thanks. Thanks a lot." Her eyes were moist. After a year of pain, the steely exterior was giving way to feelings of being normal, and Matt was responsible for that. Then she did the unthinkable. As Kareem and Ashley looked on, Cynthia walked up to Matt, threw her arms around his neck, and hugged him. He pulled her up toward him, turned her face up to his, and kissed her passionately.

"Way to go, Dad!" Ashley was delirious. This was an unimaginable joy for her. It was justice for her mother's death and redemption for her father from his lonely existence. Her dad had been stuck in a dark place for more than a year, and although she had hoped he would meet someone and move on with his life, he had not wanted to go out or meet people. Now, seeing Cynthia and her dad together, she could not ask for more. The two, best people in her life were together. Her dad was finally coming out of his shell, and they had avenged her mother's death. He and Cynthia had been lost souls but had finally found solace in each other.

"Congratulations are in order, MJ," Kareem said. He was very happy. His soldier buddy was finally back in the land of the living, after a year spent in a dark world. "Cynthia, I'm happy for you. Both of you deserve to have some fun. You guys have been miserable far too long. I know Amy is happy in heaven today. She loved Matt and would not have wanted him to waste away his life like this. Ryan too. Go on, get out of here and have some fun."

As they walked away, Matt's mind raced back to that dark night a year ago, when Amy was crossing the road. In his mind's eye, he could see his wife's terrified eyes as she was about to die. He knew deep down now that at that instant, in the millionth or billionth of a second when she knew her life was being snuffed out, his Amy knew *he* would find her killers. They had been together since they were kids and lived together for more than a quarter of a century. They had shared a bond that transcended life itself. As his soul flew back in time and he looked into those lucid eyes, Matt smiled at her—and she smiled back.

"I know I'm going, Matty," she seemed to say to him. "But I know you'll hunt down these killers and uncover the truth. I know you will. Goodbye, dear. See you on the other side."

He had spent a year in purgatory. After losing Amy, his soul had been empty. But now when he looked into her eyes, he felt the weight, lifting. He felt an inner peace as he came back from the dark place where his mind had vacillated between knowing and not knowing. *Now* he knew. Now he had found justice for Amy.

Yes, baby, he said in his thoughts. *I found Gunther and killed him. Your death is avenged, dear. You saved the world! Rest in peace, darling. I'll see you on the other side, baby.*

For the first time in a year, Matt smiled from his heart. He turned to look at Cynthia, gave her a hug, locked his hands in hers, and strode away.

About the Author

George Mathew was born in India, the youngest of five sons. His father working for the Military Engineering Service was constantly transferred to various locations around the country, leading to George being constantly on the move, picking up several languages, cultures, not being rooted to any one ethos and finding it easy to settle into his adopted country, Kenya where he has been living for four decades now. The moving also ensured he read only in English Medium schools, where the school library with additional titles from the British Council and United States information Services (USIS) helped him read extensively and helped create a world view from a very young age.

He majored in English Language & Literature with American literature as an option. So in addition to the English masters like Geoffrey Chaucer and John Milton, George also studied classical American writers like Walt Whitman, TS Elliot, Mark Twain, John Steinbeck, Ernest Hemingway, Herman Melville, Edgar Allan Poe, Pearl S Buck, Nathaniel Hawthorne among others In 1981 when he got his first job as an Advertisement representative with Delhi Press, the publishers of 'The Caravan" magazine, George did not want to sell ad's and asked the Editor to give him a chance to write articles and not to pay him if it was not good. Of course, he was published, and went on to work for a year there. One day while browsing through some old newspapers George came across an advert seeking for teacher's in East Africa. Africa excited George. He knew he had to go. He went for the interview, was hired and in 1983, George left the shores of India and landed in Kenya, where he has resided ever since.

George settled into his new country and life and taught English language & literature for some years, then switched careers to join various Kenyan, British and American companies as Administrator, Marketing Manager, General Manager and Group Chief Operating Officer. During this period, he traveled extensively in Europe, Asia, America, Africa, Singapore and Australia. He has lived in America for a year in Texas and Chicago. He also owns his own company supplying German packaging products across Africa. During this period, he still continued writing and has published several articles for a Kenyan magazine, "The Executive". He was stuck at the Westgate Mall in Kenya, when it was attacked by Al Shabab terrorists. He went to write about his experience in a local newspaper. He first book *Murder in Heaven was* published by

Locksley Hall Publishing, New Delhi. *The Last Crusade* is his second book. He is now working on his third book.

George is married to Anita has three children, Reggie, Samantha and Richie.

Made in the USA
Las Vegas, NV
18 October 2022

57555187R00156